NEPTUNE

NEPTUNE

BEN BOVA

TOR

A TOM DOHERTY ASSOCIATES BOOK

New York

NEPTUNE

Copyright © 2021 by Rashida Loya-Bova

A Tor Book
Published by Tom Doherty Associates
120 Broadway
New York, NY 10271

www.tor-forge.com

Tor® is a registered trademark of Macmillan Publishing Group, LLC.

Library of Congress Cataloging-in-Publication Data

Names: Bova, Ben, 1932–2020 author.
Title: Neptune / Ben Bova.
Description: First edition. | New York : Tor, 2021. |
    Identifiers: LCCN 2021009152 (print) | LCCN 2021009153 (ebook) |
    ISBN 9781250296627 (hardcover) | ISBN 9781250296641 (ebook)
Subjects: GSAFD: Science fiction.
Classification: LCC PS3552.O84 N47 2021 (print) |
    LCC PS3552.O84 (ebook) | DDC 813/.54—dc23
LC record available at https://lccn.loc.gov/2021009152
LC ebook record available at https://lccn.loc.gov/2021009153

Our books may be purchased in bulk for promotional, educational, or business use. Please contact your local bookseller or the Macmillan Corporate and Premium Sales Department at 1-800-221-7945, extension 5442, or by email at MacmillanSpecialMarkets@macmillan.com.

First Edition: August 2021

Printed in the United States of America

0 9 8 7 6 5 4 3 2 1

To the beauteous Rashida,
with all my love

Damn the torpedoes—full speed ahead!
—*Admiral David Glasgow Farragut*

BOOK 1

+++
++++++++++++++++++

earth

on a very clear day from the top floor of the unfinished glass-walled tower you could see the dark smudge on the northwestern horizon that marked the capital, Budapest.

Even in its incomplete state the tower was of course the tallest building in the city of Budaörs, a slim, soaring monument to the pride and wealth of Baron Miklos Magyr, the richest man in the city, in all of Hungary, in the whole of southeastern Europe.

For slightly more than three years the glittering entrance to the incomplete Magyr Tower had been draped in black, mourning for the baron's death in the dark, ice-clad ocean that encompasses the distant world of Neptune.

The baron's daughter, Ilona, kept the funeral drapery in place, driven by grief and the prideful stubbornness that was a hallmark of the ancient Magyr family, whose ancestry could be traced back to those medieval days when the Hungarians were nomadic invaders of Europe galloping out of the endless wastes of the east, fierce and merciless. And clever. In time they settled in the fertile valley of the Danube, adopted Christianity, and became a powerful defender of the land against the new tribes of would-be invaders pouring in from the West.

Sitting alone in Castle Magyr's spacious dining hall, the remains of her breakfast nothing more than crumbs scattered across her dishes, Ilona Magyr gazed at the portraits lining the walls around her. Her ancestors gazed down at her, proud, imperious, self-satisfied.

Ilona thought for the thousandth time that she should commission a portrait of her father. She would have it hung at the head of the hall, above the seat she occupied. But she shook her head. No, that would be admitting that he is dead. I can't do that.

The chief butler, Ghulam, approached her as silently as a wraith.

"The children are waiting in the gymnasium," he said in a near whisper.

Ilona looked up into the butler's expressionless face. Ghulam was like the furniture that surrounded her, as much a part of the castle as its foundation stones. He was almost as tall as Ilona herself, but thickset, dark of complexion, his black hair cut in a bowl that framed his impassive face. He had been a member of the castle's staff since Ilona had been a baby, as were his father and his father's father.

"I'll be there directly," Ilona said, pushing her chair back. Ghulam guided the chair away from the table as Ilona got to her feet.

She was strikingly tall, slim, her bony long-jawed face far from beautiful but intelligent, purposeful, with a drive and a temper that matched her long, flowing red hair. She knew that her jaw was too strong for the rest of her face: some called it stubborn, even haughty. She accepted it as a family inheritance. She was wearing a fencer's uniform: a white, high-collared padded jacket and knee-length knickers.

As she got to her feet, Ghulam reminded her softly, "Captain Humbolt is due in one hour."

"Yes," said Ilona. "I know."

THE FENCING ACADEMY

Twenty-five girls and boys—aged from nine to fifteen—were waiting for Ilona in the castle's spacious gymnasium, one floor below the grand ballroom.

All of them wore fencing outfits: high-collared white jackets with matching knickers and wire-mesh helmets. Several of them were already whacking away at one another, the ringing of steel blade against steel blade almost drowned out by the excited shouts of the youngsters gathered around the duelists.

The action and the clamor died instantly as Ilona strode into the gym, dressed in her form-hugging fencing uniform. The combatants whipped off their helmets and saluted her with their swords.

"Places, everyone!" she called out, clapping her hands sharply. The girls and boys immediately lined up, pulled their helmets over their heads, grasped their sabers in their gloved hands.

For nearly an hour Ilona worked them up and down the length of the gym. "Forward!" she commanded. "Right foot, left foot—*lunge*!" And twenty-five sabers flashed out, straight and true.

At last Ilona saw Ghulam appear at the door, nodding silently to her. Humbolt has arrived, Ilona thought.

She pointed to the tallest boy among her pupils, who hurried to her side.

"Take over for me, Janos," she said. "One hour, then let them go home."

Janos—tall and gangly—grinned and nodded. He had been a member of the fencing class since Ilona had started it, more than six years earlier. She left him in the middle of the floor and headed for the door where Ghulam waited.

Then Ilona saw that another man was standing in the doorway, behind the butler. Derek Humbolt, Ilona realized.

Humbolt was known throughout the worlds as the most fearless, most competent, boldest explorer of them all. And a legendary womanizer. He was wearing a high-collared jacket, skintight trousers and calf-length boots polished to a mirror finish.

Smiling, Ilona thought he looked like a ruggedly handsome brute. His reputation must be well-earned, she told herself.

"Captain Humbolt," she called as she approached him.

With a gracious sweep of his arm, he replied, "Baroness Magyr."

Ghulam stepped back, leaving the two of them standing face-to-face.

"It was good of you to come," Ilona said.

His lips curved into a smile. "An invitation from the baroness can't be ignored."

Raising her saber, Ilona smiled back and asked, "Do you fence?"

Humbolt looked past her to the youngsters exercising noisily across the gymnasium's floor. "Not with swords, I'm afraid."

"Too bad."

"I suppose I could learn, although I imagine I'm a bit too old to start now."

"Nonsense!" said Ilona. "You're in the prime of life."

"How kind of you to say so."

Calling to the butler, Ilona said, "Ghulam, please show Captain Humbolt some of the castle while I get out of these sweaty clothes and wash up."

"Certainly, Baroness."

Turning back to Humbolt, she said, "I'll meet you on the rooftop in half an hour."

Half an hour later, dressed in a powder-blue pantsuit that accentuated her long, lean, leggy figure, Ilona sat at the table that had been set in the exact center of the spacious, nearly empty, roofless top floor of the castle and with an excellent view of the unfinished Magyr Tower. She silently studied Derek Humbolt, sitting across from her.

Humbolt was a bare two centimeters shorter than the willowy Ilona, broad of shoulder and flat of midsection, his dark thickly curled hair flecked with gray, his craggy face handsome enough to seem totally at ease even in the presence of Magyr riches. His jet-black eyes sparkled as he sipped at the wine that the robot server had poured.

"You set a good table," he said to Ilona, placing the long-stemmed wineglass down as precisely as landing an interplanetary spacecraft.

Ilona smiled minimally. "I didn't invite you here merely for lunch, you know."

"I guessed that," Humbolt said, his broad smile dazzling.

Ilona looked back at Humbolt. She could see it in his eyes: He wants to seduce me. I'm nothing more than a potential conquest, as far as he's concerned. The trick will be to get him to agree to heading the mission without submitting to his male ego.

"I intend to go to Neptune," she said flatly.

"The planet Neptune?" Humbolt asked, his brows rising. "That's a long way from here."

Ilona nodded slightly. "My father is there."

"He died there."

"I don't believe that he is dead."

Humbolt's face remained smiling, but tensed visibly. He said, "Nothing's been heard from him for more than three years. He must be dead."

"Or cryonically preserved."

"In cold storage? Not bloody likely."

For the flash of an instant Ilona wanted to lean across the luncheon dishes and slap the self-certain egotist in his smiling face. She could picture the shock that would rattle his smug confidence.

But she suppressed the impulse. You get better results with sugar, she heard her sainted mother whispering in her mind.

"My father is an ingenious man. I believe he might well have chosen cryonic preservation once he realized his submersible was beyond recovery. I believe he's waiting for me to find him."

Humbolt shook his head slowly. "The temperature of Neptune's ocean gets hotter, the deeper you go. Even if your father somehow rigged a cryonic system to freeze his body, it would have crapped out by now."

Ilona's dark gaze flashed again, but she chose again to ignore his deliberate crudity. "I need someone to pilot my ship to Neptune and enter its ocean to search for my father. I've been told you are the best man for the job."

"That's probably true," Humbolt said, his easy smile returning.

"Will you do it?"

"Will you be coming along?"

"Of course."

Fixing his gaze on Ilona's cobalt-blue eyes, Humbolt asked, "How much are you willing to pay?"

"Whatever you wish," Ilona replied, quickly adding, "Within reason."

DATA BANK

Neptune is the farthest true planet of the solar system, orbiting an average of 4.5 billion kilometers from the sun—more than forty-eight times farther out than Earth. It takes light—moving at almost three hundred thousand kilometers *per second*—slightly more than four hours to travel from Earth to Neptune.

Neptune is a blue world, due to the presence of methane in the clouds that perpetually cover the planet from pole to pole. And cold. Temperatures at the tops of its clouds run close to two hundred degrees below zero, Celsius.

Even at such a frigid temperature, Neptune's atmosphere is quite active. Belts of darkish clouds appear in it from time to time, often edged with bright white fringes of frozen methane. Weather patterns—giant storms, actually—arise and then dissipate over periods as short as a few Earth days.

Like the other giant planets of Earth's solar system, Neptune is wrapped in a globe-girdling ocean, which in turn is covered by a heavy layer of ice that runs to hundreds of kilometers thick, in places.

Although nearly four times larger than Earth, Neptune spins on its axis in a mere sixteen hours and seven minutes. Its density of 1.64 times that of water shows that it is composed largely of light elements: hydrogen, helium, methane and ammonia.

While the temperature of its cloud tops is frigid, Neptune gets warmer beneath those clouds. Earth-based experiments have shown that at the bottom of its globe-girdling ocean there exists a core of *superionic* ice, at such high temperature and density that the oxygen atoms of the water molecules are locked into an interlaced lattice through which the hydrogen ions flow like a fluid. The temperature at the planet's core approaches five thousand one hundred degrees Celsius; the pressure, more than two million times that of Earth's atmosphere.

That hot, black and dense core of unearthly ice gives rise to the odd, swirling magnetic fields observed in the cloud tops of Neptune, as the hydrogen ions racing through the superionic ice generate constantly shifting magnetic fields.

Neptune was the first planet discovered through mathematical analysis. Once the planet Uranus was found by William Herschel in 1781, studies of its motion indicated that it was being pulled slightly out of its predicted orbit by the gravitational tug of an unseen, more distant planet. Using the mathematical analysis developed by Urbain Le Verrier, astronomer Johann Galle in Berlin discovered Neptune in 1846.

Like the other gas giant worlds—Jupiter, Saturn and Uranus— Neptune is surrounded by several orbiting rings. Neptune's are slim and dark, the remains of moons that inched too close to the giant planet and were broken into crumbled chunks of rock.

In addition to its smashed rings, Neptune has a retinue of more than a dozen satellites, most of them only a few hundred kilometers in diameter or less.

But Neptune's family of moons includes Triton, slightly larger than twenty-seven hundred kilometers in diameter, roughly three-quarters the size of Earth's own Moon. Triton orbits Neptune in retrograde fashion, backward, compared to most of the other bodies in the solar system. It was probably once an independent body that strayed close enough to Neptune to be captured by the planet's gravitational pull.

Triton has a thin atmosphere of molecular nitrogen (N_2) and methane, with a high layer of haze floating above it.

Triton has a geologically "young" surface: there are surprisingly few meteor craters scarring its methane- and ice-covered exterior. Triton also has a polar cap of nitrogen frost and—most surprising of all—active geysers that expel dark plumes of erupting gases. Driven by the moon's internal heat, the geysers resurface Triton as their spewed-out gases settle on the ground and freeze there.

Neptune's global ocean bears abundant life: thousands of varieties of microscopic creatures, colonies of interlinked diatoms, local equivalents of seaweed, and bivalves and darting fish.

At the top of the food chain are gigantic squid-like creatures, large enough to sometimes attack the unmanned submersible vessels sent into that dark and dangerous sea by inquisitive researchers from Earth.

None of the native life-forms are intelligent. They live and die in that dark, deep worldwide ocean without a thought beyond feeding and mating.

And surviving.

agreement

Humbolt's heavy dark brows rose slightly in surprise.

"Whatever I wish?" His smile broadened. "I don't come cheaply, you know."

Ilona's face remained perfectly serious. "I know precisely what you earned on your last four excursions," she said.

"Those were all missions to Jupiter and Saturn," he replied, his expression unchanged. "Neptune is a lot farther . . . and much less understood. That makes it more dangerous."

"That's why my father went there. To explore. To discover."

"I would require a minimum of five million New Dollars."

At last Ilona smiled back at him. "I expected nothing less."

Humbolt broke into a wide grin. "That's agreeable to you?"

"Agreeable," Ilona answered.

With a crafty expression on his ruggedly handsome face, Humbolt asked, "And you intend to come along with me?"

"Of course."

"As crew?"

"As owner."

"Ah. No duties, then."

"The submersible is highly automated. It needs only a captain to give it directions."

"Very good." Humbolt thrust his right hand across the table. "We are in agreement?"

Ilona could see the picture in his mind: the two of them, alone together at the far end of the solar system, millions of kilometers away from any other human being.

Very deliberately she allowed him to imagine the possibilities.

She took his hand in hers. "Done."

"Done," he echoed.

They got up from their improvised luncheon table. Ilona walked slowly to the edge of the parapet looking toward the glass and steel Magyr Tower.

Standing beside her, Humbolt asked, "Do you intend to ever finish the tower?"

She shrugged minimally. "When we find my father and bring him back, he can direct the work that remains to be done."

"But if we don't find him?"

Again she shrugged her slim shoulders. "I really haven't considered that possibility."

INTO ORBIT

+++
++

Humbolt stared out at the rolling landscape, in the direction of Budapest. The afternoon was pleasantly warm and sunny, the landscape beyond the edge of the city was green and orderly, cultivated by untold generations of hardworking peasants and, in more recent decades, by industrious indefatigable robots.

"You have a beautiful country," he said to Ilona.

Without turning to look at him she replied, "We worked hard to make it beautiful. And to keep it that way."

Still gazing at the green countryside, he murmured, "Neptune is a long way from here."

"Yes, it is. I understand that."

"It will take several weeks to get there, and then we'll have to go through the encircling windy clouds, crash through the ice and dive down into that ocean. Most of it is unexplored."

"I have contracted with the Interplanetary Council; they will pay a sizable fee for whatever we find down there."

"We'll need a very reliable ship."

"I've already bought one. It's being refurbished even as we speak."

Humbolt's cocky grin returned. "Have you now?"

"Would you like to see it?"

"Certainly."

"It's at the orbital maintenance facility at the L4 station. We can ride up there tomorrow."

"You've already made arrangements for the trip?" Humbolt asked.

Pointing to a wide treeless open area on the outskirts of the city, Ilona said, "My family owns the local spaceport. I'll phone the manager and make the arrangements."

The following morning Ilona met Humbolt at the office of the spaceport's manager. The two of them were treated with great cour-

tesy and driven to a rocket shuttle, standing on its tail fins, fully
fueled and crewed, waiting for them to arrive.

Humbolt went slightly slack-jawed as they were escorted up the
ramp and into the shuttle's interior. The passenger compartment
was empty except for them and the uniformed steward.

"You travel first class," he said.

"Why not?" Ilona asked carelessly.

The steward gestured to the first row of seats, but Ilona went
past him and slipped into the third row, taking the window seat.
Humbolt slid in beside her and started pulling the safety harness
over his broad shoulders.

As Ilona reached for her safety harness, the steward said, in a re-
spectful whisper, "Liftoff is scheduled for fifteen minutes from now.
May I bring you a refreshment while you wait?"

"A glass of Tokaji Aszú, please," said Ilona, with the smile that a
noblewoman reserves for dealing with servants.

"And you, sir?" the steward asked Humbolt.

"Egri Bikavérfor me."

Ilona's smile changed. Bull's Blood, she thought. How *macho*. How
common.

The steward brought their wines and Ilona clinked glasses with
Humbolt.

The overhead speaker announced, "Liftoff in twelve minutes." It
was a robot's flat emotionless voice, Ilona knew.

They sat in growing anticipation as they finished their wine and
allowed the steward to take the empty glasses away. Humbolt sat
back in easy anticipation; Ilona tried to hide the slight edge of ner-
vousness that always crept over her during the endless moments of
a countdown.

At last the speakers announced, "Three . . . two . . . one—*liftoff.*"

Even through the passenger compartment's heavy acoustic insu-
lation, the rocket engines' thunderous roar filled the air. The shuttle
shuddered as it lifted, slowly at first and then with growing acceleration, pressing them into their cushioned seats. Ilona stared through
the small oval window as the Earth fell farther and farther away.
Within seconds a cloud cover obscured her view.

"We're off!" Humbolt said needlessly, and Ilona realized the man
was just as excited, just as nervous, just as thrilled as she was.

For the first time since boarding the shuttle, she relaxed.

* * *

Ilona listened attentively to the prerecorded safety lecture as the robotic voice warned that the shuttle would be effectively in zero gravity for the few moments it took to connect to the L4 station's hatch. Humbolt grinned at her as he unclicked his safety harness and floated up out of his seat.

"Don't like zero gee?" he asked.

Ilona shook her head, slightly annoyed. "It's okay. I've experienced zero gravity several times." She did not bother to explain that she'd flown into orbit a half-dozen times to acclimatize herself to weightlessness.

She let the safety straps float up off her shoulders and then rose gracefully out of her seat, taking care to grasp the back of the seat before her.

The steward floated along the aisle toward them and led them to the main hatch. They waited in expectant silence until the lights beside the hatch turned green and the overhead speaker announced, "You are now free to leave the shuttle. Have a pleasant visit to the L4 facility."

The hatch popped open slightly. The steward reached out and pushed it fully open.

"Welcome to L4," he said, with a mechanical smile.

Grateful for the feeling of gravity that made her innards feel normal once again, Ilona stepped out of the shuttle and into the reception area of the massive L4 space station. With Humbolt at her side she headed out to the passageway and the nearest observation blister.

The blister was empty, of course, cleared of other visitors by the station's staff. It was a longish enclosure, dimly lit, with a row of comfortable armchairs running along its middle. Its curving roof was transparent, and through it Ilona saw the beautiful blue and white curve of Earth sliding by.

"Aahhh," Humbolt sighed, staring out at it.

Ilona was standing with her back toward him. "This way," she instructed.

Humbolt turned. Hanging there in space was a huge metallic sphere. Sparks glinted here and there across its wide metallic surface: robots at work.

"That's your ship?" Humbolt asked.

Ilona heard surprise in his voice. And, for the first time, respect.

"Yes," she replied. "*Hári János.*"

Staring at the globular ship as it floated in orbital space, Humbolt's handsome face now contracted into a puzzled frown.

"She looks familiar."

"You flew her to Saturn," said Ilona, "back when she was known as *John F. Kennedy*."

Humbolt's bewilderment vanished. "Of course! The *JFK*! I rode that bird into Saturn's ocean. Twice."

Ilona allowed the beginnings of a smile to curve her lips. "I bought her from the Astronomical Association. She's being refurbished now, brought up to date."

"Under a new name."

Nodding, Ilona explained, "*Hári János* is a Hungarian national hero."

"A myth, isn't he?"

"Is he? He kept Napoleon from invading Hungary."

"By bedding Marie Louise."

"According to the tale," said Ilona.

"A rogue. A braggart. A barroom drinker."

"A national hero," Ilona repeated.

Humbolt shook his head.

Ilona asked, "Would you like to go aboard and see how we have updated the ship's equipment?"

"Of course!"

THE HÁRI JÁNOS

From the observation blister Ilona led Humbolt back down to the docking area, past the berth where their shuttle was moored, and to a smallish debarkation port. A team of six—two men, two women and two human-sized robots—were waiting there. They all snapped to stiff attention as Ilona stepped through the port's entrance hatch.

Behind the team ran a row of lockers. Glancing at Humbolt, Ilona said, "You are size eleven-A, so I was told."

He nodded, grinning. "You've done your homework."

Pointing to the lanky, redheaded man standing nearest her, Ilona said, "My assistant has."

It took several moments for them to pick suitable nanofabric space suits from the lockers and worm into them. The suits were light and transparent, like rain gear, except for the thick-soled boots and the glassteel bubble helmets.

With the robots standing inertly to one side, the four human crew members helped Ilona and Humbolt into the suits, hung the life-support backpacks on their shoulders, then quickly checked them.

"You are good for EVA," said the red-haired team leader, gesturing toward the airlock hatch at the locker room's far end.

Without a word Ilona clomped in the heavy boots toward the hatch, Humbolt behind her. Her heart was thumping with a mixture of excitement and fear, but she didn't want Humbolt to notice her emotions.

They stepped into the smallish, almost claustrophobic airlock, Ilona first. Once Humbolt stood beside her, the inner hatch swung slowly closed.

The airlock was bathed in lurid red light. An automated voice announced, "Evacuation initiated." Ilona heard the clatter of a pump that dwindled as the air was sucked out of the enclosure.

"Opening outer hatch," the mechanical voice announced.

Ilona stared wordlessly as the outer hatch swung open. She saw a spattering of stars, hard and bright, against the utter blackness of space. To one side hung the curve of Earth, green swaths of land and glittering blue ocean with a parade of purest white clouds marching across it.

And before them, slightly higher than their hatch, rode the huge sphere of *Hári János*, gleaming with reflected sunlight.

Without a word to Humbolt, she stepped to the edge of the airlock hatch and clipped the safety line coiled at her waist to one of the bolts ringing the airlock's hatch.

Humbolt said, "You know what you're doing, don't you?" She heard approval in his tone and was glad he couldn't hear her heart thumping beneath her ribs.

"Ready?" she asked him.

"Ready," Humbolt replied as he snapped his safety tether to one of the bolts along the opposite rim of the hatch.

Ilona stood for an endless moment at the edge of the hatch, then launched herself toward the massive globular spacecraft hanging a few dozen meters away. She made it to its oval entrance, gripped a bolt to keep herself from bouncing away, then pressed the stud that opened the outer hatch.

Humbolt glided up to her as the hatch slid open. He helped her connect her tether and then did his. With an exaggerated gesture, he pointed into the hatch's interior and said, "Ladies first."

Suppressing a flare of anger at his chauvinism, Ilona instead forced a smile and murmured, "Thank you, kind sir," as she disconnected her safety line from the shuttle's hatch and felt it reel up at her waist.

He disconnected himself from the shuttle too and entered the airlock behind her, waited until its display light turned green, then cracked the seal on his glassteel helmet.

With a pleasant smile he nodded and said, "Air's okay."

They floated through the inner hatch into a long tubular passageway that delved into the heart of the enormous spacecraft. Waiting in front of them was an open trolley that seated four people.

Humbolt grinned as he pushed his bubble helmet up and over his head, leaving it dangling at the back of his neck. As Ilona did the same he commented, "This is an improvement. When I rode this bucket we had to slide along a guide wire, like tourists on a zip line."

As she pulled herself into the waiting trolley, Ilona replied, "This is better."

"And safer," Humbolt added, sliding into the tiny car beside her and snapping his seatbelt.

Once they were both seated Ilona commanded, "Trolley *go!*"

The car started slowly down the long tube, picking up speed until the tunnel's walls became a blur. Overhead lights turned on as they rushed by, and turned off as they passed.

"This is fun!" Humbolt hollered as they raced down the featureless tunnel.

Ilona smiled, amused.

"Twelve spheres, nested inside each other," Humbolt said, in a schoolteacher's lecturing tone.

"That's how the ship deals with the increasing pressure as it goes deeper into Neptune's ocean," Ilona took up, to show she wasn't ignorant of the concept.

"Right."

"Theoretically, we can go all the way down to the ocean's bottom."

"I got about two-thirds of the way down to the bottom on Saturn, but one of the supporting pistons jammed and I had to go back up to the surface."

Ilona saw the frustration that still etched his face, so many years after that mission.

She said, "The pressure you faced there was more than what we'll have to deal with on Neptune."

As if he hadn't heard her, Humbolt muttered, "Two of my crew died on that mission. I've always wondered if it was something wrong that I did."

Their little trolley was slowing down noticeably.

"Almost there," Ilona said.

Humbolt nodded silently. She realized he was reliving the expedition to Saturn that had killed two of his crew.

They sat in silence as the trolley glided smoothly to a stop at the end of the long tunnel. They were at the heart of the massive spacecraft, Ilona knew. The place where they would spend weeks searching for her father's submersible. Would he still be alive inside it, Ilona wondered, waiting for me in cryonic suspension?

Humbolt floated onto the platform that ran the length of their little trolley. His smile looking a bit forced, he bent slightly and extended his hand to Ilona. She gracefully grabbed it and moved next to him. Both felt the magnetic pull of the platform on their boots.

"Here we are," he said.

Ilona nodded to the metal hatch at the end of the platform. "Ready to inspect our command center?" she asked.

He grinned at her. "After you, boss."

Command Center

with Humbolt a step behind her, Ilona walked to the end of the platform and said in a firm voice, "Hatch open, please."

The metal hatch immediately slid back. Ilona stepped through the open doorway and the interior chamber lit up brightly.

"Everything's voice activated within the twelve spheres?" he asked.

"Almost everything."

Humbolt brushed past her, then hesitated as his head swiveled, taking in the command center.

"You've really improved it," he murmured.

It was a circular chamber, its walls lined with display screens and rimmed with a continuous long, low sofa. At its center was a high-backed black-leather command chair, its armrests studded with control buttons, flanked on either side by two smaller chairs. Identical doors stood on either side of the compartment; the curved ceiling was the milky gray of still another set of display screens.

Dipping her chin toward the command chair, Ilona said, "You can run the entire ship by yourself." She pointed to a shining metal circlet studded with electronic receivers. "The sensor ring will connect all the ship's systems directly with your cerebral cortex."

"And all those control studs in the armrests?" he asked.

"One of many backups."

Jabbing a finger at the door to the left, Humbolt asked, "What's behind them?"

"Crew quarters," Ilona replied. "I don't intend to spend the next few months of my life without my comforts."

Humbolt brushed past her and went to the door. Opening it and walking along a short hallway. He came back a few minutes later and exclaimed, "Like a first-class hotel!"

Ilona said, "Two mini-suites on this side, two more in the other."

"But there's only the two of us."

She could see it in his eyes: the thought of sharing her bed.

Pointing across the command center to the other door, she explained, "Your quarters will be on that side. I'll bunk in here."

He looked more thoughtful than disappointed. "That still leaves two bedrooms unoccupied."

"One," Ilona corrected. "We're picking up a planetary scientist at Mars."

Humbolt's ruggedly handsome face registered surprise. And curiosity. "Male or female?"

"A young man from the University of Munich. His name is Jan Meitner. Very brilliant, I've found."

With a lascivious grin Humbolt asked, "Ménage à trois?"

"Nothing of the sort," Ilona answered sharply. "This mission is to find my father. And do some exploration. You can forget about your erotic imaginings."

To her surprise, Humbolt's grin did not shrink by as much as a millimeter. "Hearkening and obedience," he said, with a slight bow.

She knew what was going through his mind. Time is on my side, he was thinking.

The two of them returned their attention to the command center's equipment. Eying the food dispensers at the rear of the compartment, Humbolt seemed satisfied that he had everything he needed, even more. The ship was well equipped, and stocked with enough food stores to last three people for half a year, at least.

Standing behind the central command chair, he nodded approvingly. "You seem to have thought of everything."

Ilona responded, "I hired a team of the most renowned mission planners on Earth. They've thought of everything for me."

Humbolt lowered his head in silent acknowledgment. He checked the sensor ring.

"Have you seen enough?" she asked.

"For the moment." Casting his gaze around the viewscreens lining the circular chamber, he added, "I'd like to schedule a run-through tomorrow. Familiarize myself with the layout, get accustomed to the equipment, that sort of thing."

"Certainly," Ilona said.

As they stepped back to the hatch and the trolley waiting outside the command center, Humbolt asked, "This planetary scientist . . . how much do you know about him?"

Climbing down into the trolley, Ilona said, "I met him last year, at a seminar on Neptune's life-forms that I attended. He is a very fine young man, from a good family. He's studying the remains of the Martian civilization, digging through the ruins, that sort of thing."

"And he's giving that up to go to Neptune?"

"For what I'm paying him, I imagine he would go to the end of the Milky Way galaxy."

Humbolt lowered himself into the trolley seat next to her, in silence. But the expression on his face looked thoughtful, almost worried.

BOOK II

Neptune

Jan meitner paced slowly across the spaceport's passenger waiting area, casting his eyes skyward from time to time as he waited for the shuttle to arrive.

The waiting area was an amorphous enclosure up on the surface of the Red Planet, its dome-shaped ceiling made of transparent glassteel. It was empty except for him and his carefully packed travel bag, resting on one of the rickety little red chairs that lined the gray floor. Beyond its transparent dome the rusted sands of Mars marched out to the disturbingly close horizon. Beyond that was the butterscotch sky, empty and quiet.

Am I doing the right thing? Meitner asked himself again and again. The money is irresistible, he knew. But to leave the dig, to fly all the way out to Neptune. For what?

He knew why he had agreed to join this half-mad mission to Neptune. For the chance to see Ilona again, to be with her, to breathe the same air she would be breathing. To hear her voice again.

Jan Meitner was a young man in love, totally, hopelessly, endlessly. The chance to be with Ilona once more, to spend weeks with an actual baroness flying out to distant Neptune and then diving into that planet's deep ocean—it was more than he could have hoped for in his wildest dream.

Meitner was slight of build, a lifelong asthmatic who during his school days had been the butt of the other boys' jokes and cruel abuses. He stood precisely 177.8 centimeters tall, never able to achieve the full two meters that he longed for. Even if he had, he knew, he would still be several centimeters shorter than Ilona.

His body was slim, his arms bony and slender. He had almost been rejected for membership on the Mars exploration team because of his meager stature and fragile health, but he had squeezed past the medical team's examinations. Barely.

His face was lean, bony, his hair a nondescript brown, his eyes small, but inside his skull was an alert, eager, first-class brain. He had won honors in every school he attended, and even gained the grudging respect of the other scientists on the Mars team.

Now he paced the waiting room floor, looking anxiously up into the reddish-brown Martian sky for the shuttle that would take him to Ilona's ship as it passed on its way to distant, alien Neptune.

They had met at Harvard University in the United States, at a class in planetary geophysics they were both attending. Ilona was the center of attention wherever she went, pursued by a horde of eager young men, most of them attracted by her money rather than her boyish looks.

But after only a few weeks of the class they shared Jan found himself completely in love with Ilona Magyr. She was the brightest woman he had ever met: sparkling, lively, totally adorable.

He had never spoken of his love for her, fearful of her laughter; she seemed not to notice it. But they shared lunches together, gossiped about their professors and other students, discussed their studies, even went to dinner together occasionally.

Now Ilona was on her way to Neptune, searching for her lost father.

And she had invited Jan to come with her.

Two months alone with her. Probably more than two months. There'd be another person with them, a pilot Ilona had hired to run the ship. But he didn't matter, Jan thought. Two months or more buttoned into the spaceship, facing the unknowns and dangers of Neptune. Together. Side by side. Sooner or later he'd be able to confess his love to her.

Would she laugh at him? Scorn him? He didn't think he could survive a rejection from her. But sooner or later he would have to tell her of his love. Sooner or later he would make the biggest decision of his life.

"Shuttle 23F's arrival in twelve minutes," the overhead speaker announced.

Jan froze where he stood. This is it, he told himself silently. Like a legendary knight of old about to face a dragon, he stood erect and squared his lean shoulders.

But she's not a dragon, he told himself. Ilona is an angel. And I'm going to make her *my* angel.

The rocket shuttle landed on the pad nearest the spaceport's dome, settling tail-first into a billowing cloud of reddish dust. A long, curving automated tunnel inched from the dome to the shuttle's hatch, like a blindly groping caterpillar. One of the spaceport's staff came up from the warren of offices belowground, stepped into the waiting area and gestured Jan to the tunnel's hatch.

"Have a pleasant flight," she said automatically as he grabbed his travel bag and headed wordlessly to the tunnel's open hatch.

She doesn't know where I'm going and she doesn't care, Jan told himself. Then he thought, What if Ilona doesn't care? What if she invited me to go to Neptune purely as a junior science member of her expedition?

As he strode alone into the tunnel's slightly yielding plastic tubing, he shook his head stubbornly. No, that's not possible. She could have picked any planetary young scientist in the solar system she wanted and she picked me. Me!

By the time he reached the tunnel's end and stepped into the waiting shuttle he was actually smiling.

Aboard the *Hári János*, Ilona sat in one of the contoured seats that flanked the central command chair. Humbolt occupied that chair, the sensor ring atop his curly grizzled hair, his eyes sweeping the viewscreens surrounding him. Ilona saw on one of the screens a shuttle rocket roaring up from the surface of Mars.

Jan Meitner is on that bird, she told herself. He'll be an effective chaperone for me. He'll make Humbolt realize I'm here to find my father, not to play sex games with his oversized ego.

Suppressing a smile, she asked aloud, "Are they going to match our velocity?"

Humbolt nodded absently, his eyes never leaving the screens. "They're accelerating as scheduled," he said tightly.

He's all business now, Ilona thought. He puts his sex drive away when he's piloting. Good.

In truth, there was little piloting for Humbolt to do. *Hári János* was passing Mars, and the shuttle had to catch up with it and make rendezvous. Ilona watched the viewscreens as the two spacecrafts played their pas de deux in the emptiness of orbital space.

Ilona knew the shuttle had only one chance to make a successful meeting with her spaceship. It didn't have the fuel for a second attempt.

RENDEZVOUS

Ilona watched the central viewscreen as the shuttle neared and took form: stubby swept-back wings, rakish tail fin, chubby little fuselage like a sharply pointed torpedo.

The shuttle captain's voice sounded through the command center's speakers. "Matching your velocity." The woman's voice sounded tight, tense.

This isn't an ordinary rendezvous for her, Ilona realized. *Our velocity is much higher than anything she's had to match.*

But match it she did and within moments the shuttle was alongside *Hári János*, seemingly hovering beside Ilona's craft. She got up from her seat and went to the hatch in the compartment's rear.

"Going to be the welcoming committee?" Humbolt asked from the command chair, a cocky grin on his rugged face.

Ilona nodded, knowing he could see her in one of the viewscreens spread before him. She stepped through the hatch, closed it and went to the waiting trolley.

It took only a few minutes for the trolley to whiz her to the ship's main docking port. Jan Meitner was just stepping through the airlock hatch as the little car slowed to a halt at the end of the tunnel.

She got to her feet and climbed up onto the tiny platform as Meitner lugged his travel bag through the airlock's inner hatch.

His eyes widened at the sight of her. "Ilona!" he cried, loud enough to echo off the tunnel's metal walls.

He dropped his bag and strode toward her. Ilona stood at the edge of the platform, smiling, happy to see him.

"Jan," she said. "How are—"

He wrapped both his arms around her in a bear hug. Ilona's smile widened. "How are you?" she asked, almost breathless.

"Fine," he answered, then added, "Now that we're together again."

"Come on," she said, pointing to the little trolley. "Let me show you the ship."

He reached down and hefted his travel bag again, then followed her into the trolley, tossing the bag onto the empty cargo carrier behind them.

"I've studied your vessel's layout from the images on the news nets, impressive," Meitner said.

Ilona grinned at him. "I should have guessed."

As the trolley started accelerating he stared at her. "You look beautiful."

Ilona lowered her lashes and replied softly, "I'm not beautiful."

"I think you are."

For one of the rare times in her life, Ilona didn't know what to say. They whizzed through the long tunnel in silence.

At last, as the trolley began to slow down, Ilona said, "Derek Humbolt is captaining the ship."

Meitner nodded. "I know."

"I'll introduce him to you."

Meitner nodded, far less than enthusiastically.

The trolley stopped at last and they both got to their feet, then stepped up onto the platform.

"This way," Ilona said, heading for the hatch at the end of the area.

Ilona opened the hatch and held it while Meitner stepped through. Humbolt was still sitting in the command chair, his back to them.

"Derek?" she called.

"One minute," Humbolt answered, unmoving. "The shuttle's moving off, heading back to Mars."

Ilona saw the main viewscreen's image of the shuttle; it seemed to be dwindling, moving away.

"Disengagement successful," the shuttle captain's voice came through the speakers. "We're on our way home."

"Happy trails," said Humbolt, with a smile in his voice. Then he got up from his command chair, the sensor ring on his head, and turned to Ilona and Meitner. Jan saw that he towered over him. Stepping around the high-backed chair, Humbolt extended his right hand.

"Welcome aboard, Dr. Meitner."

Grasping the offered hand, Jan replied, "Thank you, Mr. Humbolt."

"*Captain* Humbolt."

"Oh. Yes, of course. Captain Humbolt."

Ilona glanced back and forth from Meitner to Humbolt. Rivalry? she asked herself. Competition. Two males, sizing up each other.

There wasn't much of a comparison, Ilona realized. Humbolt was taller than Jan, bulkier, his face set in rigid determination. Jan looked almost like a little boy next to him.

A little boy with hard-edged, purposeful eyes the color of a summer sky . . . just before a thunderstorm.

ON TO NEPTUNE

Things settled into an almost boring routine as *Hári János* cruised out toward Neptune.

Humbolt spent most of his time in the command center, watching over the vessel's highly automated systems. How does he stand the monotony? Ilona asked herself as day after day the man sat there idly, his eyes flicking from one viewscreen to the next, his fingers fiddling impatiently over the armrests of his command chair.

Meitner also made himself scarce, closeting himself in his quarters, next to Humbolt's. When Ilona asked him what he was doing, alone in the mini-suite, Jan answered that he was studying all the available information about the conditions of Neptune's planet-wide ocean.

"My father's ship is somewhere in that ocean," Ilona told him, more than once.

"Yes," Meitner would reply. "I've got the tracking data on his vessel."

"Will we be able to find him?"

"We'll try."

The only bearable times for Ilona were the meals that the three of them shared together. The rear of the command center served as an informal canteen, where the three of them would gather to select meals from the dispensers lining the bulkhead and sit at the ample table on the chairs to eat and chat.

It's an ancient ritual, Ilona knew, sharing food and stories. At first Humbolt dominated the talk with tales of his missions to Jupiter and Saturn.

Over the weeks of their travel out to Neptune, Jan gradually began to speak up about his own experiences.

"The Martians were certainly intelligent," he insisted, over dinner one evening. "They built cities—"

"Cities?" Humbolt challenged. "You call those collections of mud huts *cities*?"

"Well . . . villages, at least."

Humbolt nodded. Ilona thought he looked satisfied that he had maintained the dominant alpha position of their little trio.

"They knew they were going to die," Meitner said, his voice low, almost mournful. "They saw the vegetation around them withering away after the meteor swarm struck. Their homes were smashed. Their civilization destroyed."

A tragedy, Ilona said to herself.

"And there was nothing they could do about it," Meitner mourned.

With a cocky grin, Humbolt said, "Too bad they hadn't developed spaceflight."

"They hadn't even developed internal-combustion engines," said Meitner. "They depended on draft animals."

"Fly or die," Humbolt said. "With spaceflight, we've detached the fate of the human race from the fate of planet Earth."

Meitner nodded dumbly. But his face still looked grief-stricken.

Ilona spoke very little when the two men disputed, content to let them compete. Smiling inwardly, she thought that as long as they contested for leadership she could maintain some measure of control over both of them.

The ship's prefrozen meals were pretty good, Ilona thought. Prepared by one of the finest chefs in half-drowned Venice, they offered a variety of Italian, French and even gourmet Mexican dishes with suitable wines.

It was as the three of them were finishing a pleasant dinner together one evening that the emergency alarm suddenly started hooting.

"What's that?" Jan shouted over the loud blaring.

Humbolt pushed his chair back and got to his feet. "Probably a malfunction somewhere . . ."

He turned and walked back to the command chair, placing the sensor ring back on his head. Ilona also stood up and noticed that several of the viewscreens around the curving bulkheads were flashing red EMERGENCY warnings.

Meitner looked alarmed. "What is it?" he repeated as he got up from his chair.

Humbolt plopped down onto the command chair. "This could be serious," he shouted over the warning Klaxon's wailing.

"What's wrong?" Ilona demanded.

"Looks like a failure in the oxygen feed," Humbolt shouted. His fingers grabbed tightly to his chair's armrests. The viewscreens around him blinked from one image to another in a frenzied flashing display.

"Get into your emergency suits!" Humbolt bellowed. "*Now!*"

Jan grabbed Ilona's wrist and pulled her toward the hatch that led to the emergency supplies.

"Quickly!" he screamed at her.

Through the hatch and down a short passageway they dashed. Jan pushed through the hatch at its end. There the emergency suits hung, empty, lifeless. He led Ilona to the suit that was hers.

"Into it," he commanded. "*Quickly!*"

As she reached for the nanofabric suit hanging in its cabinet, Ilona asked, "What about you?"

"You first," he snapped. "Come on!"

Ilona stepped into the suit and wormed her feet into its boots, then pulled the sleeves on and started to seal its front. The warning Klaxon seemed to be blaring louder, screaming in her ears.

At last she was able to pull the glassteel helmet over her head, tuck her hair inside and finish sealing the suit's front. She felt Jan, behind her, hanging the air tanks onto the hooks on her back.

"Good!" he said, approvingly.

"Now you," she told him.

Ilona helped Jan climb into his own suit, watched him wriggle his arms through the transparent sleeves, pull the helmet over his head and seal it to the suit's neck ring. She hefted the backpack and hung it onto him.

"Done," she said.

Meitner was breathing heavily. Even through the suit's helmet Ilona could hear his asthmatic wheezing.

But he grinned at her. "We're okay," he said, his voice a painful croak.

Decked in the emergency suits, the two of them went back through the hatch into the command center. Humbolt was standing beside his command chair, fists on his hips, a wide grin splitting his face.

The Klaxons stopped wailing. The viewscreens' red warnings disappeared.

Humbolt glanced at his wristwatch. "Two hundred and fifteen seconds," he said, still grinning. "Damned near five minutes. You're going to have to do better than that. A lot better."

Ilona felt her brows knitting in puzzlement. Meitner grasped the situation immediately.

"It was a test," he said. "Not a real emergency."

Nodding, Humbolt replied, "That's right. And the two of you flunked it. If we'd had a real oxy failure you'd both be dead by now."

Ilona felt a flare of anger. "A test?"

"A drill. Emergency-procedure drill. And two of you flunked it."

DEBRIEFING

Humbolt could see Ilona's face reddening as she said, in a barely controlled voice, "You scared us half to death for a goddamned *drill?*"

Humbolt's easy smile didn't waver. "I had to see how you'd react to a real emergency. It's standard shipboard practice, emergency drills."

"Standard shipboard practice," Meitner growled as he lifted the bubble helmet off his head.

As she too began to pull off her emergency suit, Ilona said, "Jan nearly had an asthma attack."

With a careless shrug, Humbolt answered, "Imagine how the two of you would've reacted if it'd been a real emergency."

Before Ilona could respond, Meitner held up a hand. "He's right," Jan said. "It was a drill and we flunked it." He shrugged out of his backpack and unsealed the front of his suit.

"But . . ." Ilona got no farther. She realized she had really nothing to say.

Looking totally relaxed, at ease, Humbolt suggested, "It might be better if we stored the emergency suits here in the command center, instead of down the passageway."

"Where?" Ilona demanded, as she wriggled out of her backpack.

Pointing, Humbolt replied, "Back there, beside the food dispensers. That'd cut thirty seconds off your response time, at least."

Meitner nodded wordlessly and finished pulling his feet out of the suit's boots. Draping the empty suit over one arm, he said, "I'll go back and get the hangers, and set them up beside the dispensers."

He turned and went to the hatch. Once he was through it Ilona turned back to Humbolt. "That was cruel, Derek."

"So would a real emergency be cruel. We've got to be ready for anything that happens."

Ilona saw rock-hard determination on his face, heard it in his tone of voice. She said, "I suppose so. But still . . ."

"As captain of this ship my job is to keep the three of us alive, no matter what happens."

Ilona nodded, but inwardly she still thought that Derek Humbolt had enjoyed frightening her. And Jan.

For one of the few times in her life, Ilona felt bored. The *Hári János* was speeding toward Neptune, she knew, but as far as she could tell the globular vessel was hanging motionless in space, suspended in the star-spattered darkness, achingly far from Earth, from home, from all that she had taken for granted all her life.

They passed Jupiter's orbit, but the giant planet was on the other side of the Sun, too far from them to be anything but a gleaming star. Saturn was a better sight: they passed close enough to it to see its brilliant rings and even a few of its orbiting moons, thanks to the ship's telescopes. By the time they crossed Uranus's orbit they had reached the turnaround point, where Humbolt started the ship's long deceleration that would end in establishing orbit around their target, Neptune.

Ilona had expected Derek Humbolt to show interest in her, but the ship's captain paid her no romantic attention at all. He probably has all sorts of porno vids and sex simulations in his quarters, she told herself, disappointed at his lack of interest and angry at herself for being disappointed. Jan Meitner is working too well, she thought. His presence is interfering with Derek's male libido.

So the vessel plowed on through the dreary emptiness of interplanetary space, not another ship within several million kilometers, not another person to talk with except Humbolt and Jan.

Ilona found herself fantasizing. What if I showed Derek that I was interested in him? Could I lure him away from his vids and his simulations? How would Jan react to that?

She even found herself wondering how it might be if both men were attracted to her.

But neither of them was, she thought. I'm all alone a billion kilometers from civilization with two adult males and neither one of them has shown the slightest interest in me.

A memory of Shakespeare rose in her mind: "I all alone beweep my outcast state."

Outcast state, she repeated to herself. You've outsmarted yourself, madame.

arrival

For several days now Ilona stared, fascinated, at the image of the planet Neptune on the command center's main viewscreen.

Slightly flattened at the poles, it was a round cobalt-cerulean blue ball hanging against a background of stars. A whitish tornadic storm stood out like a fat comma a quarter of the way between its north pole and equator.

Triton hung off to one side, grayish and dead-looking. Neptune's other moons were too small to be seen without telescopic amplification.

"There she is," Humbolt said as Neptune finally covered almost all of the viewscreens.

Standing to one side of the high-backed chair, Ilona nodded wordlessly.

She was staring at the viewscreen image now, it was so close. Father is there, somewhere in that serene-looking sphere, beneath the ice, at the bottom of the ocean. Is he still alive? Is he waiting for me to find him and bring him home?

Today, Jan Meitner was standing beside Ilona, all but forgotten as she gazed at the planet, their destination, their goal.

Over the next few hours, the gravitational pull from Neptune started to make the trio feel heavy and their movements awkward. However, Captain Humbolt was able to control the ship's balance. He checked and rechecked the entry point, antigravitational maneuvers and shields.

"Vacation's over," Humbolt said, his voice ringing through the command center. "Now we go to work."

Meitner said, "I have all the available data on where Baron Magyr's ship was when its last message capsule was released."

"So do I," Humbolt said, his eyes—like Ilona's—riveted on the viewscreen image of the planet.

"I believe we can use the positional data to predict where his ship went after he'd sent his last message capsule to the surface."

"Do you?" Humbolt's tone dripped disbelief.

"Yes, I do," said Meitner, either missing the tone of challenge in Humbolt's voice or deliberately ignoring it.

Meitner continued, "The baron's last message said he had picked up a trace of a magnetic anomaly, a fairly powerful magnetic signal—"

"This whole ocean is filled with magnetic blurps and beeps," Humbolt grumbled.

"But this one was quite strong," Meitner countered. "So strong that the baron went searching for its origin."

Ilona asked, "Jan, do you have the data on that anomaly?"

Meitner nodded. "Yes, I do."

"I'd like to see it."

His face flushing slightly, Meitner replied, "It's . . . it's on my personal data disk. In my quarters."

Turning toward him, Ilona said, "Could you show it to me, please?"

Humbolt said, "I can pull it up on a screen here."

"No," said Ilona. "I'll go with Jan."

And she followed Meitner out of the command center. She could feel Humbolt's eyes on her back.

They went through the door and into the short passageway that fronted the mini-suites that Meitner and Humbolt occupied. Jan's hands trembled slightly, "open door," he said, and gestured Ilona inside.

His living room was an almost exact duplicate of her own, but spotless. Everything was in its place: even the built-in desk opposite the small sofa was clear of papers or any other sign that someone had been living in this suite for weeks.

Ilona looked around, saw through the open door to the bedroom that Jan had made his bed neatly.

"You're such a perfect housekeeper," she said, smiling. "My rooms are a complete mess."

"The robots do most of the work," Meitner said, almost sheepishly. He went to the minuscule desk and stood beside its padded chair.

"I have all the data that your father sent up to the ocean's surface," he said.

Ilona remained standing before the sofa, on the other side of the tiny room.

"How did you get that?" she asked.

"From the Astronomical Association," he replied. "Once I showed them the employment contract you sent me they were only too happy to help me."

"I see."

For an awkward moment he stood there at the desk. Then at last he sat in its chair and commanded the desktop computer to show the data he'd been working with onto a large viewscreen. The viewscreen glowed to life and Ilona saw a map of Neptune's virtually featureless ice-covered surface and the track of her father's submersible through the planet-wide ocean.

"That's his last reported position," Meitner said, pointing to the image floating in midair. "The last of his message carriers came to the surface at that point."

Ilona stared at the dot in the vast ocean. She knew its location as well as Meitner did; better, she thought. She had every message her father had sent up to the surface burned into her memory.

"His last message contained no information on where he was heading," she said.

"Not quite," Meitner corrected. "The message was filled with extraneous information about the magnetic anomaly."

Despite herself, Ilona sighed. "He could be anywhere, then, couldn't he?"

With a stubborn shake of his head, Meitner replied, "I don't think so. He'd been following a rather straight course through the ocean, as though there was a specific spot that he wanted to reach. . . ."

"You think so?"

"Look at the record. He piloted his sub on a more or less straight line, halfway across the ocean."

"More or less," Ilona echoed.

"He had a destination in mind, I'm sure of it."

"A destination? What destination?" Ilona demanded. "There's nothing in that ocean that could be a destination. It's empty. We know that from the earlier exploration missions."

Meitner turned in his swivel chair to face her. "I'm certain he was heading for a specific location."

Ilona shook her head.

Still in the desk chair, Meitner asked, "Why did your father go to Neptune? What was he seeking?"

"He considered himself an amateur scientist," Ilona replied. "Like the great ones in the old days, Humphry Davy, Faraday, Darwin . . . gentlemen scientists. Before science became an academic specialty."

"But he must have had some goal in mind," Meitner insisted. "Some reason to trek all the way out to Neptune."

"Knowledge," said Ilona. "He was seeking new knowledge." And glory, she added silently. Father wanted the world to recognize him.

"Knowledge of what?" Meitner insisted. "He must have had some goal in mind, some objective that he wanted to reach."

With a slight shrug, Ilona half whispered, "We'll have to ask him once we've found him."

Meitner stared at her for a long moment, then turned back to the viewscreen. Ilona knew what was going through his mind: finding a lone submersible in an ocean almost four times bigger than the entire Earth was a well-nigh impossible task.

Well-nigh impossible. But she was determined to try her best.

INTO THE OCEAN

++++++++++ +++ +++++++++ ++++++++ +++ +++++ +++++ +++++
++++ +++++ +++ +++++ ++++ ++++++++++++++++ +++++ ++++

тhe three of them sat in the command center, Humbolt in his central chair, ιlona and meitner in the cushioned seats flanking him on either side.

The main viewscreen showed Neptune's all-encompassing sheath of ice hurtling by below them, creeping closer and closer as their ship dipped toward it. Ilona saw that the ice heaved and buckled as the ocean below it surged restlessly.

"Altitude fifteen thousand meters and decreasing steadily," announced the ship's automated navigation system.

His eyes riveted to the main viewscreen, Humbolt said tightly, "We're approaching the spot where Baron Magyr's last message carrier broke to the surface."

Ilona nodded wordlessly.

"Insertion point in three hundred twenty seconds," the nav system said.

"Strap in," Humbolt commanded.

All three of them pulled their safety harnesses over their shoulders and across their thighs, then clicked the fasteners shut.

"Releasing the nuke," Humbolt said.

Hári János carried a pair of small missiles, each armed with a ten-kiloton nuclear weapon, to break the ice that covered the ocean. Ilona had spent several weeks convincing the Interplanetary Council's governing board to allow them to carry the nukes and to use them. She had even slept with one of the Council members, to assure his vote.

She felt nothing as the nuclear-armed missile separated from their ship and plunged toward the ice.

"Trajectory looks good," Humbolt muttered. Ilona saw a red line tracing across the main screen, hugging the green line that represented the missile's planned trajectory.

"Hang on!"

The viewscreen erupted with a star-hot fireball. Ilona squeezed her eyes shut; the afterimage of the blast glowed against her closed eyelids. She heard Meitner gasp.

The shock wave hit them, and *Hári János* bucked and shuddered like a thing alive. But within moments the jouncing smoothed out and the ship was back to normal.

Humbolt's voice, sounding pleased, said, "Now we go into the water."

Opening her eyes, Ilona saw a wide swath of foaming water spread across the main viewscreen. She glanced at the screen on her left: radioactivity in the atmosphere was minimal. The missile had penetrated the ice before triggering its bomb.

Humbolt was counting down, "Thirty seconds to impact . . . twenty-five . . . twenty . . ."

Ilona squeezed her eyes shut again and clutched the seat's armrests in a grip of steel.

She heard Humbolt's powerful voice. "Here we go!"

Ilona felt a jolting force slam against her, rattling every bone in her body. She tasted blood in her mouth. Her eyes snapped open and she saw Humbolt sitting rigidly beside her and, beyond him, Jan Meitner—his eyes wide, his face white with shock.

Humbolt shook his head, as if trying to clear it after a heavy blow. The viewscreens arrayed around the command center showed nothing but bubbling, frothing water.

"We made it!" Humbolt shouted, a cocky grin breaking across his chiseled features.

Meitner was gulping air, his chest heaving. Ilona felt as if some barbarian had pummeled her from crown to toes.

"We made it," she echoed, in the tiny voice of a frightened child.

"Everybody all right?" Humbolt asked.

"Yes," said Ilona.

Meitner wheezed, "I think so."

Humbolt was already checking the ship's maintenance screens. "Compression pistons came through okay. No permanent damage. Number sixteen's jammed a bit but the robots are already working on it."

"That was . . ." Meitner seemed to grope for a word.

"A jolt," said Humbolt.

"A shock," Meitner corrected, his voice almost back to normal.

"I tried to warn you," Humbolt said, almost testily. "I gave you both several briefings."

"Briefings don't prepare you for the real thing," Ilona said.

With a nod and a grunt, Humbolt said grudgingly, "Well, we got through it okay. We're in the ocean now, let's turn on some lights."

Meitner agreed. "Now we can follow the extended track of Baron Magyr's vessel."

As the lights adjusted, Ilona glanced at the viewscreens that half surrounded them. Hundreds of creatures were floating and swimming through the ocean, thousands of them. Millions. The ocean was teeming with animals flicking past their submersible, the bigger ones chasing the smaller ones.

Then she noticed swarms of dead creatures, killed by their nuclear icebreaker. The living fish were feasting on them.

Kill or be killed, she thought. The eternal, mindless cycle of life and death. What else will we kill down here in this ocean? What will kill us?

After diving deeper and setting their course, Humbolt rubbed his hands together and declared, "It's past time for lunch. I'm starving!"

He got up from the command chair and headed back to their makeshift galley. Ilona rose to her feet, somewhat shakily, and followed him. Meitner, after remaining seated long enough to make Ilona wonder if he was going to join them, pushed himself up to his feet. Slowly.

Humbolt selected soup and a sandwich from the dispensers, then sat down and took a healthy bite from the sandwich. Ilona sat next to him, Meitner on his other side.

"We're cut off from the rest of the universe now," Humbolt said without preamble. "The seawater cuts off radio and laser communication with the world beyond this ocean."

"We have the communication capsules," Meitner said. "We can send messages through them."

"Yes," Humbolt agreed. "But we can't get any messages back from the outside. We're in a communications blackout."

"We knew that from the outset," said Ilona. "We're on our own."

"No help if we run into trouble," Meitner grumbled.

"No one to share the glory with," Humbolt amended.

"If we die," Meitner said, "no one outside will know what happened to us."

Ilona stared at him, remembering a line from a dreary Teutonic saga she had read as a student: *We'll all be buried in unmarked graves.*

PErFLUOrIDE

After more than half an hour of staring in fascination at the ocean scenes that the viewscreens were showing, Humbolt asked, "Well, let's see . . . where do we go from here? Deeper, or should we stay at this level a while longer?"

"Deeper," Ilona replied immediately. "My father intended to go all the way down to the bottom."

"Did he?" Humbolt muttered.

"That's what killed him," said Meitner. "The pressure became too powerful for his submersible to handle."

"You don't know that," Ilona snapped, as if the scientist had just insulted her. "He calculated the pressures his ship would face. He knew what he was doing."

"Then why did his vessel fail?"

Her face radiating irritation, Ilona answered, "We'll find out when we reach his ship."

Meitner looked as if he were going to reply, but instead closed his mouth and remained silent.

His face dead serious, Humbolt said, "I want to remind you, Ilona, that our chances of actually finding your father's submersible are pretty damned close to zero."

Ilona stared at him, her expression icy. "We go deeper," she said, in a whisper that could cut steel.

Humbolt nodded. "Aye, boss. After I check out all the ship's systems and make certain everything's working as it should."

Silence enveloped the command center. Humbolt patiently reviewed all the status reports on the submersible's various control systems while Meitner studied the data that the cameras and other sensors were reporting on the sea life in the ocean outside. Ilona, with nothing to do, wanted to ask Humbolt for an assignment, any assignment that would keep her busy, but instead she sat rigidly silent.

Suddenly Meitner shouted, "Look!" as he pointed to the viewscreen at his right.

Ilona turned and saw a large creature undulating through the water, more than a dozen sucker-lined tentacles waving before it.

"A squid!" she shouted.

"The Neptunian equivalent of a squid," Meitner corrected.

Humbolt said, "Sure looks like a squid to me."

"Superficial resemblance," said Meitner. Then, as if reciting from a textbook, "Neptunian cephalopods are six to ten times larger than the biggest terrestrial varieties. They are born with two tentacles but grow eight to twelve additional ones as they age. Each tentacle has an eyestalk at its tip . . ."

Ilona tuned out his droning voice as soon as she realized that Jan was indeed reciting from a text he had memorized. She focused her attention on the screen as the squid-like creature undulated closer to the ship.

"Looks like it's checking us out," Humbolt said. "I'd better activate the stun system."

Meitner interrupted his own recital. "Don't harm it! It's merely investigating something it's never seen before. It's curious!"

But Humbolt muttered, "Just a warning jolt . . ."

The squid swam even closer, its many arms snaking out to ensnare the submersible and blocking 5 of the 30 cameras. The three humans watched, fascinated, as the creature slowly, cautiously approached.

One arm stretched out toward them. Ilona could see the eye at its end, unblinking, as blue as the surrounding gel-like water.

It's going to touch us, she said to herself, with an uncontrollable shudder.

The command center's lights blinked and the viewscreens went blank momentarily. When they came on again the squid was hovering alongside the submersible, its long arm recoiled, its eye blazing red.

"You hurt it!" she shouted at Humbolt.

"Just a little bit," he said back to her. "A lesson. Don't touch us. Keep your distance."

In a hollowed voice, Meitner said, "I think it's learned the lesson."

The squid dived beneath their submersible and shot away with the speed of a torpedo.

"By god, it's got a jet propulsion system, just like squids on Earth!" Humbolt exclaimed.

"Similar environments give rise to similar adaptations," Meitner quoted.

Ilona watched the squid rapidly disappear into the depths of the ocean. Can they communicate with one another? she wondered. If they can, that one has an intriguing tale to tell its comrades.

The hours dragged by. Ilona watched the viewscreen displays. Plenty of fish-like things darting past and amorphous creatures that looked like blobs of shapeless jelly. But no other squid.

Maybe they actually do have communication capability, Ilona thought. The one we shocked must be telling its tale to the others of its kind.

Gradually she realized the command center was becoming uncomfortable. The air felt thick, heavy enough almost to knead with your fingers, like putty. Meitner's chest was heaving noticeably and even Humbolt looked unhappy as he sat in the command chair and studied the viewscreen displays.

"How deep are we?" she heard herself ask.

One of the viewscreens flashed a depth meter. "Two-thirds of the way to the bottom," Humbolt replied, his voice sounding deeper than normal.

"Pressure's building," said Meitner, almost gasping.

"Will we be able to go lower?" Ilona asked.

"Yes," Humbolt responded. Then he added, "But we'll have to go on the full-immersion mode."

Ilona knew what that meant and dreaded it. She saw from Meitner's anxious expression that he understood, too.

Full immersion. Swallowing high-density perfluoride-laced liquid, filling your body with the slimy stuff so that you could stand up to the increasing pressure that you'd be immersed in. It was inhuman, perverse, sadistic. But necessary if they were to descend further into the higher densities at the lower levels of the Neptunian ocean.

"When . . ." Ilona hesitated, then went on, "When will we have to make the transition?"

Humbolt tried to smile, almost made it. "Now is as good a time as any," he said.

She nodded wordlessly.

Turning in Meitner's direction, Humbolt said, "You can be first, Dr. Meitner."

Meitner nodded uncertainly.

Humbolt grinned. "Actually, all three of us will have to swallow the perfluoride mix at pretty much the same time. I'll be increasing the density of the air around us, turning it into soup steam, sort of." They all went to the transition room and took their seats while the room was pressurized.

Meitner's face clearly showed fear. And Ilona saw that Humbolt was enjoying it.

"Come on, Jan," she encouraged. "The sooner we start the process the sooner we'll get through it."

Meitner nodded again. In Ilona's eyes the poor man looked terrified. He knew we were going to have to go through this, Ilona said to herself. Then she realized, But that doesn't mean he's happy about it.

Abruptly three breathing masks dropped down from the ceiling, bouncing and dangling in front of their faces. Humbolt grabbed his in both hands and began strapping it over his nose and mouth. Ilona did the same, and noticed that Jan's hands trembled visibly as he followed suit.

Courage is not the lack of fear, she told herself as she fixed the straps round her lower face. Courage is acting in spite of your fear.

Jan has courage, she realized.

At first she thought the perfluoride liquid would choke her. It felt cold and slimy as she gulped it down. Her insides seemed to chill, to freeze, almost, as the chemical spread through her body. She tried to relax. This must be what hell feels like, Ilona thought: inhumanly cold, the loss of warmth, the spark of life smothered in frigid bleakness.

It took nearly an hour, but at last the three of them could unfasten the masks and let them snake back up to their compartments in the ceiling. Ilona felt distressed, uncomfortable, as if she had a headache that extended all the way down to her toes.

Then Humbolt said, in a strangely low-pitched voice, "Pressurizing the command center."

Neither Ilona nor Meitner made any reply.

Gradually, Ilona felt better. After some ten minutes the command center seemed almost normal. She could breathe with hardly any effort, and the compartment looked the way it did before they'd started to inhale the perfluoride mixture.

"Congratulations, people," said Humbolt. "We're now capable of going down to the bottom of the ocean without crushing our bodily cavities."

Meitner nodded and even smiled. Weakly.

BATTLE

The viewscreen displays of the ocean around them showed an almost empty deep blue wasteland. No, not wasteland, Ilona told herself. We are surrounded by seawater, water that contains a high ratio of methane and ammonia and god knows what other admixtures.

The water looked hazy at this depth, but it seemed almost empty of active life. A few amorphous creatures drifted by, no larger than terrestrial polyps. There must be microscopic organisms out there, too, Ilona thought, too small to be seen. Now and then a larger fish-like animal swam sleekly by, smooth and purposeful.

She turned and studied the medical readouts displayed on one of the screens to her left. No red displays, she saw. The three of us are in good physical condition, despite the pressure. She realized that she was breathing normally now, and so was Humbolt. Jan's chest was still heaving, but noticeably less than earlier.

"How far to the bottom?" she asked, surprised at how deep her voice sounded.

"A little more than an hour," Humbolt replied, also in a bass tone.

Meitner looked almost normal, glancing from one viewscreen to the next, tapping out notes on his personal handheld. Why doesn't he use its voice-recognition system? Ilona wondered. But he looked so intent as he fingered the handheld's miniaturized keyboard that she refrained from questioning him.

All at once Meitner visibly stiffened. Nearly dropping the handheld from his lap, he pointed to a viewscreen off in the far right corner of the display area.

"What's that?" he whispered, fearfully.

Ilona saw that Jan was staring at a gigantic amorphous mass of jelly, many times larger than their vessel. It glowed in the darkness of the watery depths, undulating slowly as it approached their submersible.

"Don't know," Humbolt answered, sounding more annoyed than frightened. In a louder voice he commanded, "Display listing of known Neptunian organisms, by size, largest first."

The central screen showed an image of one of the squid-like animals, then pictures of smaller Neptunian creatures.

Ilona stated the obvious: "It's not on the list."

Breaking into a crooked grin, Meitner exulted, "We've discovered a new life-form!"

"Zippity-doo-dah," said Humbolt, his tone ironic, sarcastic.

The thing was extending long, finger-like extrusions in various directions, and then pulling them back into its shapeless main body. Ilona saw that its surface looked splotchy, dotted with squirming, pulsating cells.

"It looks like a giant amoeba," she said.

Humbolt's gaze was fixed on the approaching creature. "Heading our way."

"More likely just territorial behavior," Meitner said.

His voice awed, "It's *huge*!"

"Ten-twelve times bigger than we are," Humbolt estimated.

Ilona felt a cold clutch of fear in her gut. "Maybe it wants to eat us."

"We'll give it a shock," Humbolt said.

This time Meitner nodded agreement.

"Here it comes!" Ilona shouted.

The huge creature's shapeless mass filled the viewscreen. The submersible shuddered as the monster began to engulf it.

Humbolt leaned forward. The command center's lights blinked out, then came on again. But the viewscreen showed the giant amoeba-like mass was engulfing the ship.

"It's not reacting to the electric shock!" Humbolt shouted.

"Increase the voltage!" Meitner yelled.

"I've used the maximal current!"

"Do something!"

"What?"

The submersible jounced and shook as the amoeboid's gelatinous mass swallowed it. Ilona stared wide-eyed at the diagnostic viewscreen. It showed that the sensors arrayed along the sub's outer skin were reporting highly acidic chemicals flowing across them.

Is this what happened to Father? Was his ship gobbled up by one of these giant creatures? Swallowed and digested?

Her mind recoiled at the idea.

"Do something!" Meitner screamed again.

And again Humbolt shouted back, "Do what?"

Still staring at the sensor screen, Ilona saw the level of the acidic chemicals was receding rapidly. The amoeba's slimy mass retreated from the ship's outer skin.

"It's going away!" she yelled, pointing at the screen.

"Thank god for small miracles," Humbolt muttered.

Meitner crossed himself, rapidly, several times over.

Still staring at the sensor screen, Ilona said in a shaking voice, "It didn't like how we taste."

"It spit us out!" Humbolt agreed.

The main viewscreen showed the amoeboid creature slinking away.

The three of them slumped in their chairs, gasping as if they'd sprinted hundreds of meters.

"We're all right," Ilona said, more to herself than the two men. "We're safe."

Humbolt recovered some of his male ego. "The damned thing decided we're not food."

More calmly, Meitner said, "But our electric-shock system didn't seem to bother it at all."

"Was it working correctly?" Ilona asked.

"Yes," said Humbolt. "Diagnostics show it worked as designed. At full power."

"We're going to need something better for the next time we meet one of those creatures," said Meitner.

Humbolt cocked a brow at him. "You tell me what you think will work, *Doctor* Meitner, and I'll try to build it for you."

Ilona sat in silence, watching the two men glaring at each other. Back to normal, she thought. Then a shudder of memory ran through her. I don't want to run into one of those amoeba things again, she knew.

Pressures

"Approaching the bottom," Humbolt announced.

Needlessly, Ilona thought. She could see the ocean's floor, a broad surface of flat, almost feature-less gray, glowing slightly through the murky seawater.

Sweeping her eyes across the command center's viewscreens, Ilona saw that all the submersible's systems were operating within tolerable limits. The vessel's multiple layers of compressible shells surrounding them were protecting them from the tremendous pressure outside, she realized gratefully.

It wasn't the pressure down at this depth that destroyed Father's vessel, she told herself. Maybe it's still intact down here on the bottom.

Strangely, that thought did not cheer her. She felt the weight of the ocean's pressure as if it were squeezing directly upon her, clutching her, crushing her.

She shook her head, trying to clear her mind of such dreadful thoughts. We're here at the bottom of the sea, she thought. The vessel protects us. We're safe. And we have a task to complete.

Where is Father's submersible?

Humbolt asked the same question, aloud. "Which way, Dr. Meitner?"

Meitner glanced at the handheld computer on his lap, then called out a course setting.

"Okay," said Humbolt, "here we go."

We're here, heading toward Father's vessel, Ilona reasoned. We're on our way.

Jan Meitner's voice broke into her thoughts:

"The sea bottom is composed of superionic ice," he said, in a flat, lecturing voice. "The pressure down at this level forces the oxygen atoms of the water into a lattice, stronger than steel, while the hydrogen atoms flow like liquid through the lattice."

Humbolt responded, "Pretty hot for ice, Doc." Nodding toward one of the viewscreens at his right, he went on, "Temperature of that stuff we're seeing is more than forty-five hundred degrees Celsius."

"It's ice," Meitner insisted. "Not like any ice you see on Earth, except in a specialized laboratory."

Humbolt shrugged.

"I'd like to measure the electromagnetic fields generated by the hydrogen atoms' motion," Meitner went on. "They probably have an important influence on the storms that have been observed up on the surface."

Sounding bored, Humbolt replied, "Be my guest—as long as your measuring doesn't interfere with any of the ship's systems."

Nodding happily, Meitner said, "I'll be careful."

Humbolt turned and grinned at Ilona.

The male ego, she thought. Derek's got to show that he's in command of everything.

Ilona cleared her throat, then said, "Jan, our primary goal is to find my father's ship, and—"

"I won't interfere with that," Meitner interrupted. "But you promised the Astronomical Association you'd give them the results of whatever we find down here. Well, connecting the electromagnetic activity down here at the seabed with the storms up on the surface would be a real achievement, a significant discovery."

Nodding, Ilona replied, "Okay, I understand."

But one look at Humbolt's sudden unsmiling expression showed that he didn't. And he didn't care.

The hours dragged by. Humbolt sat in his command chair, the sensor ring tilted slightly atop his mop of curly dark hair, his eyes half-closed. He's drowsing, Ilona told herself. He'll snap into full awakeness if anything unusual pops up on the screens.

Or so she hoped.

The screens showing the outside view presented a scene of nearly complete desolation: the ocean seemed almost totally empty of life down at this level, except for an occasional tiny crustacean floating aimlessly past. The ocean floor itself was utterly bare: not a form of plant life in sight, not even a leaf of kelp or any kind of algae.

"It's a desert out there," Meitner whispered.

"Not much life," Ilona agreed.

Humbolt made no reaction. To Ilona he seemed to be fully asleep, although his eyes were still half-open.

At last the master clock on the central screen showed 1800 hours. Dinnertime. But neither Humbolt nor Meitner got up from their seats.

"Aren't either of you hungry?" Ilona asked.

"Not very," Meitner replied, although he started to push himself up from his chair.

Humbolt didn't move.

As she rose to her feet, Ilona called sharply, "Derek, are you awake?"

His eyes snapping fully open, Humbolt answered, "Of course I'm awake. Bright and eager."

"It's dinnertime," she said.

Humbolt blinked twice, then said, "You go ahead. I'm not hungry."

"But—"

"I'll grab something later. You two go ahead."

Meitner made a halfhearted salute. "Aye, aye, Captain."

Humbolt grinned at him, but remained seated and half closed his eyes again.

Meitner joined Ilona at the food dispensers and opened the infusion storage cabinet and grabbed a bag of fish and rice.

Ilona realized she had little appetite. She settled for a bag of yogurt with fruit, then sat on one of the three chairs arranged in front of the dispensers and connected her bag to the infusion pump on her arm.

Pointing to Meitner's fish and rice bag, she sat next to him and connected herself, she said, "A hearty meal, Jan."

With a slight frown, Meitner said, "I feel cold. Deep down inside. I can't seem to get warm."

"It's this chemical thick air we're immersed in, I think. It makes everything seem cold."

"Psychosomatic?" he asked.

"I don't know," Ilona answered. "Maybe I should look it up in the medical files."

Jerking his head slightly toward Humbolt, sitting half-slumped in his command chair, Meitner asked, in a near whisper, "What do you think about our noble leader?"

"Humbolt?"

"Humbolt," Meitner confirmed. "He should be here with us, having dinner."

Ilona shrugged. "He said he's not hungry."

"Why not?"

"Why should he be?" she countered. "We've had nothing to do but sit for most of the day."

"Still," Meitner insisted, "as captain of this vessel he should take a break to be more awake, high-spirited, and alert at all times."

Ilona's only reply was a halfhearted shrug.

Ilona and meitner finished their meals, placed their bags into the disposal slot and returned to their seats flanking the command chair.

Humbolt stirred to life. Wiping a hand across his face, he said, "I think from now on we should keep one person awake and on duty here at all times."

With a frown, Meitner replied, "But the ship's instrumentation is programmed to wake us if—"

"The ship's sensors," Humbolt interrupted, "are programmed to wake us if they detect anything that's in their existing lists of observations. They're machines, Jan. They follow their programming but they don't—*can't*—go beyond their instructions to account for the unpredictable."

"They didn't warn us about that amoeba thing," Ilona agreed.

With a nod, Humbolt said firmly, "We keep a pair of human eyes awake and alert from now on. I'll take the first watch, Baroness Magyr the second, and Dr. Meitner, you can take the third watch. That should get us through the night."

With obvious reluctance, Jan muttered, "Very well."

"All right," Humbolt said briskly. "Off you go, both of you. Sleep well. Baroness Magyr, you relieve me at midnight."

Ilona rose from her chair, feeling totally unready for sleep. She saw that Jan looked equally cheerless.

But she said to the two of them, "Goodnight, then."

"Until midnight," said Humbolt.

Meitner went wordlessly toward his quarters.

To her surprise, Ilona fell asleep quickly. But when her alarm buzzed she snapped fully awake at once. She took a quick sponge bath, dressed, and stepped out into the command center.

Humbolt was sitting in the control chair, his head lolling and his eyes fully closed. The viewscreens decked around him were flashing from one image to another. Ilona saw that everything was in fine condition, except that their captain was fully asleep.

She stepped up to the command chair and touched his shoulder. "Derek?"

His eyes snapped open and for an instant he looked alarmed, frightened.

"Wha . . . ?"

Then he regained control of himself. "Oh. Is it midnight already?"

"Yes," said Ilona, bending over him.

Stretching in his chair, Humbolt admitted, "I guess I fell asleep."

"That's all right," Ilona said, as she sat in her chair, next to his.

Humbolt shook his head. "No, it's not all right. Aboard the old sailing ships a man could get himself flogged for falling asleep on duty."

With a slight smile, Ilona answered, "It's not the nineteenth century anymore, Derek."

"Good thing," he said.

For several long moments neither of them spoke a word. The screens beeped and clicked. Ilona could even hear the faint clickety clack sounds from the air vents in the ceiling that circulated the thick air they were breathing in . She felt the cold perfluoride liquid in her lungs.

"Aren't you going to sleep?" she asked Humbolt.

He nodded mechanically. "I guess I should."

But he made no move to lift the sensor ring off his head or to get out of the command chair. Ilona stared at him, wondering what he was up to. *If he intends to get romantic—*

But before she could finish the thought, Humbolt said softly, "This is my last mission."

"Your last . . . ?"

"Do you know how old I am?" Humbolt asked, dead serious. "Yesterday was my hundred and fiftieth birthday. One hundred and fifty years old."

She blinked. "You don't seem that old."

"But I am. I feel it inside. Oh, with modern pharmaceuticals and medical regimens I could keep going for a few more decades, I suppose." He sighed. "But I just don't feel like I want to. What the hell for? What's all of it add up to?"

Ilona felt a tendril of warning. Is this some elaborate ploy of his? Is he trying to use sympathy to get me into his bed?

Humbolt went on, "None of it means anything to me anymore. You want to find your father. Meitner wants to make scientific discoveries. But what do I want?"

"What do you want, Derek?"

With a shake of his head, Humbolt admitted, "Nothing. I don't want a goddamned thing. I've made my discoveries. I've seen the worlds. I just want to go home to New Mexico and spend the rest of my days watching the sunsets."

"New Mexico?"

"It's one of the states in the U.S.," he explained. "I've got a home up in the mountains, right on the edge of the Navaho territory. It's really beautiful up there."

Ilona nodded.

"That's where I'm heading when we get back to Earth. That's where I want to spend my last days."

Living off the money I'm paying you for this mission, Ilona thought. But she said nothing.

Humbolt lifted the sensor ring off his head and passed it to Ilona. Despite herself, she hesitated to accept it.

He broke into a crooked grin. "Go ahead. It won't hurt you. Just pipes the data from the ship's systems directly into your cerebral cortex. It's like you become a part of the ship's systems."

"I know what it does," Ilona said. Despite herself, though, she sounded uncertain.

Humbolt's grin faded. "I should have let you and Dr. Meitner try a couple of practice sessions before this."

Steeling herself, Ilona reached for the sensor ring and planted it resolutely on her head. "I'll be all right," she said firmly.

"Of course you will," Humbolt replied, his smile returning. Lowering his chair to a reclining position, he said, "I'll just stretch out here. In case you need me."

"Thank you," said Ilona, actually feeling grateful. Then she wondered how Jan would feel if Humbolt decided to stay in the command center when it was his turn to take over.

On Watch

The sensor ring was composed mainly of lightweight alloys, but Ilona felt it pressing down on her skull as if it weighed a thousand kilos.

Nonsense, she flared at herself. You're being a psychosomatic fool. Besides, there's Derek right beside me, ready to take charge if anything unusual happens.

She leaned back in her chair and tried to relax. But she couldn't. The safety of this vessel depends on me, she realized. For the first time in her life she felt the weight of responsibility pressing upon her.

And more. Much more. She sensed the power of the ship's nuclear engines. She could *feel* the atoms in its core meeting, merging, shattering to yield pure energy. She could see with the penetrating vision of the ship's external sensors, peer deep into the murky depths of the ocean, see farther and more clearly than her unaided eyes ever could.

Each bolt and weld across *Hári János*'s spherical body she felt like a stitch in her own flesh. The vessel groaned and sighed like a living creature, straining against the titanic pressure of the deep ocean. She could feel the flickers of electromagnetic energy racing through the ship, reporting on the status of each and every mechanism and sensor within its workings, moment by moment, nanosecond by nanosecond.

I am the ship! Ilona realized. I can sense every pulse of the ship's equipment, every throb of its makeup.

She felt power pulsating through her. And beyond the vessel's outermost shell she could see, she could *feel* a world of alien, inhospitable forces and creatures and pressures trying to crush her, destroy her, kill her.

But the ship—Ilona herself—held fast against those forces, kept the machinery functioning, striving against the power that would press the life out of it, fighting against doom.

"Ilona."

She heard the voice faintly, as if from far, far away. Like her mother calling to her when she was a child.

"Ilona!" More sharply, urgent.

She opened her eyes and saw Humbolt and Jan leaning over her. Meitner reached for the data ring.

"Not yet!" Humbolt cautioned, pushing Meitner's hand away.

Ilona focused on their faces. "Is it time already?"

Gently, Humbolt reached both hands to her head and lifted the data ring away.

"It's midnight," he said softly.

"My turn," said Jan, with a grin.

Ilona blinked her eyes. "It's . . . it's an overwhelming experience."

"I should have warned you," Humbolt said. "It can be pretty . . . powerful."

Rubbing her eyes, Ilona nodded. "Powerful," she agreed.

"Are you all right?" Meitner asked.

Ilona nodded. "Yes. Yes, I'm quite all right."

But she thought that now she knew how a drug addict must feel. The power. The ecstasy. She wanted to grab the sensor ring out of Humbolt's hands and plant it on her own head once again.

Ilona slowly rose up from her chair, almost surprised that her legs could support her. She looked down at Jan, the sensor ring now seated squarely on his head, like a halo that had slipped down from above him. His face seemed relaxed, almost blissful, as he leaned back in his chair.

Humbolt sat next to him, his expression taut, like a father watching his son's first attempt to ride a bicycle.

Derek can be fatherly? she asked herself. Yes, came the answer. Humbolt looked tired, weary of the responsibilities he shouldered, but he eyed Meitner closely, obviously ready to take over if any emergency arose.

Softly, Ilona said, "Goodnight, gentlemen." Then she turned and headed across the command center toward her own mini-suite.

She stepped into her bedroom, saw that the robots had cleaned the cramped chamber and freshened her bedcovers. Everything is as it should be, she told herself. We're thousands of millions of kilometers from home, from safety, from comfort, but everything is as it should be.

Yet she felt lonely, terribly alone in a foreign, alien world.

Slowly she undressed, pulled on a nightgown, and lay down on her bed. Alone. Far, far from safety and comfort and warmth.

She expected that she'd have trouble getting to sleep, but she seemed to drift off within moments of laying her head on the pillows.

She dreamed, of course. Dreamed of home, of the wooded hills and sparkling rivers of Hungary. Of the family castle that she had taken so much for granted before starting out on this mission to an alien world. She was sitting in the dining hall, a seven-year-old girl listening to her father singing boisterously at the head of the table, waving a stemmed glass of red wine while he sang of daring deeds of old.

Suddenly she was at the top of the castle's tallest tower, with a servant standing rigidly before her as she read her MirrorCom telling her of her father's possible death on distant, dangerous Neptune.

She stood in the afternoon sunshine racked with tears, weeping for the father that she loved so completely. The father that she had lost.

And then she was standing in the castle's main court, announcing to the servants that she intended to go to the planet Neptune and find her beloved father.

Or die trying.

WRECKAGE?

Jan's tour of duty at the ship's command ended quietly, with no alarms or alerts as the *Hári János* plowed through the murky waters at the bottom of Neptune's all-encompassing ocean.

Humbolt had left Meitner alone in command and gone to his quarters to freshen up. When Ilona returned to the command center and saw Jan sitting there alone she grumbled to herself, Male chauvinism. He stayed in the command center beside me all through my turn at command, but he left Jan to himself.

Humbolt returned from his quarters, and as he reached for the sensor ring that fitted somewhat loosely on Meitner's close-cropped brown hair, he asked, "Nothing to report, Jan?"

"Quiet as a grave," Meitner reported, as he allowed Humbolt to lift the ring from his head.

With a crooked grin, Humbolt muttered, "Not the most appropriate metaphor, Jan."

Meitner smiled back, faintly. "I suppose not."

Ilona stood by her chair.

"Did you have a good sleep?" Meitner asked.

"Good enough, I suppose," she said, then turned and headed for the food dispensers.

Humbolt reminded Ilona of a medieval king as he fitted the sensor ring atop his head. Then he joined Ilona and Meitner at the dispensers. "All systems functioning normally," he reported, with a half-hearted smile.

"Nothing out there to report," said Ilona.

"Not much life at this depth," Meitner corrected. "And what there is looks different from the species we saw up near the surface."

Humbolt shrugged. "Only to be expected, I suppose. Different biota down at this extreme depth."

Before either of them could respond he stiffened. "Wait a minute."

"What?"

"Something . . ."

"What?" Meitner repeated.

Without answering Humbolt stepped back to the command chair and dropped into it. "Display," he directed.

The main screen showed a view of the ocean bottom: a broad stretch of almost featureless gray spread out before their eyes.

"Focus on area 4-B, zoom in," Humbolt said.

The central screen narrowed its view to a close-up of the seafloor. A rolling grayish expanse, dead, lifeless except for a few tiny floating creatures ringed with writhing, flailing hairlike fringes.

"What is it?" Ilona asked, in a near whisper.

Humbolt replied, "I thought I saw . . . *there!*"

Ilona stared at the central viewscreen as its camera zoomed in on an odd shape lying on the nearly featureless seafloor.

"What's that?" Meitner gasped.

"Don't know," said Humbolt. "But it doesn't look natural to me."

"Like a scrap of metal," Ilona murmured.

"It's not natural," Meitner agreed, his voice firmer, surer. "It's not like anything we've seen so far."

Humbolt focused on it like a hunting dog fixed on a trembling rabbit.

Ilona felt strangely repulsed. That's not Father's ship, it's merely a twisted scrap of metal. To come all this way and find nothing but this . . . this crumb, this fragment.

Yet she heard herself asking, "Could that be from my father's vessel?"

Humbolt answered, "We'll have to take it aboard for chemical analysis."

"That could be dangerous," Meitner warned.

"The chem lab's sealed off, isolated from the rest of the ship."

"But still . . ."

"Let's do it," Ilona said.

Humbolt sat in his chair, eyes intent on the main viewscreen.

Hári János slowed, then hovered over the scrap of metal. Her eyes focused on the central screen, Ilona could see mechanical arms extend from the ship's outermost shell and quickly, efficiently grasp the object, then pull it inside.

"The sampling equipment will relay it to the chem lab," Humbolt muttered, more to himself than to Ilona and Meitner. The viewscreen showed the ship's systems encasing the metal shard in a clear plastic wrapping, then depositing it in the waiting trolley. With a satisfied nod, Humbolt shifted back to the outside as the trolley whisked off into the vessel's interior.

Ilona slowly sat herself in her chair, her eyes never leaving the main viewscreen.

"The procedure is all automated," Humbolt muttered, watching alongside her.

Meitner said, "Whatever that thing is, it's not natural. It didn't originate on Neptune."

"Maybe," said Humbolt, tightly. Before Meitner could argue, he added, "Most likely."

The three of them watched in breathless silence as the chemistry laboratory's equipment searched the sample with laser beams, sonic probes and other diagnostic tools.

It took only moments but Ilona felt as if hours were plodding by while they watched.

At last the main viewscreen showed the chemical analysis: iron, carbon, nickel, a half-dozen other elements in decreasing percentages.

Meitner burst out, "That's steel! It's a form of steel!"

Without taking his eyes from the viewscreen Humbolt commanded, "Show composition of vessel *Illustrious*."

Another list appeared on the screen, alongside the first one. Humbolt leaned forward, studying it.

"Close," he muttered.

"But not the same," said Meitner.

Ilona felt her breath sigh out of her. "It's not from my father's ship."

"No, it's not," Humbolt agreed.

Unsteadily, Meitner asked, "But . . . from where, then?"

Almost smiling, Humbolt replied, "That's the big question, isn't it?"

Ilona felt a surge of anger flow through her. "We're here to find my father's ship."

"And we've found evidence of extraterrestrial visitors," Humbolt countered.

His voice still hollow, Meitner wondered, "Do you really think . . . ?"

"It's not from Baron Magyr's ship. It's not like any alloy from a terrestrial vessel. The local life-forms on this planet haven't shown any capacity for even the simplest industrial activity. What does that leave us?"

Ilona shook her head. "But extraterrestrial visitors? That's a huge leap."

A slow smile crept along Humbolt's face. "I believe it was an English writer's character, Sherlock Holmes, who said that when you've eliminated all the reasonable possibilities, the answer must lie among the *un*reasonable ones."

Neither Ilona nor Meitner had a reply to offer.

"All right, then," Humbolt said, wiping the lists off the main viewscreen, "let's proceed further and see if we can find the source of that magnetic anomaly that Baron Magyr was searching for."

"Yes," said Ilona, realizing that the source of the anomaly would be where her father's vessel lay waiting for her.

Most likely.

SEEKING

Ilona twitched and fidgeted in her chair as the *Hári János* crept across the seabed. *Come on,* she urged silently. *Faster.*

But Humbolt was content to creep along, cameras and laser beams and all the ship's other diagnostic sensors playing out ahead of its slow, deliberate course across the barren sea bottom.

As if he could read her impatient thoughts, Humbolt said softly, "We don't want to miss anything that might be out there."

"I understand," Ilona replied—through gritted teeth.

Meitner was on the edge of his chair, peering intently at the viewscreens. "Nothing," he muttered. "Empty."

Humbolt grumbled, "Damned seawater absorbs the laser's beam in a few hundred meters."

"Nothing we can do about that," Meitner said, with a sigh.

Glancing at Ilona, Humbolt asked, "Are you sure this is the right heading?"

With an unconscious nod, she answered, "This is the direction his ship was heading when he sent his last message capsule up to the surface."

Ilona said, "But he might have changed course."

"We'd have no way to know that," Humbolt murmured.

"He'd have no reason to change his course," Meitner objected.

"None that we know of," Humbolt corrected.

With a shake of his head, Meitner said, "It certainly looks empty out there."

"It *is* barren," Humbolt agreed, his eyes still glued to the viewscreens. "Hardly even a polyp in sight."

"This is the way he went," Meitner said, certain that he was right.

Neither Humbolt nor Ilona contradicted him, although Ilona looked dubious and Humbolt visibly clenched his jaw.

Time stretched out like a man being tortured on the rack. Ilona stared at the viewscreens.

"Look." Ilona pointed at the viewscreen on the far right, which was monitoring the electromagnetic activity.

"The ship is picking up a strange peak of magnetic waves . . . looks like forty five degrees east," Humbolt said and veered the ship in that direction.

Nothing but the empty seabed, undulating slightly, glitters of electrical activity sparkling here and there, but no trace of Father's vessel was in sight.

"Are we still getting the signal from the magnetic anomaly?" she asked, in a half whisper.

With a nod, Humbolt responded, "Weak but clear."

"You'd think," said Meitner, "that the signal would get stronger if we were getting closer to its source."

"Yes, you'd think that," Humbolt agreed.

"But it's not."

Ilona challenged, "Is it getting weaker?"

"No," said Humbolt. "It's just about the same intensity as it was halfway across the planet."

That's an exaggeration, Ilona knew. He's trying to humor me. But she said nothing as their vessel inched ahead, slowly, across the bare, nearly lifeless seabed.

They took turns monitoring the ship once again that night. This time, though, Humbolt actually left Ilona by herself in the command center and went to his quarters.

He's given up, she thought as she sat by herself, surrounded by screens that showed nothing that she wanted to see. Humbolt thinks we're on a wild-goose chase. He thinks Father's ship is gone, totally destroyed, nothing left for us to find.

What if he's right? she asked herself. How far are you willing to go before you give it up and go back home, defeated, alone, destroyed?

Sitting by herself in the command center with the sensor ring perched atop her head, feeling the ship's components as if they were actually parts of her own body, Ilona strained to find the wreckage of her father's ship.

But the viewscreens showed nothing except the empty seabed:

bare, silent, mocking her, answering her hopes with bleak emptiness. No sign of the *Illustrious*.

There's nothing out there, she told herself. Nothing. Face it: Father is gone and you're never going to find him.

Meitner entered the command center, freshly scrubbed, wearing a set of coveralls that looked crisp and new.

One look at Ilona's face and he knew that she had found nothing.

Settling into his own chair, with Humbolt's seat between them, Jan asked, "Anything?"

She was so close to tears that she couldn't answer. She merely shook her head, then lifted the sensor ring off her hair and handed it to Meitner.

He settled it onto his short-cropped light brown hair, his face looking almost as dismal as she felt.

"Ilona," he began, then hesitated.

"What is it, Jan?"

"This probably isn't the best time to tell you . . ."

"Tell me what?"

"I . . . Ilona, I love you."

She blinked. Then she saw that Jan was totally serious. His face looked as if he were facing a gallows.

"You love me?"

His expression somewhere between hope and despair, Jan Meitner replied, "I've loved you since we were students together."

"You love me?" Ilona repeated. Somewhere inside her mind a voice was telling her that she was being stupid.

He nodded solemnly. "I want to marry you, Ilona."

He wants to marry your money, warned a voice in her head. He wants to marry into the Magyr fortune.

But the look in Jan's eyes gave the lie to that notion. No, not Jan. He's not like that. He's serious. He means what he's saying.

For the third time she asked, "You love me?"

"Totally," Meitner replied, his expression still dead serious. "Completely. Absolutely."

"Jan, I . . . I didn't know."

"Now you do."

Ilona stared at him, feeling dim-witted. What should I say? she asked herself. What can I say?

Meitner went on, "I know you don't love me. That would be

impossible. But maybe, over time, you might come to care for me a little . . ."

He ran out of words and just stared at her, his whole life hanging between the two of them.

And Ilona heard herself admit, "I do care for you, Jan. I think you're a very dear friend. But love . . . romantic love, with marriage . . . I've never even thought about that."

Breathlessly, he begged, "Would you think about it? Could you think about it?"

She smiled at him, almost shyly. "I suppose I should."

His face lit up bright as a supernova. "Oh, thank you, Ilona. Thank you!"

And he leaned across Humbolt's empty chair and pecked at her lips.

Ilona didn't know whether she should laugh or cry.

FINDING

++
+++++++++++++++++++++

ilona got up and went to her quarters, leaving Jan smiling contentedly, the sensor ring perched atop his head at a jaunty angle.

He's in love with me, she kept repeating to herself as she undressed and slipped into bed. She thought about the lovers she had been with over the years: the smiling, self-confident ones; the nervous, uncertain ones; the braggarts, the intellectuals, the lost souls, the fortune hunters. Seldom had she gone to bed with the same man twice.

Jan was none of those. He was a sweet, somewhat shy young man who meant what he said.

But what do I say back to him? Ilona asked herself. He wants to marry me! That ancient custom. He wouldn't try to lord himself over me; I couldn't imagine him even thinking of that. He's just a sweet, old-fashioned boy . . .

She stopped herself for a moment. Yes, she thought, Jan is a boy, despite his age. A boy. I wouldn't be happy with a boy. I want a man, a male who could be a partner to me, a person I could share my life with.

And the vision that arose in her mind was a picture of her father as a youth.

She sat on the edge of her bed and broke into tears.

When she returned to the command center, Ilona had put those thoughts behind her. Jan watched her as she said hello to him and to Humbolt and took her seat. Humbolt gave her his usual cocky grin; Meitner looked halfway between expectant and terrified.

Obviously unaware of what had happened between them, Humbolt said, "Now that we're all here, how about some breakfast?"

Instead of answering his question, Ilona asked, "Did anything interesting show up while I slept?"

Meitner shook his head as Humbolt responded, "Nothing but a

hundred kilometers of empty ocean. A few small organisms paddling about, but nothing that you would call interesting."

She nodded, then got up and wordlessly stepped back toward the food dispensers. Meitner got up from his chair, then Humbolt rose to his feet also.

"How long are we going to stay on this track?" Humbolt asked, as he joined them at the dispensers. His tone was easy, nonconfrontational. But Ilona could sense the tension behind his question.

With a minimal shrug of her slim shoulders, Ilona said, "Until we reach the source of the magnetic anomaly, at least."

"At least?"

She nodded.

"What's it going to take to make you give up this search?"

Ilona hesitated a moment, then answered, "I'm here to find my father's vessel."

"But when will you admit that we can't find it?" Humbolt pursued.

Again she shrugged. "We'll see."

With a shake of his head, Humbolt grumbled, "Aye, aye, ma'am."

Putting on her sweetest smile, Ilona corrected, "Mademoiselle."

Jan giggled softly. Humbolt broke into a reluctant grin.

On they went. Humbolt sat in his control chair, sensor ring clamped on his thick salt-and-pepper hair, silently watching the viewscreens half surrounding the three of them.

Meitner kept his eyes on the screens, too, except for occasional swift glances at Ilona, who sat tensely searching the screens for a view, a glance, a momentary glimpse of the wreckage of her father's *Illustrious*. She expected nothing more than wreckage now. Meter by meter, as they glided across the barren sea bottom, her dream of finding her father somehow alive and waiting for her was dissolving, dissipating, dying.

"What's that?" Humbolt muttered.

Ilona and Jan both stiffened in their chairs.

Humbolt pointed at one of the screens on the left of the array. It showed a telescopic view of the area slightly to the port side of the course they were following.

"Looks like a cloud," Meitner said.

Ilona saw that it did indeed look like a cloud, hovering on the distant horizon: vague, dark, throbbing noticeably.

She turned her gaze to the screen that showed the intensity of the magnetic anomaly. "The magnetic signal is coming from that direction!"

"Guess we'd better go take a look," Humbolt said.

Ilona felt the submersible swing in the direction of the cloud.

We've found it! she said to herself, too edgy, too anxious to speak aloud. That's where Father's vessel is! It's got to be!

It took more than an hour for them to inch close enough to the cloud to discern what it really was. An hour of slow, deliberate, careful approach. Ilona wanted to scream with impatience, but she clamped her teeth shut and sat patiently as Humbolt cautiously approached the cloud.

Slowly she made out that the cloud was alive. It was composed of thousands of small fish-like organisms and tiny floating gelatinous bodies hovering over . . .

Wreckage!

Spread across the ocean floor was the crumpled wreckage of a huge metallic body, curving spars spread across the sea bottom, pieces of what looked to her like equipment, fragments of what once had been sensors and viewscreens and furniture. Blackened, twisted, ruined.

Don't jump to conclusions, Ilona warned herself. Don't impose familiar identities on strange new discoveries.

The wreckage covered many hectares of the sea bottom. Much of it seemed burnt, scorched. It was difficult to get a clear view of it because of the swarms of sea life swimming around it.

And something more. A thin, filmy skin seemed to be stretched across the wreckage, pulsating slowly, rhythmically.

"That's one of those amoeba-like creatures!" Meitner cried out, pointing at the screens.

Humbolt nodded. "It's enormous."

It was spread across the wreckage, covering it like a thin glowing carpet, unmoving except for its steady slow throbbing.

"Don't get any closer," Meitner warned, his voice high with dread.

Humbolt said nothing, but he slowed the ship's forward motion and actually edged slightly away from the amoeboid. While they stared at the screens, the creature suddenly exuded a pseudopod and snared an eel-like creature undulating a meter or so above it. The eel struggled briefly, then went limp.

"Lunch," Humbolt said grimly, as the amoeboid pulled the eel into its body and began to digest it.

Staying well above the amoeboid, which lay spread over the wreckage like an opalescent carpet, Humbolt maneuvered the *Hári János* slowly around the edges of the wreckage field.

Glancing toward Meitner, Humbolt asked, "Have you figured out a defensive weapon to protect us against these giant amoebas?"

Frowning, Meitner shook his head.

"What is this wreckage?" Ilona asked.

"It's not anything from Earth," Humbolt replied. "All our research satellites are either still in orbit, or they've been recalled by the Astronomical Association."

"Then it's extraterrestrial," Meitner concluded.

"Has to be."

"How old is it?" Ilona asked.

With an elaborate shrug, Humbolt answered, "No way of knowing, unless we can get a chunk of it into our chem lab for analysis."

"Not with that amoeboid draped across it," Meitner said, his voice shuddering with dread.

"We have the sample we picked up yesterday," Ilona said.

With a nod, Humbolt said, "Yes, we could try to get an age from it . . . radioactive dating, that sort of thing."

Meitner said, "But it would be better to take a sample from this wreckage field, wouldn't it?"

"If that amoeboid will allow us to," said Humbolt.

"We've got to chase it away," said Ilona.

Meitner nodded. "Or kill it."

+ +

meitner turned to Humbolt and asked, "what about the lasers we're carrying?"

"The lasers?"

"As weapons," Meitner explained. "They're high-powered, aren't they? Megawatts of output power."

With a shake of his head, Humbolt replied, "Kilowatts. They're specialized sensors, not for weaponry."

"But we could focus all the beam's energy onto a small spot, couldn't we?" Meitner asked. "We could concentrate several megawatts of energy onto a tiny area."

Humbolt objected, "The ocean water absorbs the laser's energy, Jan. We'd have to get awfully close to the creature . . ."

Ilona realized what he was thinking of. "At a close enough range the lasers could burn metal!"

"Or amoeboid flesh."

Still shaking his head, Humbolt objected, "You'd have to get so close that the amoeboid could catch us in one of its pseudopods. Too dangerous."

"But that other amoeba didn't like the way we tasted," Meitner pointed out.

"Maybe this one will like us," said Humbolt. "Or do enough damage to the ship to cripple us before it decides to spit us out."

"We could zap the beast from a safe distance and see how it reacts," Meitner suggested.

"And what if it reacts by extending a few pseudopods and enveloping us?" Humbolt demanded.

Before Meitner could reply, Humbolt added, "And starts *digesting* us?"

"We'll sizzle the beast with the lasers," Meitner insisted.

"That's crazy."

"Do you have any better ideas?"

They argued back and forth as the vessel continued maneuvering a safe distance around the amoeboid creature and the wreckage it was draped over. As Ilona listened to their growing argument she turned her glance back to the viewscreens and—

"Look!" she cried out, pointing.

Startled out of their intensifying argument, the two men turned to look at what she was pointing to.

It was one of the viewscreens on the left side of the compartment. In the midst of the wreckage strewn across the seabed was a globular shape.

"My father's ship!" Ilona shouted. "That's his ship!"

Humbolt and Meitner stared at the viewscreen image for what seemed to Ilona to be an eternity.

Then Humbolt said in a steely voice, "I'm enlarging the image on screen seven and moving it to the central screen."

Ilona saw that the globular vessel was battered, one side of it staved in, as if a gigantic hammer had smashed it.

"That's his ship," Ilona repeated, in a whisper.

"That's where the magnetic anomaly is centered," Meitner said.

"He's in there!" Ilona felt a sense of triumph, mixed with fear, dread of what they would find inside the half-crushed *Illustrious.*

"Another amoeboid is draped over it," said Meitner, his voice hollow, awed.

Humbolt said matter-of-factly, "Well, we've found it. Now what do we do?"

"We see what's inside," Ilona answered immediately.

"But that amoeba thing is wrapped all over it," Humbolt pointed out. "We'll have to move it out of our way."

Meitner said, "With the lasers."

Reluctantly, Humbolt agreed. "With the lasers."

"First we should send a message capsule up to the surface," said Meitner, his voice trembling with excitement. "We've got to inform the Astronomical Association about this."

"Right," Humbolt agreed. "Ilona, prepare a capsule. Upload into it all the data we've collected so far."

She nodded, glad to have something to do, some duty, some activity to keep her occupied.

But as she programmed the message capsule she could not keep her eyes from drifting to the image of the battered submersible on their central screen. Unlike the rest of the wreckage strewn about the seabed like the blackened fossil of a gigantic ancient creature, the spherical submersible looked clean, shining, almost new—except for the huge dent that had buckled its skin on one side.

"Something struck it," she thought, surprised to realize that she had spoken the words aloud.

"Something massive," Meitner agreed.

Humbolt challenged, "Have you programmed the data capsule?"

Glancing at the viewscreen directly in front of her, Ilona replied, "Almost finished, Captain. . . . There! It *is* finished."

"Good. I'm sending it off."

Meitner announced, "I've programmed the lasers, narrowed their beam outputs to milliradians. They'll effectively deliver about ten to twelve megawatts to whatever they touch."

With a single curt nod, Humbolt said, "That ought to make our amoeboid friend out there uncomfortable."

Or angry, Ilona thought. But she said nothing.

Taking in an obviously deep breath, Humbolt said, "All right, let's see if we can move that hunk of slime from the baron's ship."

CONTEST

Ilona knew that *Hári János*'s outer skin was studded with a dozen laser heads that could be fired in any direction. The vessel actually bore only one laser, whose energy could be directed to any one of the output heads at the command of the captain.

Will this be enough to make the amoeboid retreat off Father's ship? Ilona wondered. Or will it merely arouse the beast to fight against us?

Humbolt was edging the vessel gradually closer to the wreckage of Baron Magyr's ship, coming in above the wreckage and the amoeboid that lay draped over it. Ilona could see the translucent shape pulsating slowly, slowly, as they approached.

"Yon beastie's found a good spot for himself," Humbolt muttered, a grim smile on his face. "He just sits there and lets the other creatures come here to feed off the wreckage and *zap!* he snags his dinner."

Let's make sure we don't become his dinner, Ilona thought. But she said nothing.

Slowly, slowly the *Hári János* settled closer to the translucent sheen of the amoeboid. Ilona watched, fascinated, almost hypnotized. A snatch of an old poem sprang into her mind: "Come into my parlor, said the spider to the fly."

Suddenly the amoeboid extruded a pseudopod. Its gelatinous arm oozed onto the *Hári János* and spread across nearly half of the globular submersible.

"Use the laser!" Meitner shouted, his voice octaves higher than normal.

"Firing," said Humbolt, calmly.

Ilona heard the muted rumble of the laser, down in the ship's equipment bay. Staring at the central viewscreen, she saw that the pseudopod had been neatly sliced off of the amoeboid's main body. It clung to the submersible for a few eons-long moments, then slipped away. A bevy of tiny sea creatures swarmed over it, gobbling it away.

"They're eating it!" Ilona said.

"Food is where you find it," muttered Humbolt.

"Kill or be killed," Meitner added.

Humbolt turned the laser beam onto the main body of the amoeboid. It writhed and slithered away.

We're hurting it, Ilona realized. Pain is the master of the universe; it rules every creature, large or small.

"Prepare an inspection team," Humbolt ordered.

Ilona knew that the *Hári János* carried several dozen miniaturized robotic probes, palm-sized, equipped to see, touch, even taste environments where it was unsafe for a human to go.

"I've got five of the probes ready to go," Meitner replied.

Humbolt nodded without taking his eyes off the central screen.

Glancing at one of the screens alongside it, Ilona saw a pseudopod rising slowly, warily, from the amoeboid's filmy body.

Before she could say anything, Humbolt activated the laser again. Its blood-red beam struck the wavering arm squarely, making a crimson splash against its pulsating translucent arm. In the flash of a second it disappeared back into the amoeboid's main body.

"Persistent cuss," Humbolt grumbled.

He maneuvered their ship to the bashed-in side of Baron Magyr's vessel, then told Meitner, "That should be close enough. Release the probes."

Meitner nodded once and pressed a stud set into his seat's armrest. Ilona saw a quintet of tiny spherical objects appear on the lower viewscreen and jet through the jagged opening in the baron's ship.

As the probes disappeared into the wreckage of the *Illustrious* Ilona stared at the screen as if she could make her father appear by sheer willpower.

The central screen blinked once, twice, then cleared to show five views of the interior of the wrecked vessel.

Ilona saw a long, narrow tunnel, similar to the one in their own ship. It leads from the outer hatch down to the command center, she told herself, as the probes jetted along its length.

Father will be in the command center, she knew. He's there, waiting for me!

The hatch at the end of the tunnel was closed, sealed, of course.

Humbolt grumbled something low and obviously uncouth.

"Is the data you fed into our system correct?" he growled, without taking his eyes off the viewscreen.

"As far as I know," Ilona answered.

The hatch remained stubbornly sealed. Ilona knew that Humbolt was sending the codes that should make it open . . .

And open it did. Slowly, reluctantly, the hatch swung outward to where the miniature probes were bobbing in the water.

Without realizing what she was doing, Ilona inched forward on her chair, eyes fixed on the central viewscreen.

Father's in there! she shouted silently as the tiny probes entered the core of the shattered vessel.

The screens before her searching eyes showed five views of the same scene.

Devastation.

Illustrious's command center was thick with fish-like creatures that scattered and fled as the probes glided in. Ilona saw that the globular compartment was wrecked, stripped to bare metal. What had once been seats and controls and viewscreens was now almost unrecognizable. The creatures of Neptune's deep ocean had eaten almost everything.

"It's destroyed," Humbolt said, his voice hollow with shock.

In an equally awed tone Meitner said, "They must feed off the metals in the alloys."

Ilona could not see anything even vaguely recognizable. "It's all gone," she whimpered.

A tiny gelatinous creature, fringed with wavering blood-red cilia, scurried up from the floor and slithered to the open hatch.

"How did they get in there?" Meitner wondered.

"Through the ventilation pipes, probably," said Humbolt.

But where is Father? Ilona asked herself.

For long wordless moments the three of them stared at the visions that the probes were showing them: desolation, ruin, crushed hope.

Then—

"What's that?" Ilona cried, pointing to the leftmost of their viewscreens.

"Where?"

"Beneath the remains of that . . . it looks like a chair," she choked out.

Humbolt switched the scene to the central viewscreen and immediately set it for maximum magnification.

Wedged into the crumbling metal framework of what had once been a padded chair was a part of a space suit.

"An arm," Meitner breathed.

Humbolt directed two of the probes to examine the remnant. The obedient little robots glided to the skeleton of what had once been a chair. Several tiny creatures swam out of the disembodied arm, fleeing as if some predator had discovered them.

Ilona recognized the emblem emblazoned on the relic. It was faded, eroded, but she could still make out the remains of the Magyr family seal.

"It's my father's," she choked out. "My father's pressure suit."

Both the robotic probes attached their extensible grippers to the disembodied arm, but as soon as they tried to pull it free of the chair frame it dissolved into a cloud of tiny powdery particles that spread out in the water.

"Catch some of those particles," Meitner snapped, then added, "For analysis."

As the robots chased after the specks Ilona stared openmouthed at the scene the viewscreens showed.

Meitner turned away from the screens and looked at her. Humbolt sat rigidly in his command chair, wordless, his eyes fixed on the screens.

Ilona struggled to hold back her tears. But when Meitner whispered, "I'm so sorry, Ilona," her restraint broke and she sobbed uncontrollably.

Her vision blurred by tears, Ilona watched as the tiny robots chased down a few of the specks floating through the water-filled compartment.

"There's nothing left," Meitner whispered.

"The local fauna have cleaned it out," Humbolt agreed.

"They've eaten it all," said Meitner.

Wiping at her eyes, Ilona agreed, "He's dead. My father is dead."

For a seemingly endless moment none of them spoke. The command center was silent, except for the background hum of the pumps and electrical equipment.

Humbolt broke the silence. In a low, almost reverential voice he said, "I've commanded the probes to pick up as many of those floating scraps as they can. We should examine them."

"There might be traces of the baron's DNA on them," Meitner added.

All that's left of Father, Ilona thought, as the tears surged through her again. But she fought them back. No more crying! she commanded herself. He's gone and nothing you or anyone else can do will bring him back. You've tried your best to find him but you were too late.

She realized it had been too late to save her father by the time she had first learned of his vessel's disappearance.

Too late, she told herself. Too late.

Baroness Magyr. Both her parents were dead. She was the eldest of her siblings. She was now head of the Magyr family. What was left of it. The family's fortune. The family's estates. The family's responsibilities. The staff, the employees, and the people who depended on the Magyrs' wisdom and kindness for their livelihoods. It was all on her shoulders now.

Wiping at her eyes with the backs of her hands, Ilona sat up straighter in her chair and squared her shoulders.

I will face the future the way my father taught me to. Standing straight and tall.

And alone.

Once Humbolt was satisfied that the tiny probes had collected adequate samples from the tatters of Baron Magyr's glove and sleeve, he announced, "It's time to leave. Time to get out of this dismal ocean."

"Not yet," Ilona countered.

"But—"

"We have to examine this alien wreckage," she said, nodding toward the viewscreens.

Humbolt said, "That's not what we came for."

Meitner, looking disturbed, almost frightened, nodded his agreement.

Her eyes red, but her heart steady and determined, Ilona pointed out, "We have the wreckage of a possible extraterrestrial visitor spread out before us! I don't intend to leave until we've taken some samples for analysis."

ARGUMENT

Humbolt leaned back in his command chair, a slight smile—a smirk, nearly—on his rugged face.

"May I point out," he said softly, but with iron behind his words, "that the wreckage you're so interested in is covered by that first amoeboid creature. He probably won't take kindly to our poking around his territory."

Sitting rigidly in his chair, Meitner stared at Ilona. "We should get away from here while we can," he agreed.

"Not until we've brought some samples of the wreckage into our ship for analysis," said Ilona.

"That's an unnecessary risk," Humbolt countered.

Lifting her chin a notch, Ilona insisted, "It's a risk I'm prepared to take."

"I'm not."

"This is my vessel. You take your orders from me."

An almost crafty grin edged across Humbolt's handsome features. "I'm the captain of this vessel."

"And I'm the owner," Ilona shot back.

Meitner broke into their argument. "Ilona, do you want to die here, like your father?"

The question shocked her. She stared at Meitner.

Humbolt took up the point. "You may want to join your beloved father, but I intend to make it out of here alive."

"Me too!" Meitner added.

Jabbing a finger at the viewscreens, Ilona argued, "We have possible evidence of an extraterrestrial visitor to our solar system, and you want to leave it here without examining it?"

"Yes!" Humbolt shouted. "Leave it for someone else to study. Let's get the hell out of here while we can."

Ilona stared at him for a long, silent moment. Then she looked past Humbolt to Meitner.

"Jan," she said, "you're a scientist. Can you leave this discovery for someone else to claim?"

Meitner glanced at Humbolt momentarily, then returned his gaze to Ilona. "It's awfully dangerous here. . . ."

"We can deal with that amoeboid thing," she insisted.

"Maybe. Maybe not."

Allowing a hint of a smile to curve her lips, Ilona coaxed, "We have a great discovery here. Do you really want to run away from it? Turn your back on it?"

She could see Meitner's inner struggle mirrored on his face: Safety versus the fame of discovery. New knowledge versus personal security.

Meitner's gaze shifted from Ilona to Humbolt and then back again. Obviously ill at ease, he muttered, "I suppose we could stay here for a few minutes more, collect some samples."

"And risk getting swallowed by that amoeboid?" Humbolt demanded, pointing toward the viewscreens.

Meitner nodded slowly.

Good for you, Jan! Ilona said to herself.

Humbolt shook his head. "You're both crazy."

Ilona allowed herself to smile brightly. "Come on, Derek. You'll end your career in a blaze of glory."

"More likely I'll end it as that damned amoeba-thing's dinner." But he edged their craft away from the ruined *Illustrious* and out toward the wreckage strewn across the seabed.

The amoeboid slinked away as *Hári János* edged forward.

Grinning, Meitner said, "Looks like he's learned his lesson."

"Think so?" Humbolt disagreed. Pointing to the leftmost of their screens he suggested, "Look at the rear view."

Ilona had to lean forward to see the screen. The amoeboid's slimy, viscous body was inching forward back there, covering again the ruined *Illustrious*.

"Our friend hasn't given up on us," Humbolt said.

"But it's keeping its distance," said Meitner, his voice quavering slightly.

As they approached an area where the strewn wreckage stood bare and blackened on the seafloor, Ilona pointed and said, "There. We should take some samples from there."

Humbolt nodded agreement and commanded the ship to hover over the curving ribs. Between the ribs the seafloor was littered with scattered chunks of metal and the remains of what looked like in-strumentation.

For nearly an hour they picked up bits and pieces, their ship's equipment grappling them and tucking them inside their own vessel.

At last Humbolt asked, "Do you think we've got enough?"

Ilona glanced at the screen that showed the rearward view. The amoeboid's glossy mass hunched across the ruins of the dead wreck-age, pulsating slowly, waiting, waiting.

She shivered involuntarily. "Yes," she answered Humbolt. "Let's get out of here."

Humbolt's smile showed plenty of teeth. "And awaaay we go!" he bellowed.

Ilona felt the lurch as *Hári János* lifted up off the wreckage, leav-ing the amoeboid draped over it, and started to rise toward the dis-tant surface of the Neptunian ocean.

An hour later, Meitner hunched tensely in his chair as he stared at the analysis displayed on the viewscreen to his right.

"It doesn't make sense," he muttered. "Some of the components of steel are present in the sample, but there are obvious gaps in the composition."

Ilona looked at the list too. Humbolt ignored both of them, in-tent in piloting their vessel toward the surface of the sea.

"There's practically no carbon in the samples," Ilona murmured, as much to herself as to Jan.

He nodded. "And hardly any potassium. Or sulfur."

"The sea creatures must have extracted those elements. They're important biological elements, aren't they?"

"Yes, I believe so."

"So the local fauna must have ingested them for their own me-tabolism."

"But how?" Meitner bleated. "How can fish and worms extract individual metal components from refined steel?"

With a slight smile, Ilona answered, "That's for the biologists to determine . . . once they get here."

Humbolt broke into their conversation. "Are you two ready to send up a message capsule?"

"No," Ilona snapped. "Not yet."

"Well, you'd better get busy and prepare one. It'll be hours before we breach the surface. You don't want your good work to be lost, do you?"

Ilona realized that they were still hundreds of kilometers deep in the alien sea. Derek is right, she said to herself. Get the data on its way toward Earth. Even if something happens to us, the data must get through.

Meitner said nothing, but he started tapping out commands onto the capsule's memory cell.

Breakout

The *Hári János* surged upward, toward the surface of the all-encompassing sea. Meitner sent off a message capsule as Ilona watched. The two men kept themselves busy: Humbolt with piloting the ship, Meitner with studying the results of the analyses of the samples they had taken aboard.

Left to her own thoughts, Ilona found herself remembering her father. She saw him as she had when she had been a child: tall, self-assured, active, handsome. Inwardly she smiled at her memories. She felt tears gathering in her eyes but she fought them back. A Magyr does not cry about the past. Her memories were happy, warm. Even her recollection of the later years, when Father became obsessed with his passion to make a name for himself and his family, when he became fixed on the mad idea of flying out to distant Neptune and showing the world that he was a brave adventurer.

It was Mother's death that drove him to that decision. Ilona knew that now. She remembered a conversation she had had with her father, the week before he left their home.

With his gambler's smile, Father had told her, "If I succeed in exploring Neptune, I'll return home a famous man. If I fail, I'll join your mother. Either way, I win."

But what about me, Ilona had wanted to ask. What happens to me if you fail?

She never asked him. She feared hearing his answer.

Upward through the hundreds of kilometers of Neptune's icy ocean they rose.

"Pressure's low enough for us to get the perfluoride out of our systems," said Humbolt. "Ilona, you go first."

Dreading what she knew was coming, Ilona rose wordlessly from her chair and made her way back to her quarters. Locked into its tiny bathroom, she swallowed the disinfectant pills and excreted the perfluoride mixture that pervaded her body, clearing her bowels and urinary tract, vomiting disgustingly into the toilet time and again.

It was worse than she had imagined it would be, but at last her convulsions eased and she began to feel nearly normal once again.

By the time she finished showering and pulled on a clean set of coveralls she felt almost normal. Almost. But a glance into the mirror above the bathroom sink showed a hollow-cheeked, pale and weary-looking vision of herself.

A little shakily, she reentered the command center and resumed her chair.

"Welcome back," said Humbolt.

Ilona merely nodded at him.

In a low voice Meitner asked, "How was it?"

Forcing a smile, Ilona replied, "Two steps up from hell."

Meitner's face turned grim, but he got to his feet and headed for his quarters.

"Not very pleasant, is it?" Humbolt groused.

"Not very," said Ilona.

Eventually Meitner returned, his face chalky, his hands trembling. Eying Ilona, he grumbled, "*One* step up from hell."

With his usual grin, Humbolt asked, "Jan, can you handle the controls for a while?"

Meitner nodded and said, "Yes, certainly."

"We're on a fixed course up to the surface. Shouldn't be any problems."

"I'll take care of things," Meitner said.

And Ilona complained to herself, Male chauvinists, the two of them. He didn't even think of asking me to take command. But she kept her resentment to herself.

With nothing else to do, Ilona put up on one of the viewscreens the analyses of the samples they had taken from the wreckage on the sea bottom. Most of the scraps of metal were very much like steel; it puzzled her that carbon and a few of the other metallic elements were lacking.

We should have taken some of the fishes and other organisms down there for analysis, she told herself. We should have tested them to see if they have elevated levels of potassium or sulfur.

Too late now, she knew. The scientists who'll come to Neptune to study the wreckage will do that, I suppose.

Eventually Humbolt returned and resumed his place in the command chair. He looked bright and clean, smiling his usual charming smile, as if the begrudging routine had hardly bothered him at all.

But Ilona thought Humbolt had taken more time than either she or Jan had. She studied the man's handsome face. He puts up a brave front, she told herself. I suppose he feels he has to show that he's beyond fear.

"Approaching the surface!" Humbolt sang out.

Their rise to the top of Neptune's ocean had taken nearly ten hours. The three of them had poked at spare lunches together while the *Hári János* had steadily climbed up from the depths.

"Strap in," Humbolt commanded. "This might be rough."

Ilona pulled the safety harness over her slim shoulders as Meitner and Humbolt did the same.

"Releasing the icebreaker," Humbolt muttered, almost as if he were talking to himself.

Hári János barely shuddered as the nuclear-tipped missile shot into the ocean and angled steeply upward, toward the ice-covered surface.

"Trajectory looks good," Humbolt said.

Ilona nodded, and saw Meitner do the same. She felt the vessel slowing, her body surging against her safety harness.

Humbolt murmured, "Don't want to get too close to the nuke."

Meitner nodded vigorously.

The central viewscreen suddenly flashed with the explosion of the nuclear bomb. Ilona held her breath, and within a few seconds felt *Hári János* rock from the impact of the blast's pressure wave.

"Woof!" Humbolt exclaimed. "Some ride."

Glancing to either side, he asked, "Everybody all right?"

Ilona managed to gasp, "That was a jolt."

"I'm okay," said Meitner.

"Good," Humbolt said. "Now we go through the hole in the ice. Breakout in three minutes."

Her seat back pressed against Ilona's spine as the vessel surged upward.

"Breakout in five seconds . . . four . . ."

Ilona felt her body tensing. Relax! she demanded silently. But her body refused to obey.

A hard sideways jolt slammed them against their safety straps. The screens showed bubbles of froth and suddenly they were shooting into the air, the methane-tinged clouds of Neptune high above looking bright and somehow reassuring.

"We're out of the sea!" Meitner cried.

"We're on our way home," said Humbolt.

Ilona stared at the screen that showed the ocean below them, the sea mantle that encompassed the entire planet, the watery grave that had killed her father.

Homeward Bound

Hári János rose smoothly through Neptune's heavy atmosphere, arrowing toward the thick clouds that blanketed the entire planet.

"Better stay buckled up," Humbolt warned. "We'll get some turbulence in those clouds."

Silently, Ilona tightened the safety straps around her. We're not really safe until we've cleared those clouds, she knew, her body tensing involuntarily. Meitner looked edgy also. Humbolt seemed more at ease, grinning enough to show teeth.

Is he really so relaxed? Ilona asked herself. Or is this a show he puts on? The big macho captain, afraid of nothing. Then she realized that if it was a show, its intent was to keep her and Jan from going hysterical. The big brave captain will get us through this. He's not afraid, why should we be?

Inwardly he must be just as scared as I am, she reasoned, but he won't let us see it.

Their vessel shuddered as it rose into the clouds; all the viewscreens showed nothing but darkness.

"Switching to radar," Humbolt muttered, loud enough for Ilona to hear.

The screens showed a vast emptiness. The skies were empty. No, wait, Ilona told herself. There was a speck of an image on one of the screens.

"Looks like we're not alone up here," Humbolt said, transferring the image to the central screen.

An ungainly-looking bird was soaring through the clouds on wide, outstretched wings.

"Ugly-looking cuss, isn't he?" Humbolt said.

Meitner recited, "Albatross analogue. Much larger than any terrestrial bird. They live completely airborne, never come to roost."

Humbolt grinned at him. "Did you swallow the zoology reports, Jan?"

"Memorized them," Meitner replied.

"How do they have sex?"

"They don't. Each animal has both male and female organs."

With a glance at Ilona, Humbolt muttered, "That's no fun."

She smiled faintly.

After nearly an hour of jouncing and shuddering in the clouds, Humbolt announced, "We'll be clearing the clouds in five minutes. I've maneuvered us to break out in a location that's away from the jet streams, but it might still get pretty bouncy for a while."

Ilona nodded as she checked her safety straps once again. Meitner did the same.

Just in time. The vessel slammed sideways, then suddenly lurched downward so hard that Ilona had to clamp her teeth shut to prevent herself from crying out. As the ship struggled upward again Meitner gasped audibly and even Humbolt seemed to tense in his command chair.

And then they were free of the clouds, soaring aloft, leaving Neptune behind them. Ilona saw thousands of stars shining in their viewscreens.

"We made it!" Meitner shouted.

Humbolt cautioned, "We're not entirely clear of the atmosphere yet. Might still be some turbulence."

But Ilona stared at the screens, at the myriads of stars scattered across the blackness of infinity, and a memory from her childhood spoke in her mind:

"The heavens declare the glory of God; and the firmament showeth His handiwork."

We've made it, she said to herself. We're free of the planet's grip. We're on our way home.

The vessel's communications system displayed more than a hundred messages. Everyone seemed to want to hear from them, from the Astronomical Association to the local news outlet at home in Budaörs.

Ilona arranged the messages by the importance she felt each one deserved and composed a simple reply to them: "We've come up from the ocean and are now in orbit around Neptune." Then she attached their data files to each response.

Humbolt made a direct call to the Astronomical Association. Since messages needed more than four hours to cross the distance to Earth, he sent an abbreviated account of their accomplishment, together with their full data records.

Ilona stretched languidly in her chair, the tension of the past days easing away from her body. We made it, she told herself. We went into that hellhole and survived.

That's more than Father did, she realized. For a flash of a moment she felt a pang of guilt. But then she told herself, I survived the ordeal and he didn't. There's no blame for that.

But no glory, either, she realized. Father's reunited with Mother now. And I'm still alive.

She understood that she should feel no guilt. No remorse. I've lived through the ordeal. But a tendril of disquiet vibrated through her consciousness. Father's dead. The reality of it, the utter implacability of it, burned in her deepest consciousness.

Father is dead and I'm alive.

Where do I go from here?

BOOK III

++
++++++++++++++++++

The Return Home

accepting reality

The long trek back to Earth became boring. Ilona realized how tiny, how confined their vessel was. She tried to busy herself by analyzing the DNA from the fragments they had salvaged from Baron Magyr's gloved sleeve.

The analyses were positive. It was her father's DNA. No matter how many times Ilona ran the tests, the answer was the same. The DNA was from her father.

He's dead, Ilona knew. But something in her refused to accept that conclusion. She ran the tests again and again, day after day as *Hári János* cruised through the solar system, heading inward, away from Neptune, speeding toward Earth.

Meitner and Humbolt seemed busy enough, Jan studying the analyses of the samples they had picked off the ocean floor, Derek keeping watch over the ship's innumerable systems.

Finally, as they neared the orbit of giant Jupiter, an old saying popped into Ilona's head:

"Insanity is doing the same thing over and over again, and expecting different results."

Shocked by the rationality of its creator, Ilona asked herself, Am I going insane?

And her answer was, Maybe. But that stops *now*. I have to accept the fact that Father is dead. Rerunning the DNA tests is not going to bring him back to me. He's dead and there's nothing anyone can do about it.

She sat up straighter in her chair. Face the future. You can't change the past. The future is the only part of the universe that you can influence.

Wordlessly, she got up from her chair and went from the command center to her quarters. She closed the door and locked it, then stepped into the minuscule bathroom. For a brief moment the thought of suicide flicked through her mind. But only for a moment.

Staring at her sunken-cheeked image in the bathroom mirror, Ilona squared her shoulders and stiffened to her full height.

I will face the future, she told her grieving image. I will go forward. No tears. No regrets. Look forward, not back.

She washed her face, then returned to the command center and sat in her chair again. Humbolt gave her a quizzical glance, then returned his attention to the ship's diagnostic screens. Meitner kept his eyes focused on the data screens he'd been studying when Ilona left the bridge.

Ilona almost smiled. Jan says he loves me, but he loves his work more.

The days slipped by as *Hári János* cruised steadily closer to Earth. Ilona put away the data from the fragments of her father's DNA and finally helped Meitner to scan the metallic samples.

Ilona spent more and more of her time with Meitner back by the food dispensers, with their emergency suits hanging off to one side. Sample after sample of the scraps of metal they had picked off Neptune's seabed told the same story.

"They all date around two million years old," Meitner said, his voice low, perplexed.

With a nod, Ilona said, "That shows that the aliens were at Neptune about two million years ago."

Meitner nodded back at her. "Give or take a few millennia."

"And the wreckage on the seafloor?" Ilona wondered.

Meitner shrugged. "I think it must have been a satellite that the aliens had placed in orbit around the planet. When they left the solar system they deorbited the satellite. They didn't need it anymore."

"It must have been a very large satellite," she said.

"Yes. A manned satellite." Then Meitner amended, "Crewed, that is."

"And it crashed into the ocean."

Meitner nodded his agreement.

"I wonder if that's the right conclusion," Ilona mused.

"What other conclusion can you come to?"

Before Ilona could reply, Humbolt called from his command chair, "Hey, you two. Come up here and take a look."

"At what?" Meitner asked.

"Come and see."

With a resigned shrug, Meitner pushed himself up from his chair. Ilona got to her feet too.

As they approached Humbolt's command chair Ilona saw what the captain had put on the central display screen.

"That's Earth!" she cried.

"It sure is," said Humbolt, with a crooked grin.

Ilona slipped into her chair without taking her eyes off the viewscreen.

Earth.

"Purty, ain't she?" Humbolt drawled. "The blue marble."

Only the daylit half of the planet was visible, but it still took Ilona's breath away. Curving before her eyes, Earth looked solid and familiar. Deep blue sea rimmed with bright white clouds. The brown sweep of what she recognized as India and part of Southeast Asia peeking out between cloud masses.

Earth. Home. Warm and welcoming. Ilona felt her entire body relaxing. Safety. Friends. Family. Home.

INTERPLANETARY COUNCIL HEADQUARTERS

copenhagen was an old city, but in the midst of its narrow, winding streets and rococo palaces and museums rose the slim, graceful tower that housed the headquarters of the Interplanetary Council, the tallest building in the city.

The entire top floor of the headquarters building was devoted to the offices of the Council's president, Yancey Darbin, a big rawboned Texan, his tanned, weathered face topped by thick white hair and a puzzled, almost annoyed expression.

Sitting in front of Darbin's airport-sized silver-inlaid mahogany desk were Harvey Millard, the Council's executive director, and Alberto Machado, chief of the Council's Astronomical Association.

"Invaded?" Darbin said, his angular face reddening. "By aliens?"

Machado nodded unhappily. "Some two million years ago, apparently."

Darbin's expression narrowed into an angry scowl. "Are you pullin' my leg?" he demanded.

Millard was much smaller than the Council president, a slim welterweight of a man, fashionably dressed in dark blue carefully creased trousers and a fitted off-white jacket. He seemed perfectly at ease despite Darbin's glower as he tried to explain, "That's what the Baroness Magyr's team has reported from Neptune."

Darbin glared at the two men sitting before his desk. "The solar system was invaded by aliens two million years ago," he muttered.

Machado—his bald, round head beaded with perspiration—said in a soft voice, "That's what the data sent to us reports."

"Bullshit," Darbin growled.

Millard smiled disarmingly.

"Yancey," he said softly, "they found wreckage on the sea bottom.

Wreckage that they've dated at some two million years old. Plus the remains of Baron Magyr's ship. It's real."

"It's really real?"

His smile widening slightly, Millard confirmed, "It's really, actually, truly real. They're bringing back samples from the wreckage."

"Two million years old?"

Machado said, "It seems that our solar system was visited by intelligent aliens about two million years ago, and they . . . they . . ."

"Spit it out, Alberto!" Darbin snapped. "They what?"

The astronomer glanced at Millard, then replied in an almost guilty voice, "They apparently sterilized the planet Uranus."

"Sterilized the whole planet?"

Millard took up the explanation. "They wiped out the intelligent civilization of Uranus, and every other trace of life there."

Darbin gaped at him. "Wiped out everything? Everybody?"

Nodding ruefully, Millard answered, "That's what seems to have happened."

"Seems," said Darbin.

"The evidence is very strong," Machado said, his voice still quavering.

"Seems, what is the evidence for that?" Darbin repeated.

It took almost another hour, but at last Millard felt that the Council's president understood what they were trying to explain to him.

"Two million years ago," Darbin was muttering. "Alien invaders came into our solar system and wiped Uranus clean of all life-forms."

Machado, looking as if he'd rather be locked in a cage with a gang of hungry lions, said, "I'm afraid there's something more."

"More?" Darbin growled. "What more?"

"The Pleistocene ice age here on Earth began approximately two million years ago. The aliens may have caused it."

"The frickin' ice age?"

"It's not all that certain, Yancey," said Millard, calmly, "but it might not be a coincidence."

Scowling, Darbin asked, "What makes you think so?"

"They might have wanted to destroy us," said Millard.

"The human race didn't even exist two million years ago," Darbin growled. Then he added, "Did it?"

"Our particular species, *Homo sapiens*, hadn't arisen yet. But our progenitors were alive in Africa and elsewhere."

"So these aliens caused the ice age?"

"To prevent the prehumans that existed on Earth from developing into us," said Machado.

Darbin grumbled, "Holy Jesus Christ on a goddamned crutch."

"*Homo habilis* and such," Machado half whispered.

Calmly, Millard said, "I know this is a lot for you to swallow—"

"Swallow?" Darbin roared. "I can't even get my goddamned teeth around it!"

RECEPTION

TWO days later *Hári János* settled into a parking orbit around the moon, hovering alongside the lunar space station that serviced returning interplanetary vessels. The station was a series of huge slowly revolving wheels, nested within each other, linked through their middles by a connecting structure.

"Docking established," a robotic voice announced, quickly followed by a woman's smiling image and a cheerful "Welcome home, *Hári János*."

"It's good to be back," Humbolt responded, smiling ear to ear.

The three of them had showered and put on new sets of clothing, unused until their safe arrival. Humbolt had shaved; Ilona had become accustomed to the dark shadow of an incipient beard shading his face, but now he looked fresh and clean.

Jan hadn't shown a trace of a beard all through their mission; Ilona guessed he had undergone depilatory treatment while still at university.

"You are clear to leave your vessel and enter Station One," said the woman. Ilona saw that she was quite young, good-looking in a wholesome, collegiate way. Blond. Toothy smile.

Once Humbolt shut down all the ship's systems—except for housekeeping and life support—they put on their space suits and helmets and rode on the trolley out of the twelve encircling spheres in silence. The three of them got up from their seats and trooped to the ship's main airlock: Ilona first, then Humbolt and finally Meitner. Ilona stumbled slightly, and Humbolt grasped her arm to steady her.

Humbolt reached past Ilona and tapped out the code that unsealed the airlock hatch. It swung slowly open.

Beyond the hatch, in the receiving area of the orbiting lunar station, stood a small crowd of people.

"Welcome home!" one of them shouted. And they all cheered.

Surprised, and more than a little delighted at their reception, Ilona blurted, "It's good to be back."

A diminutive man impeccably dressed in a perfectly fitted chocolate-brown jacket over tan slacks stepped forward and extended his hand to Ilona.

"Welcome back, Baroness Magyr," he said, with a warm smile as he helped her over the hatch's coaming. "I am Harvey Millard."

The Interplanetary Council's executive director, Ilona knew. He's come up here to the lunar orbit to greet us?

Millard was small and trim, a compact man with a finely sculpted face that was smiling warmly at Ilona. Dapper little moustache. Bright light brown eyes.

Ilona stammered, "I . . . we . . . we didn't expect a reception committee."

Millard's easy smile widened. "Why not? You've returned from an arduous journey. You've made significant discoveries. The whole world is excited about your safe return."

And Ilona thought, But I didn't save my father. The mission failed.

Millard was going on, "You've certainly complicated my life. Half the astronomical community is pushing for a chance to go to Neptune and study the ruins you discovered."

"My father discovered them," Ilona corrected. "We merely traced his path."

"You located the ruins and reported the information to the worlds. Remember what's-his-name's dictum: 'Science is to make discoveries *and to publish them.*'"

From behind Ilona, Jan Meitner said, "Michael Faraday."

Humbolt shook his head. "I don't think it was him."

"Who, then?"

Millard broke into their incipient argument. "It doesn't really matter, does it? The thing is, you're home, safe and sound."

Without Father, Ilona thought. With nothing of Father except a few scraps of DNA samples.

But she said nothing aloud.

Gesturing the trio into the crowded receiving area, Millard told them, "We've arranged a dinner party for you tonight. Tomorrow you meet with the board of directors of the Astronomical Association. And there are a few thousand news reporters who want to talk to you."

Ilona managed to say, "I'm overwhelmed."

With his sunny smile Millard replied, "It's my job to see that you're not overly taxed by all this. But I must say that you've certainly earned all the attention."

"It's . . ." Ilona searched for a word, but ended up with repeating, ". . . overwhelming."

"Fame can be a burden," Millard said, as he took Ilona gently by the elbow and led her through the crowd toward a hatch at the rear of the reception area.

The throng parted like the Red Sea as Millard guided Ilona, Humbolt and Meitner toward the hatch.

He hesitated as they approached it. "I'm afraid the medical staff has first claim on you. They have to certify that you're fit to mix with the rest of humanity."

Ilona glanced questioningly at the crowd on either side of them.

"Oh, them?" Millard said, grinning. "Officially, they're not here. Neither am I, officially."

With a grin that showed teeth, Humbolt raised his voice. "I hope we're not carrying any alien bugs."

Meitner said firmly, "We haven't been outside of our spacecraft; we didn't visit the Black Hole of Calcutta, for God's sake."

THE QUESTION

The medical team's physical examinations seemed perfunctory to Ilona, but she told herself that was probably because it was highly automated. Diagnostic machines scanned their bodies, tested their reflexes, sampled their fluids—quickly, efficiently, almost painlessly.

It took little more than an hour for the medical staff to pronounce the three returned travelers physically healthy, clear of potentially infectious agents and mentally astute.

The dinner that Millard had arranged was smaller than Ilona had expected: merely the three of them, Millard himself and five others—all members of the Interplanetary Council's board of directors.

The food was good, the wines better. Ilona drank sparingly, though, feeling somehow that she was still under examination, that Millard had arranged everything to test her.

Humbolt had no such fears, apparently. He drank and ate as though being feted was nothing less than he deserved. Even Meitner seemed to loosen up happily after a few glasses.

Sitting at Ilona's right, Millard congratulated the three of them for their "epic voyage" and found several reasons to toast them all. Humbolt took it as nothing less than his due; Meitner smiled and nodded at all the congratulations. Ilona's smile was much more guarded.

At last the dinner ended and Millard walked them to their quarters, halfway around the huge metallic ring that made up the space station. Through the oversized viewscreens that studded the station's central passageway Ilona could see the Moon, seemingly close enough to touch, bleak and barren and empty.

But beyond it rode the blue and white hemisphere of Earth, vibrant with life, a shining jewel in the dark emptiness of space.

Ilona's quarters were ample: a single compartment, but it was furnished with a comfortable bed and a viewscreen that could connect with more than a thousand Earth-based visual news stations. She fell asleep watching the day's news from Earth, all upbeat, happy, purposeful stories. No bad news. Nothing gloomy.

It's all controlled, Ilona realized as she drifted off to sleep. Everything is under control.

She was awakened by an automated female figure on the viewscreen, telling her she was expected at a breakfast meeting with Millard and two other IP Council members in exactly two hours.

She showered and dressed, then used the station's information system to locate the compartment where the breakfast was to take place.

It was a modest room, she found. As Ilona stepped through its doorway she saw Harvey Millard standing in front of a man-tall food dispenser, deep in discussion with Derek Humbolt. Otherwise the room was empty.

The two broke off their conversation and turned toward her.

"Baroness Magyr," said Millard, extending both his hands as he walked toward her.

With a faint smile she said, "Please, call me Ilona."

Millard dipped his chin as he replied, "And I am Harvey."

"Good morning, Harvey," said Ilona. "And Derek. Where are the others?"

"Actually, you are ten minutes early for this meeting."

"But last night—"

Looking almost guilty, Millard said, "I gave both you and Captain Humbolt, here, an earlier time than the others. I have something to ask of you and I thought we could discuss it before the rest of the troop arrives."

Ilona glanced at the table in the middle of the room. It was set for nine.

"I see," she said.

"Would you like some coffee?" Millard asked.

Feeling slightly put out, Ilona replied, "I'd like to know what you want to discuss."

Millard's expression turned serious, almost grim. "A return to Neptune, actually."

"Return?"

"Yes."

"You want me to return to Neptune?"

Nodding, Millard repeated, "Yes."

"What on Earth for? Why should I?"

Humbolt broke in, "I'm going."

Ilona stared at his humorless face. He was serious, she realized. "But I thought you were going to retire. You told me—"

"He's made me an offer I can't refuse," Humbolt said, his expression dead serious.

"I don't understand," Ilona said.

Millard said, "Please allow me to explain."

"Please do," said Ilona, feeling somewhere between bewildered and exasperated.

As the three of them sat at one end of the table, Millard said, "we have a curious situation on our hands."

"Curious?" Ilona asked.

"Difficult, I should have said."

"How so?"

Humbolt grumbled, "Politics."

"It's much deeper than politics, I'm afraid," said Millard.

Feeling puzzled, Ilona murmured, "Please explain."

"Certain members of the Council," Millard said, "are dragging their feet about funding a new mission to Neptune."

"Dragging their feet?"

"They don't believe us," Humbolt blurted.

More gently, Millard explained, "They don't want to believe that the wreckage you found on Neptune is from an extraterrestrial visitor."

Ilona nodded slowly. It *is* a lot to accept, she thought.

"They're not willing to fund another mission to Neptune until we have shown incontrovertible evidence that the samples you've brought back to us are of extraterrestrial origin."

"What else could they be?"

Millard hesitated. But Humbolt groused, "They claim we planted the evidence just to get them to fund another mission to Neptune."

"Planted the evidence?" Ilona repeated. "That's silly. Stupid! Why?" Then she realized, "They're calling us liars!"

Humbolt nodded, tight-lipped.

"Personally," said Millard, "I think they're frightened. Scared out of their wits."

Humbolt snapped, "Ostriches. Hiding their heads in the sand."

Ilona stared at the two of them.

"It's a lot for them to swallow," Millard said, "the idea that our solar system was invaded by aliens who sterilized the planet Uranus by bombarding it with moons from Neptune."

"Sterilized Uranus?" Ilona blurted.

With a tight nod, Millard replied, "Yes. We've found that Uranus once supported an intelligent civilization. But it was wiped out, the entire planet was scoured of life. Completely sterilized."

"No," Ilona objected. "That's not possible."

"That's what I thought," said Humbolt, grimly.

"It's not only possible," Millard replied, "but it actually happened. A young astronomer named Teresa Gomez made the discovery and subsequent investigations have supported her conclusion."

"They even knocked the planet sidewise," Humbolt added.

Millard went on, "The entire astronomical profession is in a whirl over Gomez's findings. It *is* rather staggering, you know."

Ilona realized what the man was saying. "And the wreckage we found on Neptune—"

"Supports the basic idea," said Millard. "Our solar system was invaded by aliens who wiped out the intelligent civilization on Uranus, apparently two million years ago."

"That's . . ." Ilona searched for a word. "It seems outrageous!"

"Yes, quite. But if it's true, we have an enemy out among the stars," Millard said firmly. "An enemy who may return to wipe us out of existence."

"While the goddamned ostriches do nothing," Humbolt growled.

"Until the aliens return to finish us off," said Millard.

Ilona stared at the two of them. They're serious. This threat is real.

"So what can we do?" she asked.

"Go back to Neptune," Humbolt answered. "Now. As quick as we can get your ship refurbished. Before they find a way to stop us."

"Go back now?"

"Yes," Millard agreed. "Find enough evidence to convince the skeptics—"

"Ostriches," Humbolt muttered.

"Enough evidence to silence the naysayers," said Millard.

Ilona shook her head. "If they don't believe us now . . . if they think we're lying to them . . ."

"I know," said Millard. "They may never change their minds. But we've got to present enough evidence to make it impossible for them to vote against sending follow-up missions to Neptune."

"Politics," Humbolt groused again.

Just then the door from the corridor outside opened and in trooped six people: Jan Meitner and five members of the Interplanetary Council.

All men, Ilona noted.

The breakfast started well enough. Smiling introductions, then a trio of robots came in to serve orange-flavored drinks and canapés. It wasn't until they were all digging into their soufflés that one of the councilmen said to Humbolt:

"You don't really believe that the wreckage you found on the seabed is from an extraterrestrial visitor to our solar system, do you?"

Humbolt gulped down the mouthful he'd been chewing and replied, "What else could it be?"

"One of our early probes to Neptune, of course," the councilman replied. He was rail-thin, his face cadaverous, his hair white and thinning.

Humbolt glanced at Millard, then answered, "We checked all the probes sent to Neptune. None of them was that big, or that old."

The man sitting beside the questioner—younger, fleshier, smiling disarmingly—asked, "You really believe the wreckage is two million years old?"

"That's what the evidence shows."

His smiling dimming a notch, the younger man said, "Evidence can be tampered with."

Humbolt slammed his fork down on the tabletop. Pointing at the questioner, he said, "You're lucky that dueling is outlawed."

Everyone stopped eating. Ilona saw that Humbolt's face was smoldering red.

The young man got to his feet. "Oh, you're going to challenge me to a duel?"

Rising from his chair, Humbolt said, "I'll knock you on your fucking ass!"

Millard, sitting at the head of the table, stood up also. "Let's keep things civil, please. We can have a difference of opinion without a brawl."

Humbolt pointed across the table. "This stiff called me a liar!"

"I'm sure he didn't mean it that way," said Millard. To the councilman he added, "Did you, Brad?"

Keeping his eyes fixed on Humbolt, the councilman replied thinly, "No, I didn't. I guess I spoke without thinking."

Humbolt nodded once and wordlessly sat down. The councilman did the same.

Still standing, Millard suggested softly, "Perhaps we should change the subject."

INTERVIEWS

The breakfast ended in tense silence, except for a few pointless questions by the other councilmen. Few of them were asked of Ilona, for which she was grateful. She felt just as angry as Humbolt at the insinuation that the young councilman had made so blatantly.

As the group headed for the door, Millard took Ilona by the wrist. Humbolt and Meitner stopped a few steps away from him. "Time for your grilling," Millard said, almost morosely.

"Grilling?" she asked.

"News reporters. They're champing at the bit to talk to the three of you."

Ilona lifted her chin a notch. "The price of fame," she muttered. She meant it as a joke, but it sounded quite serious, even in her own ears.

Leading the three of them along the station's main corridor, Millard explained, "Your interviewers aren't here on the space station. They're all in their news offices on Earth or the Moon."

Grinning tightly, Humbolt said, "So we can turn them off if we want to."

"I wouldn't advise that," replied Millard. "Just answer their questions, be honest and fair with them. Win them to our side."

"Side?" Meitner wondered aloud.

"We want to build support for your return to Neptune," said Millard. "We need the news media on our side."

Ilona nodded her understanding, but inwardly she felt she was heading not for an interview, but an inquisition.

Alien invaders, she thought. It does sound ludicrous. But the evidence is there. We found it. And Millard says they sterilized Uranus. Wiped out an entire intelligent race. Why? What could have motivated such a slaughter, such a holocaust?

And then she realized that the aliens caused her father's death, as well. They killed Father! Had her father not discovered the wreckage and put everything on the line to reach it, he would still be alive. And a cold, implacable hatred was born inside her.

Millard showed them into a small conference room. Four comfortable chairs were arrayed around a polished oval table. Tiny cameras ringed the walls, which were bare faux-maple panels.

What's behind those walls? Ilona wondered as she sat in the chair Millard held for her. But her mind overrode such a triviality. They killed Father. They caused Father's death!

Abruptly one of the panels brightened into a viewscreen. A good-looking young brunette's slightly Mixed-Asian face appeared on it. She was smiling enough to show perfect teeth; her hair was made up flawlessly, not a curl out of place. Ilona stared at her with eyes turned icy cold.

"Good morning," she said cheerily. "I'm Cass Crucet. I'll be moderating this circus. It will be live, so please think before you speak."

Ilona nodded, and noted Humbolt and Jan doing the same.

"Please try to relax and speak to the image on your screen," Crucet continued. "We go live in three minutes."

The viewscreen went blank.

Relax, Ilona said to herself. God knows how many reporters are out there to question us and she wants me to relax. She glanced at Millard; he looked perfectly at ease. Of course he's been through this hundreds of times. Thousands, maybe.

"Live in thirty seconds," a disembodied voice announced. Ilona sat up a little straighter.

Cass Crucet's face suddenly reappeared. With a warm smile, she introduced herself and the four of them sitting around the table. Then,

"Our first interviewer is Kwame Ngono, from Lagos, Nigeria."

A handsome face appeared on the screen. With a dazzling smile, he asked, "Baroness Magyr, how did you enjoy your jaunt to the planet Neptune?"

Ilona took an instant dislike to the man and his question. "I didn't go to Neptune for enjoyment," she snapped. "I went in search of my father."

For several seconds there was no reaction. The time lag from Earth to lunar orbit, Ilona realized.

At last the Nigerian reporter asked, "And you found him?"

"I found the remains of his dead body."

Again the three-second delay. Ilona found it maddening.

"I am so sorry to hear that. You must have loved him very much."

Fighting down the fury that was rising in her, Ilona replied, "He was a great man. A magnificent person."

And so it went. Interview after interview, question after question, had practically nothing to do with what they had found at Neptune. All the reporters wanted to hear was of Ilona's quest for her father, and her devastation at finding him dead.

Millard tried to break in with, "The mission made a tremendous discovery at Neptune."

"The ruins of an old spacecraft," said Cass Crucet. Then, "Now here's Teri Winkler, from Toronto."

Another perfectly coiffed woman's face filled the viewscreen.

"Baroness Magyr, how did you feel when you realized your father was dead?"

Ilona swallowed visibly before answering, "How would you feel if you found your father's remains?"

Lowering her voice slightly, Winkler said mournfully, "It must have been devastating."

"Yes," said Ilona. "Devastating."

At last it was over. Ilona slumped back in her chair, her dress clinging uncomfortably to her perspiring body.

Cass Crucet was as cheerful as ever. "That was marvelous. Simply marvelous. I think you've shown the world that even scientists have human hearts."

"Thank you so much, Ms. Crucet," said Millard, smiling as if he really meant his words.

The viewscreen went blank.

"Two frickin' hours," Humbolt moaned, "and we hardly got to mention the ruins we found."

"They were more concerned with Ilona's human-interest story," said Millard.

Meitner, sitting across the table from Ilona, peered at her. "Are you all right, Ilona?" he asked.

"Yes. I'm angry, that's all. We didn't get a chance to tell the rest of the story."

"Not yet," murmured Humbolt.

Rubbing his hands together, Millard said, "Well, tomorrow we go to Copenhagen and make our report to the Council's assembly. They'll be interested in what we have to say, I guarantee you."

Humbolt made a sour face. "Let's hope so."

++
++

Late in the day the four of them left the space station and rode down to Earth on a private interplanetary council rocketplane. Ilona and the three men were the only passengers. Four of the ship's commodious, comfortable armchairs had been arranged to face each other. Otherwise the compartment was empty.

As the ship pushed off gently from the station, Meitner complained, "All those news reporters, all those questions, and they hardly seemed interested at all in what we found on Neptune."

"Stupid fuckers," Humbolt grumbled.

"No," said Millard. "I think they were told beforehand to stick to Ilona's story and downplay our discovery."

"Stupid," Humbolt repeated.

With a slight shake of his head, Millard explained, "There are important people on the Council who apparently don't want Earth's population to be upset by the idea that aliens invaded our solar system."

"And might come back," Ilona added.

"Precisely," said Millard. "They want to keep our story as nonthreatening as possible. They want to keep a lid on it."

"Huh?" questioned Meitner. They all explained to him the overarching impact of their discovery as they had discussed the night before.

Very seriously, Meitner countered, "Well, they won't be able to keep a lid on what we have to report to the Council tomorrow."

Millard stared at him for a long wordless moment. At last he murmured, "Let's hope so."

A long white limousine was waiting for them as their ship rolled toward the Interplanetary Council's private hangar at the Copenhagen spaceport. Ilona and the others were escorted by plainclothes guards into the limo, which whisked them to a soaring glass-sheathed hotel tower in the midst of Copenhagen's congested downtown area.

The hotel's manager personally greeted the four of them as they entered the lobby. He showed them to a row of sumptuous suites on the hotel's topmost floor.

Ilona was unimpressed with the splendor. She thought of her family residence in Budaörs: less ostentatious but more comfortable.

Looking through the sweeping windows of her bedroom, Ilona saw that the sun was setting. Lights along the city's narrow, twisting streets were turning on. People were thronging the sidewalks, heading for dinner, for meetings with friends, for romance and perhaps even adventure.

Normal people. Ordinary people. Not the Baroness Magyr. Not an explorer who had returned from distant Neptune.

She almost envied those tiny figures swarming along the streets so far below. But then a voice within her intoned, *You are the head of one of the oldest families in Europe. You have a duty to perform. A Magyr always places her duty ahead of her private desires.*

Ilona nodded her agreement.

REPORT TO THE ASSEMBLY

To her surprise, once they arrived at the sweeping modernistic building that housed the council's headquarters, Ilona and the three men were shown not to the Council's assembly hall, but to a much smaller, intimate conference room.

Almost apologetically their escort—a tall, trim young man with a thick head of hair so blond it looked almost white—gestured to the narrow conference table. Ilona saw that there were pitchers and bottles and tiny plates of food carefully arranged along the table.

"The committee will be with you in a few minutes," their guide said. Gesturing to the food, he added, "Please make yourselves comfortable."

Millard went to the head of the table and pulled out its high-backed wheeled chair. Like the other chairs along the table it was upholstered in dark brown leather.

Gesturing for the other three to sit, Millard put on a guarded smile. "When handed a lemon," he said, reaching for the bottle standing on the table before him, "make lemonade."

Ilona sat warily. "I thought we were going to make our report to the full Council," she said.

"Apparently not," answered Millard. He pulled off the bottle's stopper, took a sniff, then with a disappointed frown silently resealed it and pushed it away.

The four of them sat in tense silence. Ilona saw that the conference room was opulently decorated: its high vaulted ceiling bore a painted star map; the walls showed murals from Earth's long, often bloody history.

Humbolt reached for the silver pitcher standing in front of his place, popped it open and took a deep sniff.

"It's not alcoholic," he sighed.

Millard grinned at him. "They want us upright and sober."

Just then the door to the corridor outside slid open and a half-dozen men trooped in. Millard shot to his feet; Ilona and the other two men arose more slowly.

"Harvey," said the leader of the committee. "It's good to see you again."

With a self-deprecating little smile Millard took the man's extended hand. "I've only been away for a day and a half, Yancey."

Millard introduced the committee, starting with Yancey Darbin, the president of the Council, who would be chairing the meeting.

Darbin pulled out a chair next to Ilona's as the other committee members found seats for themselves. Once everyone was seated, Darbin asked, in a loud, almost demanding voice, "Now what's all this about the wreckage of an alien spacecraft?"

Millard nodded toward Ilona. "I think the Baroness Magyr can answer that."

All eyes turned to Ilona.

Feeling slightly uncomfortable at the sudden attention, Ilona began, "As you undoubtedly already know, we went to Neptune to search for my father."

"And you found him dead, I am sorry for your loss," Darbin said impatiently. He paused for a moment. Ilona thought his condolences less than sincere. He then asked, "What about this wreckage on the bottom of the sea?"

"The wreckage covered almost four football fields, we have not mapped it yet. Data collected by our ships computers showed that the wreckage dates from approximately two million years ago," Ilona said. "Apparently it was originally an orbital station that the aliens deorbited when they left our solar system."

"Aliens?" squeaked one of the councilmen.

"Aliens," Ilona repeated. "They apparently visited our solar system some two million years ago."

"Apparently," Darbin echoed.

One of the councilmen on the side of the table opposite Ilona asked, "How do you know the wreckage was alien? From another civilization?"

Ilona gestured to Meitner. "Dr. Meitner is better equipped to answer that than I am."

Without waiting a moment, Meitner began, "The alloy used in these structures is not earth-like by any means. We gathered more than two dozen fragments from the wreckage and used radioactive dating to establish their age. They all are from approximately two million years ago."

"Approximately," echoed the councilman.

"All of them," added another.

"That's what our tests showed."

"Could the tests be wrong?"

Meitner smiled thinly. "That possibility is very close to zero."

"But it's not zero."

"Neither is the possibility that the sun will not rise tomorrow morning," Meitner retorted. "But I wouldn't bet on it."

A few chuckles went around the table.

Millard broke in. "The point is that the wreckage shows our solar system was visited by intelligent aliens some two million years ago. And they destroyed the civilization on the planet Uranus. Sterilized the planet."

"That's hard to believe," said Darbin.

Ilona stared at the Texan. He smiles as he says it, she thought. But he says it.

The questioning continued. Ilona felt like a prisoner before the bar of justice. These men are hostile, she realized. They may smile politely but they don't believe what we're telling them. They don't want to believe.

At last she interrupted a tedious repetition of the questions they had been answering for more than an hour.

"This is getting us nowhere," Ilona snapped. "You have our full report. All the videos and photographs. Your scientific staff can review it in detail. The samples can be tested in your laboratories. The facts are there. Why must we debate the issue?"

Before any of the councilmen could reply, Millard said softly, "Because we are dealing with the most momentous issue in the history of the human race. Was our solar system invaded by aliens two million years ago?"

Ilona immediately added, "And why did they destroy the civilization on Uranus?"

Meitner added, "And cause the most recent ice age on our own planet Earth?"

A cold silence fell across the conference table.

Humbolt, who had been silent throughout most of the questioning, leaned back in his chair and smiled sardonically. "We're talking life and death here. For the whole human race. Those suckers might come back here to finish what they started."

DECISION

Darbin leaned back in his chair. "And you want us to send a full-fledged expedition to Neptune to study the ruins you found."

Nodding slowly, Millard said, "I think it's imperative."

"So does the scientific community," said one of the councilmen. "I've been getting calls from all over the world. Thousands of 'em."

"They all want to go to Neptune," said the man beside him.

"I imagine they do," Millard said.

"That would be a major undertaking," said Darbin. "We'd have to discuss it fully in the complete assembly."

"Which would take time to arrange," said another councilman.

Millard said, "I understand your problem. That's why I'm proposing that we send Baroness Magyr and her crew back to Neptune immediately, to begin a thorough examination of the wreckage they found there."

"Immediately?"

"As soon as our ship is refitted," said Ilona.

"And who's going to pay for this excursion?" one of the councilmen demanded.

"Excursion?" snapped Ilona, her eyes blazing.

"Trip," amended the councilman. "Visit. Examination."

Millard said, "Financing one vehicle's second flight to research Neptune's wreckage is well within the Council's discretionary funding."

"Yes, perhaps, but—"

Darbin interrupted, "Director Millard is correct. The Council can finance the flight."

"Not without a vote!"

His weathered face set in a stern scowl, Darbin lapsed into a Texas drawl as he said, "We have a majority of the finance subcommittee sittin' around this h'yar table. What say you?"

Obviously taken aback, the councilmen glanced at each other.

Easing into a tight smile, Darbin said, "All in favor, raise your hands."

Two of their hands shot up immediately, then another, and at last the final two.

Darbin nodded. "It's unanimous. Thank you, gentlemen." Turning back to Ilona, he added, "Looks like you're goin' back to Neptune."

Once the meeting broke up, Millard brought Ilona, Humbolt and Meitner to his office, where he ordered a luncheon from one of his assistants.

"It's a cheerful afternoon," he said, gesturing to the sunlit balcony beyond his office's sweeping windows. "Why don't we eat outside?"

From the expression on the man's face, Ilona got the impression that Millard felt they could talk more freely outside, without anyone possibly eavesdropping.

Once they were seated in the warm sunshine around a circular table with their lunches before them, Millard said, "You got a glimpse of what I'm facing."

Humbolt reached for a slice of bread as he said, "They sure don't look enthusiastic."

"They're frightened," said Millard. "You've brought them news that they don't want to hear."

"Darbin kept them in line, though."

Millard smiled grimly. "Darbin has seen to it that you won't be here to plead your case. I imagine he's half hoping that you'll break your necks while you're out at Neptune."

Ilona felt her brows knitting. "Really. A man may smile and smile and still be a villain."

Meitner stared at Millard. "You don't really think he'll sabotage our ship, do you?"

"Of course not. But if anything goes wrong with your vessel while you're alone out there, I'm sure Darbin won't shed too many tears."

"But the problem will still exist!" Ilona insisted. "Killing us won't solve anything."

Millard carefully put down his fork and replied, "If it's been two million years since the aliens left our solar system, what are the chances that they'll return while Darbin and his entire generation are still living?"

No one answered.

Breaking the silence, Millard said, "I've found that a good deal of politics consists of sweeping problems under the rug and leaving them for future generations to deal with."

Still none of them had a response to offer.

FOrCED ADDITION

Ilona turned her penthouse hotel suite into a busy, efficient office. She called in two of her servitors from Budaörs to assist her in readying Hári János for the flight back to Neptune.

Humbolt worked with her, shuttling between his hotel suite (next to Ilona's) and the spacecraft now orbiting a few hundred kilometers from the moon. Meitner, meanwhile, seemed consumed by meetings with scientists who wanted to learn what he had found at Neptune. For the first time in his young life, Meitner found himself the center of his elders' attention.

Ilona saw that Jan basked in his newfound importance. She smiled at his happiness.

The fifth day of their preparations, Millard phoned. From the expression on his face on the hotel suite's wall screen, Ilona guessed he had hit a problem.

Without a word of preliminary chitchat Millard announced, "The Council wants to send a representative along with you."

Surprised, Ilona asked, "A representative?"

"A scientist," Millard explained. "One that they pick. From one of the universities they fund."

"Another scientist?" Ilona wondered. "Why do they—"

Millard interrupted, "To keep an eye on you. To make certain you're not faking the data, or misinterpreting what you find."

"Not faking the data?"

Nodding unhappily, Millard replied, "It's their way of keeping you honest."

"Keeping me honest?" Ilona felt her blood pressure rising.

"Please don't get angry. It won't do any good."

Ilona pulled in a deep breath. It did not calm her. "You're telling me that the Council still doesn't trust us!"

"I wouldn't exactly put it that way."

"What way would you put it?"

Looking almost as unhappy as Ilona felt, Millard said, "Ilona, it's a fait accompli. Or as Darbin would put it, a 'done deal.' Either you take their man along with you or they will refuse you permission to go."

As she sat staring at the screen, Ilona realized that both her fists were tightly clenched. Slowly opening her hands, she echoed, "A done deal."

"I'm afraid so."

"Well," sighed Ilona, "we'll have to add meals for another person. That means off-loading some of the scientific equipment. Jan will be unhappy."

"Can't be helped," said Millard, his expression somewhere between gloom and seething anger.

"Who is this person?" Ilona asked.

"I don't know yet. He'll probably contact you later today, or tomorrow at the latest."

For the rest of the day Ilona kept an eye on her phone screen, but no call came through from the scientist who was to join their crew.

At precisely ten o'clock the following morning, however, the phone buzzed. Ilona read the name of the caller: Francine Savoy, Massachusetts Institute of Technology.

Taking a deep breath to calm herself, Ilona said, "Phone answer," and put on a smile.

A young woman's face appeared on the screen: a spry black woman, with the sleek looks of a Caribbean Islander. Wishing she'd been able to look up the woman's CV before speaking with her, Ilona said tentatively, "Dr. Savoy?"

Francine Savoy smiled prettily and replied, "Yes. And you must be Baroness Magyr."

"Correct," said Ilona. "Where are you? How soon can we meet face-to-face?"

"I'm in your hotel's lobby," said Francine Savoy, "and I can come up immediately, if that's all right with you."

Ilona hesitated a heartbeat, then replied, "Yes. Of course. Come right up."

"Wonderful. I'm sending you my CV, so you can look it over while I come up to your suite."

Efficient, Ilona thought. Aloud, she replied, "That's fine."

Francine's face on the viewscreen was immediately replaced by the woman's curriculum vitae. It wasn't very long, barely three pages. Ilona saw that Dr. Savoy had graduated with high honors from MIT, with a double major in astronomy and biology. Impressive, Ilona thought. Since graduation she had spent most of her time at the Institute, studying the gigantic whale-like inhabitants of the planet Jupiter.

She's never been off-Earth, Ilona realized. Strictly a lab rat. Then she noticed that Savoy had taken a hatful of psychology courses, as well.

Psychology, Ilona thought. Maybe Darbin expects her to work up psych profiles of Derek, Jan and me.

The buzzer from her front door sounded. Ilona got up from her desk, glanced at the second bedroom, where her two assistants were busily at work, and called, "Door open, please."

Francine Savoy stood in the corridor outside, looking for all the world like a lost orphan.

She was tiny, barely as tall as Ilona's shoulders, and so thin that a fair breeze might have knocked her over. Dark hair cut boyishly short. She wore a thin pale nondescript pullover sweater and a knee-length dark skirt. Her skinny legs were bare, her feet nestled in obviously shabby sandals.

But her smile was gleaming and her jet-black eyes seemed to sparkle.

"Dr. Savoy?" Ilona asked.

Extending her hand, Savoy said, "Baroness Magyr. It's a pleasure to meet you." Her voice was sharp, penetrating.

Ilona gestured Dr. Savoy into her living room, saying, "I should call the two men who make up the ship's crew. We can have lunch together, get to know each other."

"That would be fine," said Francine. "I missed breakfast on the flight from Boston."

"You must be famished!"

Nodding and grinning, Francine Savoy said, "Close to it."

Doctor savoy, Ilona said to herself as she led the elfin black woman into her makeshift office. she looks awfully young to have a phd. she must be very bright, ambitious.

For lack of anything else to say, Ilona heard herself ask, "Where were you born, Dr. Savoy?"

"Please call me Francine, Baroness."

"Very well . . . Francine. And I am Ilona."

Francine Savoy nodded happily. "Thank you, Ilona. I was born in Kingston, Jamaica, although my father came from Zambia and my mother from Saint Kitts."

Ilona murmured regrets as she gestured Savoy to one of the living room's delicate little chairs. "I'm sorry the place is in such a mess. We're—"

"Preparing for your flight back to Neptune. That's why I'm here."

"Of course," said Ilona. "I'll ask our other two crew members to join us for lunch."

"Captain Humbolt and Dr. Meitner. I'm anxious to meet them."

Looking at Savoy perched on the elegantly designed chair like a little bird, Ilona thought that this young woman didn't seem anxious about anything. Yet there was something about her, some inner tension.

"You're very young to have a doctorate," Ilona said as she sat at her room's petite desk.

Her smile fading just the slightest bit, Savoy replied, "I worked very hard. No play, just study, study, study."

"I see."

"And the occasional happy hour," Savoy added, her grin widening.

"Oh?"

"You learn a thing or two from having a wide variety of partners and dalliances."

"Really?"

Staring at the tiny figure, Ilona thought, She's painfully honest. Or is this just a ploy to gain my trust?

Turning to the wall screen, Ilona put through calls to Humbolt and Meitner. Derek was in the next suite, reviewing the meal provisions being readied for their mission. Jan was at the university, still enjoying the glow of fame.

They both agreed to meet at Ilona's suite for lunch.

Ilona studied the two men as she introduced them to Francine Savoy. Humbolt looked down at the young woman's bony figure with obvious interest. Ilona got a vision of Derek licking his chops. Meitner seemed shy, perplexed. Ilona thought he looked almost embarrassed.

The four of them sat around the circular table out on the suite's patio. The sunlight was warm, tempered by a breeze wafting in from the nearby sea.

Savoy seemed to enjoy the presence of the two men. She told them of her studies of the fauna and flora of Europa. Meitner was full of questions; Humbolt had little to say, but his eyes stayed fixed on Francine's expressive face.

As they worked their way through the salads and main courses on the table before them, Francine looked toward Humbolt and said, "I understand you've actually been to Jupiter, Captain. I was—"

"Derek," Humbolt interrupted. "Call me Derek."

"Derek," Francine echoed.

With a smile that Ilona thought looked wolfish, Humbolt said, "We're going to be cooped up together for a couple of months. Might as well be friendly."

"I appreciate that."

Humbolt's smile widened. Ilona's eyes rolled.

Suddenly Meitner stammered, "We . . . we're all . . . very happy to welcome you to our crew, Dr. Savoy."

"Francine," she corrected.

His face reddening noticeably, Jan mumbled, "Francine."

Ilona thought the two men were making asses of themselves. She decided to take control of the situation.

"Director Millard is worried that you've been added to our crew by the Council as a sort of spy."

"Spy?" Savoy blurted, her eyes going wide.

"To see if our findings were accurate . . . real."

For an instant silence fell across the table. Even the breeze stopped billowing.

Then Francine Savoy—staring into Ilona's eyes—answered, "That's entirely correct. The Council is afraid that your report of your discoveries on Neptune is . . . how should I put it? Exaggerated."

"False," Ilona insisted.

Nodding, Savoy admitted, "That's what President Darbin and some of the others suspect. That's why they added me to your crew."

"And what do you think?" Humbolt challenged.

Savoy smiled minimally. "I really don't know what to think. That's why I'm going with you to Neptune: to learn, to discover, not to spy."

Ilona nodded. Good answer, she thought. But she admitted to being a spy far too easily. It seems I can't trust her quite yet.

CREDENTIALS

++
++

The following morning, Ilona took Francine Savoy up to the orbiting *Hári János*. As their shuttle rocket approached the spacecraft Savoy stared at its image on the viewscreen built into the seat back in front of her.

"It's big," she said, half to herself.

Sitting beside her, Ilona explained, "Most of it consists of pressure spheres, to handle the depth of the ocean."

"Yes, of course."

"Our work area is in the middle," Ilona continued. "Rather cramped."

"Of course," Savoy repeated.

"Our personal quarters are quite small, as well. But as comfortable as the designers could make them."

"That's good."

Their shuttle established orbit alongside *Hári János* and the crew extended a tunnel connecting the two vehicles while the steward attending the otherwise-empty passenger deck went through the standard spiel about weightlessness.

Ignoring the fluttering of her innards, Ilona got up carefully from her seat, keeping a firm grip on the seat back in front of herself. Savoy rose cautiously beside her, her face showing more curiosity than anxiety.

"You've experienced zero gee before?" Ilona asked.

Savoy started to shake her head, thought better of it and replied in a hushed voice, "No, never."

But she handled the experience quite well, Ilona thought. The two of them floated along the shuttle's passenger compartment to the hatch that opened onto the connecting tunnel.

"Enjoy your visit," said the steward, smiling robotically.

Ilona led the way along the short, springy tunnel to *Hári János*'s main hatch. She and Savoy hovered weightlessly while Ilona asked for the door hatch to open. The hatch swung open silently, and the two of them made their way to the empty trolley waiting for them.

Ilona watched Savoy force herself down onto the trolley's seat, then pushed herself down alongside her. Once they were both strapped in, the trolley started along the long, dimly lit tunnel.

"All this area is made up of the compression spheres?" Savoy asked.

Suppressing the urge to nod, Ilona kept looking straight ahead as she replied, "Yes."

Savoy did nod, and her dark cheeks paled noticeably.

At last the trolley slid to a stop and the two women floated carefully up to the platform. A few gliding steps and they were at the hatch to the changing room and then the hatch that led into the command center.

Savoy seemed unimpressed by the empty command center. Neither the array of viewscreens, the controls built into the central control chair's armrests, nor the sensor ring that hovered above the chair raised a comment from her.

Ilona said, "The maintenance people will install a seat for you."

Savoy nodded. "That will make things even tighter, won't it?"

"We'll manage."

"Of course."

Pointing to the hatches leading to the crew's quarters, Ilona said, "You'll bunk in beside me. Derek and Jan will take the two compartments on the other side."

A trace of a smile bent Savoy's lips slightly. "Like a co-ed dorm," she murmured.

"Do you want to see your bunk?"

"No, thanks. I've gone through all this on the simulator back at MIT."

"Ah! That's why there's nothing here that's new to you."

Gripping the back of the captain's chair with both hands, Savoy replied, "Zero gravity is new to me."

"You're handling it quite well."

"Tell that to my stomach."

Ilona laughed, then realized, "Do you need to upchuck?"

"Not yet."

Sitting herself down into her regular seat, Ilona asked, "What made Darbin pick you for this mission?"

Savoy remained standing, but her eyes seemed to focus on

something only she could see. For long moments she remained silent, seemingly staring into her own past.

At last she answered, "Heartbreak."

Ilona felt her brows hike up.

"I made the mistake of falling in love," Savoy said, her voice barely above a whisper. "He didn't."

"A fellow student?"

With a barely perceptible shake of her head, Savoy responded, "My department chief. When the request for a student came from the Council he put in my name in a hot second. Great way to get rid of me."

"I'm sorry," said Ilona.

Forcing a smile, Savoy said, "It's my own fault. I knew I was nothing more than a fling, as far as he was concerned. I knew he was married . . . but I made the error of listening to my heart instead of my brain. Bad mistake."

Ilona stared at her, not knowing what she should say—what she could say.

Keeping her smile in place, Francine Savoy said, "So now I'm going to Neptune with you, whether you like it or not." She hesitated a moment, then added, her smile fading, "Whether *I* like it or not."

BOOK IV

Return to Neptune

Departure

Hári János's command center was more crowded than ever with the added seat for Francine Savoy, next to Ilona's place. The four of them sat strapped into their seats as Humbolt went painstakingly through the prelaunch countdown procedure.

At last the launch director's image on the main viewscreen eased into a tight smile. "Prelaunch procedure completed," he said. "Launch in . . . sixty-five seconds."

"Sixty-five and counting," Humbolt replied.

Despite herself, Ilona tensed as the countdown ticked away. We're going back to Neptune, she told herself. A vision of the family's castle in Budaörs flashed into her mind. Will I ever see home again? she asked herself.

The countdown clock chanted, ". . . three . . . two . . . one: liftoff!" The ancient word was still used, despite the fact that *Hári János* was already in orbit. Ilona smiled inwardly at the anachronism. Tradition, she thought. Even in spaceflight we keep to our traditions.

She felt a gentle but firm push against her spine. The main viewscreen showed Earth, half masked in shadow, the visible half bright blue and white, visibly shrinking away from them.

"And we're off!" Humbolt announced, needlessly.

Ilona felt a sensation of uncertainty enough to get her stomach feel unsettled.

"We're off," Francine Savoy echoed, almost wistfully.

Meitner grinned as he said, "Next stop, the planet Neptune."

If all goes as planned, Ilona said to herself.

Day after day was monotonously the same aboard the spacecraft, like being in quarantine. They ate, they slept, they monitored the viewscreens, they planned why and how they would collect more wreckage samples and if they should collect some living specimens.

It seemed to Ilona as if *Hári János* were standing still in the vast star-studded expanse of space, just hanging in the middle of vacuum, going nowhere, accomplishing nothing.

But the numbers of Humbolt's central screen showed that their vessel was speeding toward its rendezvous with the distant Neptune, hurtling through space like a metal-plated meteor.

Humbolt insisted that they should eat their meals together. "Time for socializing," he said. So they dutifully sat next to the food dispensers in the command center's rear each mealtime and tried to think of something new and different to talk about. Francine stayed in her chair, she simply swiveled it around to join the other three at the dispensers.

At first Humbolt monopolized the conversations with tales of his adventures in the oceans of Jupiter and Saturn. Neither Meitner nor Ilona had any reminiscences to compare with his tales, and Humbolt obviously enjoyed being the center of attention.

One night, though, Francine interrupted the captain's monologue by saying, "You're very lucky, Derek. You've had such an interesting life."

"Well," Humbolt reacted, "it hasn't been *too* dull."

Her expression intense, Francine said, "The closest thing to an adventure that's ever happened to me is the day they killed my parents."

A surprised silence fell upon the four of them.

Ilona broke the spell with, "Who killed your parents?"

"The revolutionaries. They had taken control of Port Royal, where we lived, and gangs of them were going house to house, searching for what they called contraband."

"Contraband?" asked Meitner.

"Anything they could steal," Francine replied. "They found some bread and milk that my father had hidden in the bedroom for us children. They shot him right there, left him to die on the floor."

Ilona felt her innards turning to ice.

As calmly as if she were reading from a textbook, Francine went on, "When my mother began to shout at them they shot her too."

"My god," Meitner whispered.

"How old were you?" Ilona asked.

"I was almost ten. I had been hiding in the closet, but when I heard my mother scream I came out and saw her bleeding on the floor, next to my father."

"They were both dead?"

Nodding, Francine said, "Dying. Then they all raped me."

Meitner repeated, "My god."

Humbolt's eyes were locked on Francine's. "They raped you? Ten years old and they raped you?"

"Four of them," Francine answered, her voice low, trembling.

Ilona's reaction was different from the men's: she couldn't help wondering if Francine's story was true. The data she'd read in the Council's report she requested said that Francine's parents had died in an automobile accident.

Is this little urchin making up her tale? If so, why? To impress us? To gain our sympathy?

To impress the men, Ilona decided. And she wondered what she should do about it.

Ilona waited until the four of them went to their quarters to prepare for sleep. She stopped at the door to her bedroom and asked, "Francine, would you come in here with me, please?"

Francine looked uncertain, almost startled, but she quickly recovered her usual smiling expression. "Yes, of course."

Once they were both in her cramped compartment, Ilona sat on her bed and gestured Francine to the only chair, by the tiny built-in desk.

Francine sat down slowly, looking rather like a schoolchild who had been summoned to the principal's office.

"That story you told about your parents' deaths," Ilona began. "Is it really true?"

Francine blinked once, then replied, "Yes, of course it's true."

"But the Council's report sent to me says your parents were killed in an auto accident."

The nervous Dr. Savoy seemed to relax. She said, "The government has tried to hide the murders and terrorist crimes committed in those days. It's part of what they call their reconciliation program."

"Truly?"

Looking straight into Ilona's eyes, Francine replied, "Truly. I swear it."

Ilona nodded slowly. But she thought, And they say that Hungarians are the world's best liars.

Neptune looked like a giant unblemished blueberry in the central screen. Sitting beside the captain, Ilona asked, "How far from it are we?"

With the sensor ring wrapped around his head, Humbolt said, "In two days we'll settle into orbit around the planet."

Meitner, standing by the food dispensers with Francine, called, "Then we begin our real work."

Francine added, "Into the ocean!"

Ilona thought she sounded considerably less than eager.

Under Humbolt's vigilant eyes the crew checked and rechecked all of *Hári János*'s systems, sampling robots and supplies. Ilona felt it was little more than busywork, but it kept them gainfully occupied as the vessel slowed and began to establish a circular orbit around Neptune.

Sitting at Humbolt's right, Meitner said, "We should spend some time exploring Triton and the other moons, while we're here."

Ilona immediately replied, "We're here to study the ruins at the bottom of the ocean. The moons will have to wait."

Meitner gave Ilona a sour look, but he said nothing.

The following day, Humbolt leaned back in his control chair and announced, "That's it: we have established orbit."

Ilona smiled. "Good work, Derek."

Humbolt grinned, almost sheepishly. "The nav system did all the real work, boss. Makes my life easy."

"How soon do we go into the ocean?" Ilona asked.

"Flight plan calls for us to orbit the planet for twenty-four hours before we take the plunge."

"Must we waste twenty-four hours?"

With a shrug, Humbolt replied, "Not if you don't want to. I can run through a quick systems check and head into the ocean in less than . . . eight hours."

Glancing toward Francine and Meitner, Ilona asked, "Any objections?"

Francine shook her head. Meitner hesitated a moment, then said softly, "No objections."

"Okay," Humbolt declared. His fingers tip-to-tip, he announced, "Into the deep blue sea we go!"

Ilona reached behind her and pulled her seat's safety harness from its recess in the chair's back. Humbolt and the others did the same.

Their vessel made one complete orbit around Neptune as it swung lower, toward the ice pack swathing the world-girdling ocean. Ilona pictured the fish-like and squid-like organisms they had seen down in the ocean's depths. And the vast, undulating amoeba-like creatures. She felt a shudder surge through her body.

Once they were beneath the planet's cloud deck, everyone slumped in their chairs as deceleration took hold. Humbolt checked the readings on the ice pack's depth, then selected a point to release the nuclear-tipped missile that would break open the icy sheathing.

"Hold on," he commanded. "Gonna be a kick."

Hári János bounced hard as the nuclear explosion's shock wave hit the vessel.

"Everybody okay?" Humbolt shouted.

Ilona and the others gasped their acknowledgments.

"Okay! Immersion in . . . five minutes and counting." Humbolt's voice was strong and steady.

Ilona stared at the central viewscreen. The ocean was rushing up to meet them, frothing madly from the nuclear blast.

"Hang on!" Humbolt commanded.

Hári János slammed into the water with a body-rattling shock. Ilona felt the shoulder straps of her harness cutting into her brutally. Her head snapped back against the cushioned rest. She heard a sighing whimper from Francine, a deeper *oof* from Jan.

The viewscreens showed water bubbling all around them. Their ship bobbed like a cork for a breathless moment, then steadied as it drove deeper into the ocean.

Ilona turned her head toward Humbolt. He was busy checking the screens that showed the status of the ship's systems. No red lights, she saw. We're all right.

For several minutes no one spoke. The only sounds in the command center were the hum of electrical power and a distant throbbing, gurgling of water.

Never noticed that noise before, Ilona thought. Humbolt seemed unfazed by the sound. It must be all right, she told herself. Flicking through the screens to her left and right, she still saw no red warning lights.

"In case you haven't noticed," Humbolt wisecracked, "we're in the ocean, safe and sound. All systems operating normally."

Despite herself, Ilona felt immensely grateful for that announcement.

"A fish!" Francine shouted, pointing to the viewscreen on their extreme left.

Meitner teased, "Did you expect to see an elephant?"

Humbolt chuckled and Ilona smiled. Francine paid no attention to Jan's attempt at humor. She stared at the long, many-jointed fish as it swam alongside their vessel. Suddenly it darted away and disappeared.

"Make sure you take pictures as soon as you spot them, they move very quickly," he said to Francine.

"That one didn't like our company," Humbolt groused.

"It realized we're too big for it to eat," said Meitner.

"It was curious about us," Ilona said.

"Curiosity killed the cat," Humbolt said.

Ilona immediately replied, "Curiosity is the beginning of wisdom."

"If you live through it."

Yes, Ilona agreed silently. If you live through it.

Deeper they went. Ilona watched the different forms of life that swam around *Hári János* as the submersible sank deeper into the ocean. She heard an occasional groaning sound from the vessel's compressible outer layers, but Humbolt seemed unworried by the sound, so she thought it was nothing to be troubled about.

She concentrated her attention on the fish and other organisms in the water outside their vessel. Many of them seemed almost like fish on Earth, while others were strange assortments of wriggling arms and bulbous staring eyes. Francine seemed fascinated by the organisms in the sea, as well. Then Ilona remembered that she had studied biology at university.

"Quite a zoo out there," she said to Francine.

Without taking her eyes from the screens, the younger woman nodded and replied, "Biologists on Earth will go crazy over these."

Ilona nodded back at her. "You'll be famous."

"Yes," said Francine. Then she added, "For fifteen minutes."

Humbolt announced, "I'm picking up a weak magnetic signal."

"From the wreckage?" Meitner asked.

"More likely from Baron Magyr's ship. I don't think the aliens could rig a signaling system that runs unattended for a couple of million years."

"Maybe to each other," Meitner said.

"Besides, why would the aliens want to send out a signal? They deorbited their station and set it to rest at the bottom of the ocean. They didn't want anybody to find it."

"How do you know that?" Meitner challenged.

"That's what I would do," said Humbolt.

"You're not an alien. You don't think the way they do."

"Probably not."

Meitner continued, "Maybe they planned to come back here. Maybe they wanted to find the wreckage when they returned."

"After two million years? Get real."

"They're *aliens*, Derek. They don't think the same way we do."

"Meitner is right. It could be the signal of the alloys they used. Remember, my father was also trying to find a strong magnetic anomaly," Ilona recalled.

Humbolt was quiet for a moment. Then he conceded, "Then maybe, we are still too far away from either."

Humbolt realized, If the wreckage is the remains of an alien space station, they could very well be the source of the magnetic anomaly signal. Had her father found the source? Was it the wreckage? Anything is possible. Who knows how the aliens think? Who knows why they came to our solar system? They erased the civilization on Uranus. Why? Who knows what they wanted? What might they still want if—or when—they return?

FEEDING FRENZY

+++

+++++++++++++++++++++

They descended deeper into Neptune's planet-wide ocean. Ilona watched the viewscreens and saw that the fish and other life-forms they had passed at the higher regions of the sea had almost completely disappeared from view.

"There's almost nothing down at this depth," muttered Francine, sounding disappointed.

"We'll see a completely different biota once we get down near the bottom," Meitner reassured her.

Francine nodded, but she looked uncertain.

The four of them gathered at the food dispensers and had lunch while the vessel descended deeper into the ocean. Ilona seemed somehow sensitized to every quiver and groan of the ship; she felt almost as if she could feel *Hári János* struggling against the pressures that were trying to crush the vessel.

Nonsense! she growled at herself. We made it down to the bottom before, there's no reason why we won't make it again.

Still, every shudder of the ship made her tremble, despite herself.

"We should go to the perfluoride now," Humbolt said.

Ilona nodded, although she felt the same revulsion as she had before. Yet she gulped down the cold, slimy mixture and watched the others do the same. Francine took the disgusting mixture without a whimper, and Ilona felt a new respect for the younger woman.

Deeper they went.

"Look at that!" Meitner shouted from his chair alongside Humbolt.

Ilona focused on the screen Jan was pointing at. A large, flat, round creature was undulating out there, close enough for her to make out a hideous array of round sucker-like projections lining its underside.

"Another new species," Meitner proclaimed happily.

Ilona barely suppressed a shudder.

"Flat as a pancake," Francine muttered.

"And big," said Humbolt. "That bastard's almost a third the diameter of our ship."

The creature seemed curious, Ilona thought. It swam alongside their submersible, leisurely flapping its thin round body to keep up with *Hári János*. Ilona could see a circle of brilliant blue eyes ringing its top side. They seemed to glow from within.

For some reason the creature frightened Ilona. It seemed to be pacing alongside *Hári János*, studying it.

Nonsense, Ilona scolded herself. Still, the creature made her uneasy.

Then another one swam up to the first and the two of them trailed along beside their vessel. And two more came into view. Then another half dozen.

"We're attracting a flock of 'em," Humbolt muttered. Uneasily, Ilona thought.

She heard herself suggest, "Try increasing our speed."

"See if we can shake 'em," Humbolt agreed. He focused his eyes on the left screen.

Hári János surged away from the growing assembly of beasts. But only for a moment. They increased their speed and swiftly overtook the craft.

"They don't want us to get away," said Humbolt.

One of the creatures flapped closer to the vessel and flattened itself against its curving hull. Two of the viewscreens suddenly showed nothing but those disgusting suckers of its underside.

Another of the beasts attached itself to the ship. As Ilona watched, horrified, more and more of them draped themselves over *Hári János*'s spherical shell. The vessel tilted wildly, tossing Ilona and the others about in the cabin.

"Strap in!" Humbolt shouted.

"Why are they doing this?" Meitner yelled.

"Who the hell—" Humbolt's answer cut off in midsentence. "Oh my god!" he gasped.

"What?" Ilona cried.

Pointing at the diagnostic screen, Humbolt said, "They're dissolving our outer shell!"

Ilona stared at the screen. It showed that the outermost layer of steel alloy was melting.

"Get them off us!" Francine screamed.

Humbolt was already nervously looking left and right at the viewscreens.

The clinging creatures seemed to shudder, then suddenly shot away from the vessel's outermost shell.

"They don't like electric shocks," Humbolt said grimly.

Ilona stared at the screens, her heart pounding. The vessel was again surrounded by more than a dozen of the undulating beasts.

"Standoff," muttered Humbolt.

"I think they can still sense the electric current," Meitner said. "Try increasing the voltage."

Humbolt muttered into the ship's vocal control system. For an eternally long moment nothing happened. Then suddenly the creatures vanished into the depths of the ocean.

"Good thinking!" Humbolt said to Meitner.

Ilona breathed a sigh of relief. Then she glanced at Francine, who looked almost disappointed.

Shaking his head, Humbolt studied the screens before him. "Those bastards sucked off more than a millimeter of our outer skin in spots. A couple more minutes of that and we'd've been in deep trouble."

Francine shook her head. "We could always have risen up above the level where the things live. We could have gotten away safely."

"You think so?" Humbolt challenged.

"I do," said Francine, like a stubborn student facing down the school bully.

Humbolt muttered, "one of those pancake critters is following us."

"Following?" Ilona echoed, startled.

Pointing to the viewscreen farthest on his right, Humbolt said, "It's been trailing along behind us for the past half hour or so."

"Only one of them?" Meitner asked. His voice sounded shaky, worried, Ilona thought.

With a curt nod, Humbolt conjectured, "They must've liked the metals they sucked off our outermost shell. They don't want their dinner to get away from them."

"What can we do to discourage them?" Francine asked.

With a shrug, Humbolt answered, "Not much we can do, as long as their scout keeps his distance."

Ilona nodded, but felt a distinct apprehension. We're being tracked, she told herself. Like a big cat in the jungle being tracked by a tribe of hunters. And there's nothing we can do about it.

For hours their submersible glided deeper, toward the ocean's bottom. Ilona felt the inner chill of the perfluoride mixture pervading her body. To get her mind off that, she concentrated on listening to the steady hum of the tracking beacon as they approached the wreckage. What else is waiting down there? she wondered. Is the amoeboid still there, draped over the wreckage? If those pancake-shaped creatures like the way we taste, why didn't the amoeboid? What other organisms are down there, feasting on the remains?

"There it is!" Humbolt announced.

The central viewscreen showed the scattered wreckage of the aliens' deorbited space station, with the cloud of sea creatures darting back and forth above it. And the faintly glowing gelatinous spread of the enormous amoeba draped across most of it. Ilona made out the battered sphere of her father's ship, *Illustrious*, amid the ruins.

Illustrious, Ilona thought as she stared at the image. It doesn't look illustrious. It's nothing but a bashed-in resting place for Father and all his hopes, all his dreams.

Still, she told herself, Father made an important discovery here: real evidence of an extraterrestrial visit to our solar system. Then she shuddered. An extraterrestrial *invasion*, she corrected herself. Aliens who wiped out the civilization on Uranus and triggered the ice age on Earth two million years ago.

Where are those aliens now? Will they return to our solar system? Are they already on their way back here to finish what they started in the Pleistocene epoch?

"Ilona!"

She snapped her attention to the here and now. Humbolt was staring at her.

"You okay, boss?" he asked.

"Yes. Of course."

Humbolt's jet-black eyes seemed to be boring into Ilona's soul. "You looked like you were a million kilometers away."

With a faint smile, Ilona replied, "Two million *years* away."

"Huh?"

"Nothing. Sorry. I wasn't paying attention." Ilona saw that the ancient wreckage on the ocean floor was displayed on the main viewscreen. And that Jan and Francine were staring at her.

She stated the obvious. "We're almost there."

"Right," said Humbolt.

Blinking at the screen, Ilona asked, "How do we shoo the local denizens off the wreckage?"

"The amoeba didn't like our laser shots," Humbolt said, with a thin smile.

"You think we can get it to retreat again?" Meitner wondered.

Humbolt nodded slowly. "It worked before."

The wreckage was still spread across the seafloor. Through the swarm of fish and other organisms Ilona could see her father's battered spherical ship still sitting amid the debris, tilted to one side.

Humbolt was also staring at the screens, flicking them from one view to another as they approached, shaking his head and muttering to himself. "It worked before," he repeated, "it should work again." "Francine, snap some pictures here before it moves away."

The cloud of fish-like animals scattered as *Hári János* inched closer to the wreckage. Suddenly the amoeboid slithered away, as well, clearing more than half of the wreckage.

"It remembers us!" Ilona cried out.

Francine added, more calmly, "Yes, it must have remembered you from your first encounter with it."

"It has memory," Meitner said, his voice hollow with awe.

Humbolt nodded. "Makes our job easier." Then, with a crooked grin, he added, "More good news. The pancake gave up trailing us. Guess we went too deep for it."

Good, Ilona thought, although she realized, But we'll have to face them again when we head back to the surface.

Humbolt settled *Hári János* on the edge of the wreckage field and started the ship's recovery arms plucking up pieces of the debris for inspection by Meitner and Francine. The ship was outfitted with a highly automated laboratory, specially equipped for analyzing specimens picked out of the sea.

While the two scientists studied the wreckage with the ship's remote-analyses equipment, Ilona made sure the robots rode the trolley to the vessel's outermost shell and helped stow the larger samples of wreckage onto the trolley, which swiftly carried the debris back to the automated laboratory.

Humbolt stayed in his captain's chair, his attention focused on the viewscreens, watching the deep-sea creatures milling around in the distance—and the amoeboid that waited, patiently throbbing, off at the edge of the wreckage.

Humbolt got up from his chair briefly to get something to infuse himself with, but Ilona, Francine and Meitner worked through the normal lunchtime and into the early evening hours.

"Aren't you guys getting hungry?" Humbolt asked them.

Meitner looked up from the screen he was studying. "Not yet," he replied, then returned his focus to the twisted pieces of debris that the laboratory systems were analyzing.

"Have you found anything interesting?"

Francine replied, "It's all interesting, Derek. But strange. Incomprehensible."

"Alien," Ilona added, watching the two scientists as they carefully followed the pieces in the automated lab while they were labeled and numbered on the viewscreens, one by one. Every once in a while they would ask the mechanical arms to move the objects closer to the cameras or to flip it around to take a closer look. She understood now that science consisted of long hours of boring, seemingly point-less physical labor, punctuated by moments of astounding discovery.

But they had made no astounding discovery so far.

Then Francine pointed to a long, thin piece of padded structure in the middle of one of the viewscreens.

"Jan," she said to Meitner, "pull up the image of number . . ." She ran through the catalogue they were amassing. "Number 105."

With a slight frown, Meitner put the image on the screen along-side the image Francine had been staring at.

Francine spoke into her lip microphone, and the analysis system rotated her sample and connected it to the one Meitner had recovered.

"It looks like the arm of a chair, doesn't it?" Francine said.

"Too big," said Meitner. "Unless it's for a giant."

Francine paid him scant attention; she was skimming through the catalogue numbers. Within a few minutes she had pulled up several other samples and put them together on the screen.

"It *is* a chair!" Ilona exclaimed.

"But look at the size of it," said Humbolt.

"For a giant," Meitner whispered.

a Giant's Chair

The four of them stared at the image on the central screen. A chair, Ilona saw. But a chair for a giant.

"How big . . . ?" she began, then realized that Meitner was already putting up the chair's dimensions on the screen.

Humbolt goggled at the numbers. "That chair's built to seat somebody who's damned near four meters tall."

"More than twelve feet in English units," Francine said.

"A giant," breathed Ilona.

"An alien from a low-gravity planet," Meitner amended.

"Four meters tall," Humbolt repeated, with awe in his voice. Then he joked, "He'd be a basketball star on Earth." Weakly.

Meitner countered, "I doubt that he'd be able to stand erect under Earth's gravity. Not without a supporting suit of some sort."

"That's why none of the fragments we've recovered made any sense to us," Ilona said. "We were automatically thinking that the aliens were our size."

"They're more than twice our size," Meitner said.

Francine visibly shuddered. "Huge. Giants."

"No," said Ilona. "They think of themselves as normal. They'd look at us as pygmies."

Humbolt nodded and muttered, "Runts."

The four of them fell silent as the reality of their discovery sank in on them. An alien race of four-meter-tall giants. It seemed threatening, merely on the face of it.

Ilona broke the silence. "We should reexamine every piece that we've recovered and see if we can make some sense of the debris in the light of the aliens' size differential."

"After dinner," Humbolt said, almost gruffly. "I'm starving."

Ilona realized that she was hungry too.

* * *

They had their infused meal in nearly total silence, all of them wrapped in their own thoughts, their own apprehensions. At first Humbolt tried to liven things up with a few poor jokes about giants, but no one laughed. He finally lapsed into silence and they finished their meal with hardly a word spoken.

As she dropped her bag of leftover liquid into the disposal chute between the food dispensers, Ilona said, "We should inform the Council about this."

Getting up from his chair, Humbolt replied, "The data's already in a message pod on its way to the surface. Then it'll be transmitted Earthside. Automatically."

"Yes, but shouldn't we add a message to Earth? To call their attention to what we've found?"

Humbolt leaned back against one of the food dispensers. "I suppose you could if you want to. Personally, I don't think we've got much to add to the data that's already on its way Earthside."

Ilona studied Humbolt's impassive face. He didn't seem to feel the uneasiness that she herself felt gnawing at her innards. He's got real courage, she thought. Guts.

But Humbolt broke that illusion. With a wry grin, he said, "There's not a damned thing we can do about this, one way or the other. We're sending them what we've found. Our opinions won't impress them—that is, if we really have any opinions beyond surprise and fear."

Ilona smiled at him. "Surprise and fear. That sums it up pretty neatly."

"Yeah. I guess so."

Suddenly a feeling of exhaustion nearly overwhelmed Ilona. "Derek," she said, "I'm going to call it a day."

With a nod, Humbolt agreed, "Been a pretty stressful day."

"Goodnight, Derek," Ilona said. As she went past him, heading for her quarters, she nodded to Francine and Meitner.

Humbolt let her pass. "Goodnight, boss." Shifting his gaze to the other two, he added, "I think I'll go to my bunk, too. See you in the morning." And he lifted the sensor ring from his head and handed it to Meitner.

Meitner nodded. Francine watched as Humbolt went through the hatch to his quarters and softly closed it.

Looking down at Francine, Meitner said, "We've made a major discovery, I think."

With a glimmer of a smile, Francine agreed, "A major discovery. Our alien visitors were giants."

"*Are* giants," Meitner corrected.

"You think they still exist?"

Quite seriously, Meitner answered, "Yes, I do."

"After two million years?"

"Yes. Of course."

Francine's face looked woeful. "And they might be on their way back."

"To finish what they started."

"To wipe us out."

Meitner hesitated, then murmured, "Possibly. Probably."

"God," Francine breathed.

"It makes me feel pretty helpless," Meitner admitted.

"Me too."

Forcing a grin, Meitner echoed Humbolt's conclusion: "Well, there's not much we can do about it."

"I feel like a prisoner facing a firing squad."

"We're not dead yet."

"But maybe we're . . . condemned."

He dropped the sensor ring onto Humbolt's empty chair and tucked his fist beneath her chin. Lifting her face up toward him, he repeated, softly, "We're not dead yet."

Francine slid her arms around his waist. "Jan . . . I don't want to be alone," she said as she buried her face on his chest. She could hear his heart thudding.

"Come with me, Francine," he said softly. "We'll face this together."

"Together," said Francine.

And the two of them went to Meitner's quarters, arms wrapped around each other, the sensor ring lying forgotten on Humbolt's chair.

STRUGGLE

++
++++++++++++++++++++++++

Her clock's soft buzz woke Ilona. She blinked, rubbed her eyes, then sat up in the bed. The vague unfocused memory of a dream dissolved in her mind, like an image being washed away by a gentle flow of water.

Something about giants, she recalled. Giants that loomed over her, silent, watching, judging her actions.

The more she tried to remember, the more the images dissolved into a meaningless blur.

Dreams, she thought. Memories of the past and fears of the future. She got out of bed, went to the lavatory and showered, then dressed and headed for the command center and the new day.

Humbolt was already in his captain's seat, staring at the central viewscreen. He looked grim. Then Ilona saw what the viewscreen was displaying. The dim glow of the amoeboid's slimy body was draped atop their vessel. Above its thin form, a myriad of deep-sea creatures were darting and wheeling frenziedly.

"It's covering us?" Ilona blurted.

Humbolt nodded tightly. "Must've slid itself over us while we were sleeping."

"Nobody was on duty last night?"

"I thought Jan was, but apparently he wasn't. I slept through the whole damned night. It's my own fault."

Ignoring his admission, Ilona asked, "And our sensors didn't alarm us?"

"The damned amoeba's too thin and amorphous for the sensors to notice, I imagine."

Meitner entered the command center, suddenly stopping and scowling at the central screen's display. "It's trying to keep us here?"

"Looks that way," said Humbolt.

"Can we get it off us?"

Disregarding Jan's question, Humbolt asked mildly, "Where were you all night?"

"I . . ." Meitner glanced at Ilona, his cheeks reddening, but he said nothing.

With a curt nod, Humbolt said, "We can slice it open with the lasers."

Ilona heard herself object, "But that will kill it." Then she added, "Perhaps."

Humbolt half shrugged. "The alternative is to let it kill us, by starvation."

"We've got to get out of here!" Meitner snapped.

"Yep," Humbolt agreed.

Thinking quickly, Ilona suggested, "Perhaps you could fire a few low-power laser bursts at the amoeboid. Maybe that would stimulate it to back off."

Humbolt's expression was almost sneering. "We ask it 'pretty please'?"

Meitner disagreed. "I say we hit it with full power. Slice it open. Kill it. We've got to get away from here!"

"I agree," said Humbolt. "No fooling around. I don't want to stay trapped down here one millisecond longer than we have to."

Ilona looked from Humbolt's face to Meitner's and back again. She could see that they were determined.

Almost sighing, she capitulated. "If that's your decision," she said to Humbolt.

"Let's do it," Meitner assented.

"Do what?"

The three of them turned and saw Francine standing at the hatch that led to the men's quarters. She was freshly scrubbed, Ilona noted, but wearing the same coveralls she had been in the night before.

Meitner stepped to her side. "The amoeboid has slid over us. We're going to use the lasers to get him off."

Francine's eyes widened, but she nodded wordlessly.

"It's the quickest way for us to get out of here," Meitner added.

"I understand," Francine said, in a frightened little girl's voice.

Ilona realized that Francine had spent the night with Meitner. She couldn't decide whether she should be pleased or outraged.

GETAWAY

"Better strap in," said Humbolt as he took his chair. "This might get rough."

Ilona sat in her chair, to the captain's left, and clicked her safety harness snugly around her. Francine and Meitner did the same.

"Powering up the propulsion system," Humbolt muttered.

"Laser on full power," said Meitner.

Glancing across the screens arrayed before him, Humbolt said tightly, "Here we go."

Ilona saw a splash of the laser's red beam reflect off the amoeboid's translucent body. The creature twitched but did not move away.

"More power," Meitner said.

"Pretty close to max already," Humbolt responded.

It's not moving, Ilona saw.

"It doesn't feel pain!" said Francine, her voice high, frightened.

"Maybe," Humbolt growled. "Maybe not."

Ilona saw that Humbolt was cutting a slim line along the amoeboid's underside as he muttered, "Something's got to give."

The amoeboid seemed to twitch, but did not slide away from their ship. The laser beam was cutting a thin slice through its body, but the beast stayed stubbornly draped over them.

"Come on, buddy," Humbolt snarled. "Move your stupid ass."

The amoeboid remained draped over them, glowing in a wild flashing display of colors. That must be its reaction to pain, Ilona thought. She felt a cold terror clutching at her innards. What if it doesn't get off us? What if we're stuck here?

But Humbolt had another scheme in mind. Ilona saw that he was cutting a large open square through the amoeboid's thin, glowing body.

"You're draining the power system!" Francine cried. "It's down nearly fifty percent!"

Humbolt made no reply. His face was set in a harsh grimace, his lips pulled back over his teeth, his eyes blazing with fury.

"Come on, you stupid sonofabitch," he muttered.

Ilona saw that the amoeboid was slowly sealing up the slices the laser beam made in its translucent body. Can Derek cut an escape hole for us before the beast closes it again? she wondered.

"Hang on!" Humbolt shouted. And he leaned forward.

Ilona felt a surge of power slam into the small of her back. The vessel shuddered, strained for several eternally long moments, then finally broke through the amoeboid's thin body and darted upward from the sea bottom, trailing tendrils of the slimy body as it rose through the water.

"We're free!" Francine shouted.

"Look at that," said Meitner, pointing to the screen that showed the sea bottom behind them.

Dozens of fish-like creatures were tearing at the ragged seams of the amoeboid's body. Others—hundreds of them, Ilona guessed—were pouring into the breach in the thing's body and spreading across the wreckage on the bottom.

"They're feeding off the wreckage!" Francine exclaimed.

"The metals," said Meitner, staring at the scene dwindling below them. "They want the metals."

"Like vitamins to them," Ilona murmured.

With a wry grin, Humbolt said, "Once that amoeba thing patches itself up, those fish will be trapped underneath it. It'll have a feast."

Ilona realized that he was right. In an odd, almost perverse way, they had provided a banquet for the amoeboid.

As *Hári János* rose steadily toward the surface of the planet-wide ocean, Humbolt muttered, "I have to power down a bit. Getting past that damned amoeba drained a lot of the ship's juice."

Their rate of ascent slowed noticeably. Ilona sat tightly in her chair and studied the viewscreens. The ocean seemed almost empty of life-forms at this level: nothing out there but a few crustacean-like animals swimming idly by.

Francine said, "I haven't noticed any plants out there. Nothing but animals."

"We're not on Earth," Meitner quickly corrected. "You can't expect direct correlations to our biota."

Francine hesitated a moment, then replied, "Still . . . there ought to be *something* that corresponds to plant life."

Humbolt joked, "Giant cantaloupes, maybe?"

Meitner laughed. Francine frowned. Meitner's laughter died instantly.

More seriously, Humbolt said, "We're getting high enough to purge ourselves of the perfluoride."

Ilona nodded and began to unclick her safety harness. Getting to her feet, she turned to Francine. "Come on," she said, extending a hand to the younger woman, "we can vomit together."

Francine made an awful face, but she rose from her chair and followed Ilona to the women's quarters.

Ilona opened the door to her compartment and gestured Francine inside. Looking tense, almost worried, Francine stepped in.

As Ilona slid her door shut behind the younger woman, she asked, "So you and Jan slept together?"

Lifting her chin a notch, Francine replied, "Yes, we did."

Suddenly Ilona didn't know what to say.

Almost defiantly, Francine continued, "Apparently you had your chance with him and you pushed him away."

"True enough," Ilona murmured.

"I hope you're not jealous," Francine said, in a tone that implied exactly the opposite.

"Why should I be jealous?"

With a mischievous little smile Francine said, "He's really a very nice fellow. Gentle, a little frightened, but he feels very protective toward me."

"And you need protection?" Ilona almost smirked.

"Everybody needs protection, even you."

Ilona sighed as she realized the truth of her remark. Then she said, in a near whisper, "Don't hurt him."

"Hurt him?" Francine seemed genuinely surprised.

"As you said, he's a very nice young man. Don't hurt him."

Francine's expression became quite serious. "I have no intention of hurting him. I think I could fall in love with him quite easily."

"Good," said Ilona. "Good."

But she wondered if Francine was speaking the truth. She wondered if the young woman even understood where the truth was.

PURSUIT

AS Ilona returned to her seat, she gave silent thanks that she wouldn't have to go through the perfluoride purge again. Vomiting and excreting the slimy stuff was as near to hell as she ever wanted to get.

Humbolt and Meitner were already in their seats when Ilona had returned, the captain looking just as he had before, Meitner showing signs of weariness.

Francine had gone to her own quarters, next to Ilona's, for her purging. But Ilona could hear her gagging and moaning through the ordeal.

When Francine returned to her chair in the command center she looked paler than usual, shaken. But she sat down without a word to anyone.

Their vessel was rising steadily, heading to the ocean's ice-covered surface and, beyond that, the tranquility of outer space.

"Uh-oh," Humbolt muttered.

Every nerve in Ilona's body tightened. "What is it?" she asked.

Pointing to one of the screens to his right, Humbolt said, "We've got company."

Ilona saw the distant, hazy image of one of the pancake-like creatures swimming some distance from them. But in the same direction as *Hári János*.

"It's only one of them," said Meitner.

Humbolt transferred the image to the central screen. Ilona saw that despite its seemingly leisurely flapping motion, the creature was getting closer to them.

"Can't you speed us up?" Francine asked.

"I'm trying to save power. We used a lot of juice breaking away from the amoeboid."

There's only one of them, Ilona echoed Meitner's words. But then she saw another of the flat, round creatures appear out of the

depths and join the first one. Together they undulated closer to
Hári János.

"I'm pushing for max power," Humbolt said, through clenched
teeth.

Ilona reached back for her safety harness. She noticed Francine
do the same, then Jan and finally the captain.

And the pancake creatures still were gaining on them. Now
there were a half dozen of them. And more joining the pack every
moment.

"We must taste damned good to them," Humbolt growled.

Ilona could feel the push against her spine from their increased
acceleration. Still the creatures grew closer.

"You wouldn't think they'd be so fast," Francine murmured.

Humbolt said, "They're hunters."

And they're hunting us, Ilona added silently.

"I'll activate the electric field," Meitner said.

"Not yet!" Humbolt snapped. "I need every watt of power we've
got for the propulsion system."

Meitner nodded, but his hand remained clutched on his armrest.

We're in a race, Ilona told herself. If those creatures reach us
they'll wrap themselves around the outer hull and start leaching
away its metals. They'll destroy us!

Except for the deep-throated hum of the ship's engines the command center was absolutely silent. Ilona watched the armada of flat
round monsters edging closer, closer.

"Hit them with the laser!" Meitner demanded.

"Not yet," Humbolt replied, through gritted teeth. "They're too
far away; the beam'll break up before it reaches them."

Ilona felt helpless. It's like a nightmare, she thought. Those beasts
inching closer, closer. She could see the disgusting rows of suckers
on their undersides as they glided nearer. Do something! she silently
begged Humbolt. Anything!

"Now!" Humbolt growled.

A thin red line of intense power lanced out from their vessel's
outer skin to the nearest of the creatures. It twisted and folded in on
itself, writhing in obvious pain.

"You hit it!" Meitner shouted.

"That's only one of 'em," said Humbolt.

The other pancake-like creatures pulled up short and milled
around their wounded companion.

"Start chewing on him," Humbolt muttered.

But after a few moments, they resumed their pursuit of *Hári János* and left their wounded companion struggling in the water behind them.

"They're not cannibals," Ilona muttered.

"Too bad," growled Humbolt.

"Use the laser again!" Meitner snapped.

With a shake of his head, Humbolt answered, "Not enough power. Gotta save the juice for the engines."

"But they're catching up to us!" Francine said, her voice edged with panic.

"I'm turning off our running lights," Humbolt said.

What good will that do? Ilona wondered. But she kept silent. Derek has enough to worry about without me second-guessing him.

The pancake-like brutes were drawing closer, ever closer. But then one of them fluttered, twitched, and turned away.

Ilona stared at the viewscreens as, one by one, the creatures stopped chasing them and disappeared into the murky depths of the sea.

"We've risen too high for them to follow!" Ilona realized.

Humbolt nodded, grinning. "Water pressure's too low for them up here. They try to follow us, they'll explode themselves."

"We're safe!" Francine cried out.

Meitner broke into a huge toothy grin.

"Don't count your chickens yet," Humbolt cautioned. "Our power reserve is pretty damned close to zero."

Glancing at the diagnostic screen, Ilona saw that the vessel's power curves were all slanting perilously downward.

"Will we make it?" she heard someone ask in a thin frightened voice. Her own.

Fish-like organisms flashed past, paying no attention at all to their craft. Ilona wanted to ask how close they were to the surface, but she kept silent, afraid of what Humbolt's answer might be. Instead, she started mentally counting the seconds. She gave up when she reached one thousand.

Grim silence filled the command center, broken only by the low hum of the propulsion system's engines.

Then Humbolt called out, "Everybody strapped in?"

Eager affirmatives.

"Firing our last nuke."

Ilona felt the vessel shudder as the nuclear-armed missile flashed away, toward the ice cap above them.

"Hang on!"

The blast wave rattled *Hári János*. Ilona's eyes blurred momentarily. She blinked several times as Humbolt barked, "Blue sky up ahead." She felt the ship accelerating.

Hári János popped out from the ocean's surface like a cork fired from a champagne bottle.

"We made it!" Meitner crowed.

"You've done it again, Derek," said Ilona, her voice brimming with relief.

But Humbolt was staring at the diagnostic screens, to his left.

"Don't cheer yet," he warned. "We don't have enough power left to get to orbit or for propulsion back to Earth. We're going to glide on a ballistic arc and plop right back onto the goddamned ice."

marooned

Ilona stared at the central viewscreen as *Hári János* arced high above the ocean's bluish, ice-covered surface. Her stomach suddenly lurched sickeningly, and she realized the vessel had reached the peak of its trajectory and had started to plummet back toward the icy sea.

"Everybody strapped in?" Humbolt shouted, his eyes focused on the screens.

A chorus of assenting mumbles and grunts.

"Hang on!"

The all-encompassing sea ice was rushing up to meet them. Gripping her armrests with white-knuckled intensity, Ilona could see the ice's cracked and seamed surface, rushing closer, closer.

"Firing the retro-rockets," Humbolt said, "*now!*"

Ilona felt the thruster's power like a vise squeezing the juices out of her. The view of the bobbing ice on the screens seemed to freeze for an instant.

And then the ship dropped daintily onto the ice, like a flower petal settling on the ocean's surface. Ilona felt the slightest of bumps, and then the vessel stopped, within sight of the hole blown up by their nuclear blast.

"Made it," Humbolt said softly.

"We're on the ice," Meitner exclaimed, sounding surprised.

Braced by its landing struts, *Hári János* sat on the ice steadily.

Ilona stared at Humbolt. "A wonderful landing, Derek," she breathed.

He grinned at her. "Haven't lost my touch."

For several moments the four of them simply sat in their chairs.

Humbolt's grin faded. All business once again, he told the others, "I'll send an emergency signal to Earth, tell 'em we need a rescue mission. Jan, you start a damage assessment. Francine, you—"

"I think my wrist is broken," Francine said.

Ilona turned in her chair and saw that Francine's left wrist was swollen to twice its normal size.

"I twisted it, somehow," Francine said, apologetically.

Before Humbolt could respond, Ilona said, "I'll get a medical analysis for her."

"Good," said Humbolt. "Jan, you get started on the damage assessment."

Meitner objected, "But Francine—"

"Ilona will take care of her. You need to check all the ship's systems and structures. *Now!*"

"Yessir," Meitner replied.

Ilona got up from her chair and reached a hand out to Francine. "Come on, Francine," she said. "Let's get that wrist looked at."

With only a slight wince, Francine rose to her feet and followed Ilona to the ship's minuscule medical facility.

"I don't know how it happened," Francine said, her voice small, penitent.

"Doesn't matter," said Ilona. "The important thing is to determine how bad the injury is and how we can fix it."

The ship's medical facility was little more than a closet just outside the command center. Ilona led Francine to the diagnostic chair and pulled the scanner fastened to the bulkhead toward her wrist.

The scanner hummed briefly. Ilona studied its screen.

"It's not a fracture," she said, as much to herself as Francine. The scanner's screen displayed SPRAINED WRIST.

Ilona inhaled a deep breath, feeling relieved, as the screen spelled out the proper treatment for Francine's injury. Ilona followed the written directions, sprayed Francine's wrist with an anesthetic, then poked through the supplies on the shelves lining the narrow compartment until she found the proper support and bandaging.

Francine winced slightly as Ilona placed the support under her arm and wrist and wrapped the bandage around it. Peering at the directions written on the diagnostic screen, she told the younger woman, "You should be as good as new in a few days."

"Thank you," Francine said meekly.

The two of them returned to the command center. Meitner stared worriedly at Francine's bandaged wrist. Humbolt grinned.

"We have a casualty," he said. "Something to tell your children about, Francine. Wounded in the Sea of Neptune."

Francine smiled minimally.

They waited on the ice for hours, waiting for a return message from Earth.

"Might as well get some dinner," Humbolt said, getting up from his chair.

Ilona got to her feet also, followed by Meitner, who reached out a hand to help Francine. She smiled at him as she turned her chair to face the food dispensers.

"How long do you think it will take them to reply to us?" Ilona asked, as she made her dinner selection.

"Could be several more hours," Humbolt replied sourly. "Bureaucrats back Earthside don't move very quickly."

"But we're stuck here," Meitner complained. "Trapped."

"And they're back Earthside, in their fancy offices, fat and happy."

Ilona caught the unmistakable bitterness in Humbolt's voice.

She said, "Surely they must realize that this is an emergency."

With a crooked grin, Humbolt said, "It's an emergency to us. To them it's a lot less urgent. First thing they'll do, once they get our message, is check our inventory of supplies. When they see we've got several months worth of food, and our life-support systems are working, they'll send our message up to the next level of their organization, and then—"

"INCOMING MESSAGE," announced the automated communications system.

Humbolt looked surprised, almost shocked.

Harvey Millard's trim, spare face appeared on the central screen.

"Hello *Hári János*," he said in a crisp, earnest voice. "We've just received your message. I've ordered a rescue mission to be prepared and sent to you immediately. It should take at least three weeks to reach you. Are you all all right? Do you need medical or any other type of assistance?"

Humbolt sagged back in his command chair, totally surprised, shocked.

"I'll be damned," he said. "The Big Cheese himself."

Ilona smiled inwardly. It helps to be a Magyr, she said to herself. It gets their attention.

Touching the REPLY button on his armrest, Humbolt swiftly outlined their situation, ending with, "We have food and air, but we don't know what problems the local fauna might make for us."

Then he turned back to the others. "That'll take just about four hours to reach Earth. Help is on the way."

"Thank god," Meitner breathed.

Ilona suppressed a smile, remembering a line from her military-history lessons: *There are no atheists in foxholes.*

And not in a spacecraft stranded out at the edge of the solar system, either, she said to herself.

WAITING

+++
++++++++++++++++++++++

It was a little difficult to work the food dispensers with the vessel jolting from the wind. Francine stumbled several times; each time Jan—standing beside her—folded her in his arms until she could stand straight again.

Ilona herself felt wobbly as she selected her dinner. And she noticed that Humbolt stood next to her, ready to assist her if she slipped. She smiled at him and he grinned back at her, a bit sheepishly.

"It's like being in an old canoe," he said as he selected his dinner tray.

"When were you in an old canoe?" Ilona challenged.

Humbolt lifted his chin a notch. "I grew up in a cabin on the shore of a pretty sizable lake. Spent a lot of my boyhood years canoeing."

Meitner added, "I did some powerboating at university. It was fun."

"Do you think there are any dangerous animals here?" Francine asked, as she sat in her chair and placed her tray on her lap with one hand.

Shaking his head, Meitner answered, "There's no record of anything dangerous here at the surface."

Ilona quoted, "Absence of evidence is not evidence of absence."

"Not necessarily," Humbolt agreed.

The four of them sat before the meal dispensers and turned their attention to their dinners.

"The big dangerous hunters are down at lower depths," Meitner said, as if trying to convince himself.

Whistling past the graveyard, thought Ilona.

Humbolt began spinning tales again of his earlier adventures, especially his missions into Jupiter's deep and turbulent ocean.

"Nobody's gotten to the bottom," he said. "Not even unmanned probes. Too damned deep. The pressure squashes our probes like eggshells."

That led him to start talking about the gigantic Jovian whale-like creatures that inhabit Jupiter's vast ocean.

"Big as a city, they are," said Humbolt, spreading his arms for emphasis. His dinner tray nearly slid off his lap. Ilona had to suppress a laugh.

"They have a language of their own, you know?" Humbolt continued as he deftly grabbed his escaping tray with one hand. "Pictures. They flash pictures on their flanks."

Nodding, Meitner said, "I've seen videos of them."

"First time I saw them put up a picture of my own vessel on their flanks I nearly wet myself, I was so surprised."

"So they're intelligent?" Ilona asked.

"The science guys say no, it's just imitation. But I think they're full of hooey. Those big things are smart. They just don't care about talking to us."

"We're too small and puny to be interesting to them," said Francine.

Humbolt nodded. "It's like us trying to talk to fruit flies. Or mosquitoes."

I wonder, Ilona asked herself. And she thought about the four-meter-tall aliens that had sterilized the planet Uranus.

Silence settled on the four of them for several moments. Then Meitner said, "I think I'll try to get a berth on one of the Jupiter missions. I'd like to see those Jovian whales face-to-face."

Before anyone could reply, the communications system's buzzer sounded.

"Message from Earth," Humbolt guessed, getting up from his chair. This time his dinner tray clattered to the floor. "Oh damn!" he snapped.

"I'll take care of it," said Ilona. "Go see what the message is."

It was Harvey Millard again, his thin, ascetic face looking concerned, worried.

"We're outfitting a Council ship to go out and rescue you," Millard said, his tenor voice strained with tension, "but it won't get underway for several days. If you need assistance sooner we can fire off a standard resupply vehicle within twenty-four hours. Please advise."

Humbolt glanced at the other three watching him, then leaned on his REPLY communicator button.

"We have provisions, and the ship's life-support systems are working as designed. We just won't have enough juice to get the thrusters up for propulsion back out. Used all our power to get up from the sea bottom. Had to fight off a few predators. We should be able to wait for your rescue mission, unless there are unknown killers up here at the ocean surface."

With a curt nod, Humbolt touched the TRANSMIT button on his armrest.

"That ought to do it," he muttered.

Ilona nodded agreement, and noticed Jan and Francine did the same.

Life in the cramped confines of the command center became a boring routine. The outside lights and non-essential equipment had been turned to low to conserve energy. The robots were working to repair the damage to the outer sphere. Its four occupants watched the viewscreens, recorded the life-forms that glided or flew within range of their cameras, ate and slept and talked to each other.

And waited.

Messages from Earth—most of them automated—kept them informed of the progress their rescue ship was making. They watched video of its launch, and got reports as it sped past Mars, then Jupiter, then beringed Saturn.

Francine and Meitner made no secret of their sleeping together. Ilona realized that within the confines of their vessel they couldn't have kept their romance a secret even if they wanted to.

One evening, as the two of them bade goodnight to Ilona and Humbolt, the captain grinned at their backs, then turned to Ilona.

"Ahh, young love," he said.

"Is that what it is?" Ilona asked.

Humbolt's dark brows hiked up. "What else?"

Ilona started to reply, but hesitated. What else, indeed? she asked herself. Is Jan really in love with Francine? I doubt that she actually loves him. But they both need the illusion, the fairy tale, to keep themselves from going insane while we wait in this cockleshell for our salvation to get here.

Humbolt was staring at her, waiting for her answer. Waiting for a response.

"Need," Ilona replied at last. "They need each other. They're marooned out here at the far end of the solar system, alone and frightened."

"And you're not frightened?" Humbolt asked, his voice low, soft.

Briefly, Ilona pondered his question. With a sardonic smile, she replied, "All things considered, I'd rather be in Budaörs, at home, in my own bed."

Humbolt grinned back at her. "We have beds here, you know."

RESCUE

++
++++++++++++++++++++++

I know we have beds, Ilona said to herself. But they're narrow and cramped. Youngsters like Francine and Jan might not be bothered by that, but . . .

But what? she asked herself. And noticed Humbolt staring at her, his face totally serious.

"Derek," she began. Then hesitated. What should I say to him? What can I say to him?

Humbolt's face eased into a wry grin. "You know, when you first told me about this mission, back in your castle at Budaörs, I got a vision of you and I making love together."

Ilona smiled back at him. "It hasn't worked out that way, has it?"

"It could. As the poet said, we have world enough and time."

"But not love," said Ilona. "Love is the essential ingredient."

"Is it? Isn't love something that you search for, something you find, the reward of your quest?"

"You're a hopeless romantic, Derek."

His wry grin turned slightly sad. "I suppose I am."

"But perhaps you are right. Perhaps one must search for love, in order to find it."

Humbolt's eyes widened. "Are you willing to search?"

"With you?"

He hesitated long enough for Ilona to see the yearning in his eyes. "Yes," he whispered, and he leaned from his chair toward her. Ilona leaned toward him, and they kissed.

As their kiss deepened, they rose from their chairs and Humbolt lifted the sensor ring from his head and laid it down gently on its place above the control chair. Then silently, hand in hand, they stepped across the command center to the hatch that led to Ilona's tiny quarters.

The bed was indeed narrow and cramped. But somehow it didn't matter. Nothing mattered to Ilona except that Derek Humbolt was there with her, sharing it, searching for love.

* * *

The world did not change. Ilona had no romantic fantasies about Humbolt, although he was a gentle and patient lover. In the morning they were still on Neptune's endless ice-covered sea, waiting for the rescue mission from Earth.

But somehow everything seemed brighter, warmer, as she awakened the next morning. Humbolt lay pressed beside her, wide awake, staring at her.

"Good morning," he said softly.

"Good morning."

"Sleep well?"

"Yes," she said, suppressing a smile. "Quite well."

"Me too."

"That's good."

Humbolt lay on his side, pressed against her. For long moments neither of them said anything. Then Humbolt sat up. "I'd better get back to my own quarters and wash up."

Ilona nodded.

He bent over and kissed her lightly on the lips. "Thank you," he said.

"Thank you," said Ilona.

Humbolt pulled on his coveralls and left Ilona's bedroom without another word.

It took five more days before the rescue mission from Earth reached them. Humbolt slept with Ilona on three of those nights, but—without a word to her—went to his own quarters on the fourth.

Alone in her bed that night, Ilona wondered, have I worn him out, or is he just bored with me?

She told herself it didn't matter. We've had our fling. He can add me to his list of conquests. That's all there was to our brief affair.

But she felt disappointed, saddened.

"There she is!" Humbolt cried out as the main viewscreen showed the contrail of the rescue ship blazing across the clouds high above them.

"We're saved!" Francine said, clapping her hands together like a little girl.

Ilona felt a great rush of relief. It seemed to her that she had been holding her breath for a week, and now she could breathe again.

"Hello *Hári János*," came a bright, cheerful voice from the communications speaker. "This is the salvage vessel *Orion*. How are you?"

Humbolt switched the main screen's picture to a view of the rescuer. He looked like a middle-aged man, wearing a military uniform, solidly built with flecks of gray in his crew-cut hair.

He answered, "We're a lot better now that you're here."

The officer grinned and nodded. "All alive and well?"

"Yep."

"Good. It's going to take us a little time to set up your recovery. We don't have room to take your craft aboard us—"

"We don't need that," Humbolt interrupted. "We're out of propellant, that's all."

"That's enough!"

Humbolt broke into a grin. "Hope you brought along some go-juice for us."

"Enough to fill your tanks. We'll have to come down on the ice next to you, set up, and connect the hyperbattery."

Humbolt's grin widened. "Be my guest!"

BOOK V

earth

Prisoners?

++

++++++++++++++++++++++++++

This time there was no crowd to greet them, no horde of journalists eager to interview them. Hári János arrived at the same lunar docking facility as it had the last time, but to no acclaim, no celebration whatever.

Ilona and the rest of the crew were greeted at the docking facility by a team of dour-faced officials who met them as they stepped from the tunnel that had been connected to their ship. The receiving facility was empty of welcomers—except for slim, elegant Harvey Millard.

"Welcome home," he said to the four of them, as they entered the reception area. He was smiling at them, but Ilona saw no joy in his expression.

There was no one else in the docking facility. The desks and inspection screens were bare, unmanned. No one on hand to welcome them, as there had been last time.

"Where is everybody?" Meitner asked, swinging his puzzled gaze across the empty reception area.

Looking almost ashamed, Millard replied, "I'm afraid there's only me. The Council has decided to keep your return a secret, more or less, until you report to their investigative committee."

"Investigative committee?" Ilona echoed.

With a curt nod, Millard replied, "Yes. They want to hear first-hand what you've got to report about your mission before announcing your return to the public."

Blinking with surprise, Ilona could only say, "I see."

"A medical inspection team is on its way here to examine you," Millard went on. "They should be here shortly."

"The Council doesn't want anyone to know we've returned?" Ilona said.

"I'm afraid so," said Millard, apologetically. "Frankly, you've got them frightened out of their wits."

It was awkward, standing in the nearly empty reception area. Millard seemed unhappy, embarrassed. Ilona didn't know what she should say. This is no way to treat the Baroness Magyr, she grumbled inwardly. But she kept her thoughts to herself.

Not so Humbolt. "Well, this stinks," he snapped. "We come all the way back from Neptune after having damned near died in that fuckin' ocean, and we're treated like criminals!"

"Yes," Francine agreed. "After all, I'm a representative of the Council. President Darbin himself picked me to go on this mission."

All Millard could do was shrug.

The inspection team arrived after nearly a half hour's wait. Ilona thought it was a not-so-subtle ploy to show her and her crewmates that they were under the Council's control.

One by one, the four of them went through the automated medical exams and were approved by the inspectors.

Trying to make the best of the situation, Millard told them, "The Council has set up quarters for the four of you here on this station. Tomorrow President Darbin will speak with you."

"Hot shit," Humbolt groused.

Ilona found the quarters that the Council had assigned to them were quite comfortable, but she couldn't escape the feeling that she and her shipmates were prisoners. The Council doesn't want the public to see us, hear us, learn what we have to tell them about Neptune and the giant aliens who invaded the solar system two million years ago. The aliens who sterilized the planet Uranus and caused the Pleistocene ice age on Earth.

As she paced through her three-room suite, Ilona wondered if Derek would call. No, she decided. He's had his time with me. I'm just another conquest that he can brag about.

But the bedside telephone buzzed. Ilona stared at it for an undecided moment, then stepped around the king-sized bed as she called, "Phone answer."

Derek Humbolt's craggy face appeared on the phone's little screen.

"Hello there," he said, his face unsmiling.

"Hello, Derek," Ilona replied, sitting down on the edge of the bed.

"Everything all right? Your quarters comfortable?"

With a nod, Ilona said, "Quite comfortable. For a jail cell."

Humbolt's expression deepened. "Yeah. We're prisoners, aren't we?"

"It feels that way."

"Millard doesn't like it, but there's not much he can do about it, I guess."

"I suppose we'll just have to wait until tomorrow and see what President Darbin has to say."

Humbolt agreed, "Looks that way."

"Thanks for calling," Ilona heard herself say.

With the trace of a grin curling his lips, Humbolt asked, "Are you all right?"

"I'm weary," Ilona replied. "I need a good night's sleep."

"Oh. Okay." Humbolt hesitated, then added, "I'm right next door to you . . . if you need anything."

Ilona smiled tiredly. "Not tonight, Derek, thank you."

"Okay," he repeated. Reluctantly, Ilona thought. "Goodnight, then."

"Goodnight, Derek."

The phone screen went blank.

He's really a dear man, Ilona thought as she undressed. Not at all the unfeeling Lothario image he likes to project.

As she slipped into bed and pulled the coverlet over her, a sudden thought shrilled in her mind. Have they put a soporific in the air? Why am I so tired, so sleepy?

But before she could do anything about it, Ilona drifted into a deep and tranquil sleep.

ILONA'S DREAM

It was just past midnight when the psychotechnician sitting at the monitoring board called out, "She's started REM sleep."

There were four technicians stationed at monitoring posts, in a compartment a few hundred meters down the central passageway of the lunar space station where Ilona and her crew were quartered.

The psychotechnicians' commander, a white-jacketed medical doctor, nodded. He was a short man, with thick dark hair and a trim little Van Dyke beard hiding his receding chin.

"Good," he said.

Standing alongside him, Harvey Millard said worriedly, "This is an invasion of their privacy, isn't it?"

Shaking his head, the doctor said, "Not really. Not legally. We can't tell what she's dreaming about, merely that she's dreaming."

"REM sleep on number three!" announced one of the other technicians.

Jan Meitner, Millard knew. He felt uneasy about this monitoring of Ilona and the others from *Hári János*, but Yancey Darbin himself had insisted on it.

So they're dreaming, Millard said to himself. What does that prove? Darbin's treating them like captured criminals instead of returning explorers.

Still, he wondered what Ilona might be dreaming of.

She was walking through the gardens of the castle at Budaörs, along the three-meter-high hedges of flowers and greenery, safe and serene and happy.

The sky above Ilona was a perfect cloudless blue, the summer breeze warm and refreshing. She felt happy to be home, to be back on Earth, to be safe.

Ilona knew that her father was somewhere in this lushly blooming garden, waiting for her to find him.

Briefly she thought of Derek Humbolt, and Jan and even Francine. But the one who stepped out from a side passage in the hedges was Harvey Millard, looking as trim and stylish as usual in his form-fitting jacket and slacks.

"Good afternoon, Baroness," he said, with a polite little bow.

"Hello," Ilona replied. "Have you seen my father?"

"Yes, Baroness." Turning, Millard pointed further up the pathway. "He's right down this path, not more than—"

An enormous figure suddenly blocked her way, huge, towering over her. It was somewhat human in form, but its greenish face was snarling, threatening.

"You'll never find your father," it growled, in a harsh voice heavy with fury.

Millard disappeared. Ilona faced the alien alone. Hiding the terror that boiled within her, she demanded, "What have you done to him?"

"What he would have done to us."

"Us? How many of you are there?"

"Millions. Billions!"

"Then where are all these legions of yours? How come you are here alone?"

The huge alien bent down until its menacing face was mere centimeters from Ilona's. Its thin lips twisting into a terrifying smile, it answered, "They're on their way. And they are bringing death and destruction to you puny, troublesome creatures."

Troublesome? Ilona thought. She asked, "How have we been troublesome to you? We didn't even know you existed until a few months ago."

Straightening up again, the alien said, "Don't try to lie to me. We know the truth. We know much more than you do."

"Tell me, then. Enlighten me. Educate me."

The alien made a noise that might have been a laugh. "Educate you? What good would that do?"

It suddenly struck Ilona. "You're afraid of us!"

"Afraid? Of a puny race of former apes? That's ridiculous!"

"You fear us," Ilona insisted. "That's why you want to eliminate us."

"You just don't understand," the alien said, with a weary shake of its head.

"Then help me to understand. Enlighten me!"

"Never."

"Then begone!" Ilona commanded. "Return to your own people and leave us alone."

The alien vanished. And in its place stood Ilona's father, Baron Magyr, standing tall and lean and smiling at his daughter.

"Father!"

The baron stretched both his arms out to his daughter and smiled at her.

Ilona stood rooted on the garden pathway. With every atom of energy within her she strained to cross the meter or so that separated her from her father, but she could not move. Her body was frozen, as if encased in ice. Father! she tried to cry out, but not even her voice was able to leave her mouth.

Father! she screamed silently.

And woke up in bed, in the room she had been placed in. In prison.

She bowed her head and wept.

commanding herself to control her emotions, Ilona dried her tears, got out of bed, showered and dressed. Then she phoned Humbolt.

"Derek," she asked, "are you ready for breakfast?"

In the phone's smallish screen she could see a flash of surprise on Humbolt's face.

"We're in the middle of breakfast," he replied. "I'm with Francine and Jan."

"Why didn't you call me?" Ilona complained.

Humbolt made a small shrug. "Figured you'd call me when you were ready to."

Which is precisely what I did, Ilona realized. She said to Humbolt's image, "May I join you?"

"Sure! Glad to have you. We're at my place, right next to yours."

"I'll be right there."

Once Humbolt ushered her into his suite, it was obvious that all three of them were just about finished with their breakfasts. Ilona sat between Meitner and Francine Savoy, while Humbolt slipped back into his chair at the head of the rectangular table.

Glancing at his wrist, Humbolt said, "President Darbin is expecting us in half an hour."

"Good," said Ilona, glancing at the coffee urn standing by Francine's place. The younger woman took the hint and poured Ilona a cup of strong black coffee.

"I can get you some bacon and eggs," Humbolt said.

"No, thank you," said Ilona, holding the coffee cup before her lips. "This will be fine."

The door buzzer sounded. Turning to look at the viewscreen by the entrance, Ilona saw that Harvey Millard was standing outside in the corridor.

Humbolt called out, "Door open," as he pushed himself to his feet.

Millard stepped in, his smile looking a bit forced. "Are you ready to meet the president?"

Ilona said, "And the Council?"

His smile waning, Millard said, "Only the inner cabinet members, I'm afraid."

"But I thought—"

With a little shrug, Millard explained, "Darbin wants to keep this meeting small and manageable."

"I thought we were going to make our report to the full Council," Ilona said.

"Not yet," said Millard.

There were eight cabinet members arrayed along a narrow walnut table. Yancey Darbin sat at its head. Five unoccupied seats waited at the table's foot as Millard led Ilona and the others into the conference room. The table was bare, except for individual screens set into its surface at each chair.

All eight of the cabinet members, plus Darbin, rose to their feet as Millard led Ilona's group in. She couldn't shake the feeling that she and the others were being treated like prisoners.

Once everyone was seated, Darbin smiled graciously and said, "Glad y'all could meet with us this morning."

Ilona replied evenly, "We weren't given much choice, were we?"

"No, I guess you weren't," Darbin admitted, his smile still in place.

One of the cabinet members, a waspish gray-haired woman with a lantern jaw, said, "What you've found on Neptune could be very serious."

Harvey Millard broke in, "The full set of data is being examined by the scientists. So far they've found no inconsistencies from the first report."

"Alien invaders?" another of the cabinet members asked, stark disbelief in his voice and his face.

"That's what the evidence shows," said Ilona.

Millard took up, "It's the most consequential discovery of all time."

Before anyone else could speak, Yancey Darbin raised both his hands in a calming gesture. "Now, we don't have to wet ourselves over this. The aliens—if they really exist—haven't been back in two million years. Chances are—"

"What do you mean, 'if they really exist'?" challenged Humbolt. "We've gone back and forth to Neptune twice now and brought you back more pieces of their goddamn hardware, for cryin' out loud."

Meitner added, "Isn't that enough evidence for you?"

"No, it's not," said Darbin, his smile gone. "Not until our biochemical, biophysics, and material engineer section verifies your conclusion."

"So why are we sitting here?" Ilona demanded. "Let your astronomers study the samples we've returned from Neptune."

Darbin stared down the length of the table at her. "That's just what we're doing, Baroness. We've got the best astronomers in the solar system examinin' the samples you brought back. That's not the question we're here to decide on today."

Surprised, Ilona snapped, "Then what is the question?"

His expression souring, Darbin replied, "What the hell should we do with the four of you while the astronomers are tryin' to make up their minds?"

DECISION

"what should you do with us?" Ilona echoed.

"Yup," Darbin answered. "We can't have y'all runnin' loose and scarin' everybody with stories about alien invaders."

Brushing his thin moustache with a fingertip, Harvey Millard said mildly, "It *is* rather frightening news, don't you think, Yancey?"

"That's jes th' point. We don't want to start a panic among the people."

One of the cabinet members, dark-haired and obviously younger than the others, pointed an accusative finger at Ilona. "We've just about got through the latest round of greenhouse flooding and now you're bringing news of alien invaders? People'll go crazy!"

"Panic in the streets," agreed the stern-faced woman sitting next to him.

"We can't have that kind of terror spreadin' through the solar system," Darbin agreed. "It'd cause all kinds of trouble."

Ilona's disbelief settled into a scowl. "Whatever happened to the old maxim, 'You shall know the truth and the truth shall set you free'?"

Darbin's face eased into a withering smile. "In this case, if the people knew the truth we'd have panic and riots and who knows what else?"

"We can't let the people know what you've learned on Neptune," said another cabinet member. "Not yet."

Nods and mutters of assent broke out around the table.

"And what of these fine people here?" Millard asked, gesturing toward Ilona and her crewmates.

Darbin heaved an audible sigh as he leaned forward in his seat. "I'm afraid y'all are goin' to have to stay here aboard this station for a while."

"You'd keep us prisoners?" Ilona snapped.

With a brittle little smile Darbin answered, "Guests. Not prisoners. You'll be guests of the Council."

"For how long?" Meitner demanded.

Darbin shrugged his broad shoulders.

"Prisoners," Ilona repeated.

"Just for the time being," Darbin said. "'Til we figure out how to handle this situation."

"I presume that includes me, as well," said Millard.

"'Fraid so."

Millard turned his gaze to the young man among the cabinet members. "I suppose that means that you'll be taking my place, Henri."

Henri tried to suppress a satisfied grin. And failed.

The meeting ended. Darbin and the cabinet members filed out of the conference room, leaving Ilona, Millard and the other three sitting at the end of the table.

"We're prisoners," Francine muttered, her voice sounding surprised, fearful.

"What about our constitutional rights?" Humbolt grumbled.

Millard cast him a pitying glance. "I doubt that we'll be allowed to contact a lawyer, Derek."

As if in response to his words, the door to the conference room slid open and six black-uniformed security guards trooped in. They were wearing stun wands tucked into their belts, Ilona saw.

"We're here to escort you back to your quarters," said the woman leading them, a tall, athletically slim brunette with a hard-bitten face. "Please come along with us."

Wordlessly Ilona and the others got to their feet. Prisoners, Ilona repeated to herself. We're prisoners.

As they left the conference room, Ilona saw that the passageway outside was empty of pedestrians. Stepping next to the security team's leader, she asked the woman, "Will we be confined to our quarters?"

The woman look surprised. "Oh no! Not at all. You'll have complete freedom of this entire section of the station. The restaurant, the observation blister, everything in this section." She hesitated, then added, "Think of this as a sort of vacation. You can do anything you want, as long as you stay in this section."

Ilona said, "I presume the hatches leading to the station's other sections will be guarded."

"I'm afraid so."

"I see."

"It'll only be for a little while, I'm sure."

A little while, Ilona thought: days, weeks . . . years?

ACTION

+++
+++++++++++++++++++++++++

Once they got to Ilona's quarters, she said to Millard, "Harvey, why don't you and the others come into my place?"

With a glance at the flinty security leader, Millard nodded. "I'm sure our quarters are being monitored," he half whispered. But he entered Ilona's sitting room, followed by the others.

Once the door slid shut, leaving the security guards outside in the passageway, and the five of them were all comfortably seated on the sofa and chairs, Ilona asked, "What are we going to do about this?"

Meitner, sitting next to Francine, shrugged hopelessly. Humbolt grumbled, "Not a helluva lot we can do, I guess."

With a weary little grin, Harvey Millard hiked a thumb toward the ceiling and cautioned, "Whatever we say is being monitored by the security people, you realize."

Humbolt leaned back in his web chair and said, "That makes it just about impossible to do anything."

But Meitner offered, "We can neutralize the cameras and listening devices they're using to bug us."

Millard looked surprised. "Neutralize them?"

"Sure," said Meitner, grinning. "We used to do it in college, when we didn't want the faculty to know what we were doing in our dorm rooms."

"You can do that, Jan?" Francine asked.

"Maybe."

Millard shook his head. "But they'll be watching us searching for the cameras. And they'll come in and stop us."

Meitner's cheerful grin widened. "You don't understand, sir. We bribed the guys monitoring the cameras."

"Oh!"

"A security system is only as good as the honesty of the people watching the cameras."

"But how can we bribe the security guards?" Ilona asked.

And got no answer.

Harvey Millard's light brown eyes flicked across the ceiling above them as he said casually, "Well, let's explore our prison, shall we?"

"Might's well," said Humbolt, pushing himself to his feet.

Jan and Francine stood up, too. Ilona stared at Millard, who was still focused on the ceiling. He's searching for the surveillance cameras, she realized.

Abruptly, Millard reached out his hand toward her. "Come, Baroness. Let's go exploring."

Something's going on in his mind, Ilona thought. There's a *purpose* in what he's doing. She reached for Millard's hand and let him help her to her feet.

The five of them trooped outside, beyond Ilona's front door. The security guards had gone, but a lone tall robot stood outside the door, silent, inhumanly patient. Without hesitation Millard started down the passageway; Ilona and the others followed his lead down the empty corridor, past closed, unmarked doors. The robot clumped along behind them.

"Not much to see," Humbolt muttered.

"Not yet," Millard replied.

The passageway ended at what was obviously a hatch: a heavy-looking door with a metal wheel in its middle. A sign above the wheel warned: OBSERVATION BLISTER AIRLOCK. TO BE OPERATED BY CREW MEMBERS ONLY.

Millard glanced at the sign, then turned to Humbolt. "What do you think, Derek? Should we open it?"

Stepping up to Millard, Humbolt shrugged and said, "The security guard said the blister was okay for us."

From behind them, the robot's flat emotionless voice called, "I can operate the hatch for you."

Millard smiled. "Please do," he said, gesturing to the wheel.

The robot was slightly taller than Francine, slim and gracile. It stepped up to the hatch and spun its wheel deftly. The hatch opened a crack, then the robot pushed it wide.

"Thank you," said Millard, as he gestured the others into the observation blister.

It was a narrow chamber, empty of furniture. Small dim pinpoints of light barely broke the darkness. The five of them trooped in, with the robot following them, making the place feel crowded. Above them was a metal dome.

"It's closed," said Francine, sounding disappointed.

"Not much in the way of creature comforts," Millard said, in a low voice.

"There ought to be a control panel around here someplace," Humbolt muttered.

The robot's voice, sounding almost eerie in the semidarkness, said, "The control panel is beneath the edge of the shroud, five paces to your left, Captain Humbolt."

Ilona watched Humbolt step up to the edge of the narrow chamber. "Ah! Got it!"

The shroud covering the blister's glassteel bubble split apart and peeled down. Beyond it was the universe.

Ilona gaped at the sight. Stars everywhere, staring down at them in the millions. Swarms of stars, billows of stars, unblinking, steady, solemn.

She felt her pulse quicken. They had seen the heavens on the viewscreens of *Hári János*'s command center, of course, but this . . . this was like *being* in the midst of the universe's splendor.

"Oh my god," Meitner breathed.

"It's so beautiful!" Francine voiced.

And then, from one side of the bubble, the Earth glided into view: huge, blue and white, glowing against the darkness of eternity. Ilona's knees went weak.

That's home! she thought. She could make out the sweep of Africa's coast, the Red Sea, Arabia. Up above, hidden by purest white clouds, was southwestern Europe, the Balkans, Hungary, Budaörs, home. Tears filled her eyes.

So near, she thought. It's so very near. When will I ever see Budaörs again?

Then she noticed that Millard was standing so close to the blister's glassteel canopy that he must be pressing his nose against it. Odd, she thought.

Ilona pushed past Francine and Jan to stand beside Millard. He was holding something in both his hands, down by his waist. For an absurd moment she thought he was urinating against the glassteel covering of the blister.

She started to ask, "Harvey, what—"

"Shh!" he whispered.

Ilona went silent.

"Mustn't let our robotic guard know what I'm doing," he said, so softly that Ilona barely heard him.

"What *are* you up to?" she whispered back to him.

Millard did something with his hands. Whatever he'd been holding disappeared.

With a soft smile he pointed toward the ponderous bulk of Earth. "See that pinpoint of light? Just slightly above the curve of the planet. It's a communications satellite, one of dozens in orbit around the Earth."

"A commsat," Ilona said.

"A commsat," Millard agreed. "Now we'll see if it received my signal, and if my staff in Copenhagen acts on it."

reaction

++++ +++++ +++++ +++++ +++++ +++++ +++++ +++++ +++++ +++++
++++ +++++ +++++ +++++ +++++ ~~~~~~~~~~~~~~~~~~~~~~~

The five of them—plus their robot guard—trooped back to their quarters. Jan and Francine paired off and entered Meitner's lodging together. Humbolt glanced at Millard, then shrugged and said goodbye to Ilona. Millard looked almost flustered for a moment, but he smiled at Ilona and made a little bow.

"Good day, Baroness."

"Don't be so formal, Harvey," she reproved him, gently.

"Good day, then . . . Ilona," he said.

With a smile and a nod, Ilona responded, "Good day for now, Harvey. I'll see you at lunch."

He smiled back. "At lunch."

Ilona stepped into her sitting room and let the door to the corridor slide shut behind her. Stifling a yawn, she wondered again if the air in her quarters might be laced with a soporific. It would feel good to sleep, she thought.

Then a line from her high school English classes rose in her memory: *Who knows what dreams may come once we have shuffled off this mortal coil?*

She frowned, not certain that her memory was correct. But it was good enough. *What dreams might I have, locked away in this plush prison?*

The insistent buzz of her bedside telephone woke Ilona. Shreds of a dream fluttered through her mind and disappeared into nothingness.

"Phone answer," she mumbled, pushing herself up to a sitting position on the bed. Realizing that she had fallen asleep fully clothed, she quickly added, "Voice only."

A flat robotic voice said, "President Darbin has called a meeting for nine a.m. Your attendance is required."

Squinting at the clock readout on the bottom of the screen, Ilona saw that it was 7:55 A.M.

I've slept the whole day! she realized. And night.

"Where?" she asked.

"In your quarters."

"My quarters?"

"Yes, Baroness. Nine a.m."

Nodding, she answered, "Very well."

She phoned Harvey Millard, Humbolt, Jan and Francine. They had all been already notified of the meeting.

"What does he want?" Ilona wondered aloud.

Millard's lean, ascetic face smiled grimly. "We'll find out soon enough."

The five of them gathered in Ilona's front room, sitting tensely, waiting. Ilona asked the others if they had slept the whole day and night. None of them admitted to it.

Precisely at 9:00 A.M. the doorbell buzzed. Ilona saw that Yancey Darbin was standing in the passageway outside, looking decidedly nettled. A lean, almost delicately slender man in the jet-black uniform of the security forces stood beside him, his face a mask of impassivity. He wore three stars on each shoulder.

Darbin's come up here to the station again? Ilona asked herself. What's going on? From the expression on the Council president's face, it must be something important, something that's got him upset.

"Door open," Ilona called out.

The door slid open. Darbin and the security man stepped in. From her seat on the sofa, between Millard and Humbolt, Ilona offered a cheerful, "Good morning."

"Not a good one," Darbin snarled. "Damned security goons woke me up at three in the goddamned morning."

Millard got to his feet. "What's this all about, Yancey?"

"As if you don't know," Darbin growled. He jerked a thumb toward the security officer. "This is Commander Ranau, head of the Council's security division."

Commander Ranau took one step forward. Ilona thought for a moment that he was going to salute Millard. Instead, he broke into a toothy smile and extended his hand.

"It is good to see that you are well, sir," he said, in a deep basso voice that belied his slight physique.

Grasping his hand, Millard smiled warmly and said, "Thank you, Commander. It's good to see you again, too."

Ranau's smile vanished as he let go of Millard's hand. As if reading from a formal report, the commander recited, "Last night at nineteen-forty-three hours I was informed that a signal from your emergency transponder had been earlier received aboard Station Gamma. The origin of the signal was this space station."

Millard nodded and murmured, "Good."

Darbin grumbled, "So what're you doin', Harvey, sendin' out an emergency beacon? Got the security troops halfway across the world all stirred up."

Ignoring Darbin's irritation, Millard said to the commander, "I am being detained aboard this station against my will, together with my four friends, here."

"Against your will?" Ranau's red-rimmed eyes went wide.

"By President Darbin." Millard nodded curtly at the president.

"Without a hearing? Without a trial?"

"I'm afraid so," Millard answered.

Turning to Darbin, Ranau said, "Sir, this is impermissible. The law clearly states—"

"You're not a judge, Commander," Darbin interrupted. "I have certain emergency rights."

"Emergency? What emergency? I have not been informed of any emergency."

His face reddening, Darbin said, "I don't have to answer to you, dammit! You work for me, not the other way around."

Commander Ranau's skin flushed also as he replied, "Sir, we live in a community of laws. You cannot imprison people on your personal whim."

"Personal whim?" Darbin shouted. "Goddammit, we're talkin' about the survival of the whole mother-lovin' human race here!"

Ranau was unmoved. "This is a matter for the courts to decide."

"You're fired!" Darbin snarled.

With great dignity, Ranau said, "In that case, I request a formal hearing before a qualified judge."

agreement

Towering over the commander's slight stature, Darbin glowered at Ranau. Ilona thought the council president was going to spout steam from his ears. But Ranau stood unmoving, ramrod straight, staring up at Darbin's scowling face.

Before either of them could say anything more, Millard spoke up. "There's no need to make a formal complaint, Commander. Yancey, you don't want to turn this little disagreement into a full-blown court hearing, do you?"

Turning his sizzling brown eyes toward Millard, Darbin choked out, "Not if I don't have to."

"So let's not turn this minor disagreement into a major confrontation," Millard said mildly. "I'm sure we can settle this matter without attracting the news media."

Darbin's scowl deepened as he muttered, "News media." Then he seemed to remember why he had come up to the space station again. Pointing an accusing finger at Millard, he grumbled, "You contacted your staff!"

Millard nodded agreeably. "I'm afraid I did. I didn't want them to think I'd disappeared under mysterious circumstances."

"Mysterious circum—" Darbin stopped himself, took a deep breath, then said, "You're being held here by my order, goddammit! And you know that!"

Sweetly reasonable, Millard said, "But Yancey, nobody has the authority to detain people without judicial permission. That's against our most fundamental laws."

Darbin towered over Millard, as well as over Commander Ranau. But he just stood there, his face red, his arms raised. Millard stood before him, calm, seemingly relaxed.

For several moments the two men stood facing each other, silent.

Ilona thought she could hear the wheels grinding away inside Darbin's skull. And she visualized the headlines:

COUNCIL PRESIDENT ACCUSED OF ILLEGALLY DETAINING BARONESS MAGYR!

"WE WERE FALSELY HELD AGAINST OUR WILL," SAYS COUNCIL'S EXECUTIVE DIRECTOR

Finally Darbin's angry glare eased. His arms slowly dropped to his sides.

"What do you want, Harvey?"

"I'd like this imprisonment to end," said Millard.

"Not until the scientists put out their decision."

"Then at least allow these people to return to Earth." Turning to Ilona, Millard asked, "Will you keep your silence until the council scientists announce their finding?"

With a glance at the others, Ilona said, "Yes, if you believe we should."

Darbin nodded slowly, but said nothing.

Ilona got a sudden thought. "We can stay at my family's castle in Budaörs! It is secured. And it's much more comfortable than this space station."

Before Darbin could reply, Millard added, "The castle's big enough to hold the Council final meeting there, as well."

Darbin looked from Ilona's face to Millard's, then back again. His expression eased into a guarded smile.

"Very well, Baroness," he said. "You can return to your home."

Before Ilona could thank him, Darbin added, "But no media interviews, no announcement of your return. Not until we have the final report to the Council."

Trying to suppress her sudden exhilaration, Ilona said merely, "Thank you, Mr. President." But inwardly her spirit soared.

All five of them rode back to Earth on the shuttle that had carried Darbin to the space station. They landed at the Council's spaceport outside Copenhagen and were quickly transferred to a swept-wing jet plane that flew them to the Magyr spaceport on the edge of Budaörs.

As they circled the field on their landing approach Ilona's pulse quickened when she caught a glimpse of the family's castle, rising high above the town's clustered buildings. It's still there, she thought, strong and firm, waiting for my return. Then she glimpsed the unfinished tower in the middle of the town and her heart sank. I didn't bring Father home, she told herself sadly. All I have of him is a few samples of his DNA.

From the spaceport the five of them—plus three armed security guards—were bundled into a waiting stretch limousine and whisked to the castle. The limo clattered over the drawbridge and passed through the big arching gate in the castle's wall. It squealed to a stop in the courtyard and the security guards helped them out into the sunshine.

The courtyard was empty. Ilona realized that no one had alerted the staff that she would be arriving home.

"Wow," said Jan Meitner, as he climbed out of the limo and looked around. "A real castle!"

Then Ilona saw a trio of servants running out into the sunny courtyard, led by Ghulam, her chief butler.

"Baroness Magyr!" he shouted as he ran up to her. "No one informed us—"

The butler was reed-slim, his skin swarthy, his dark eyes wide with surprised consternation. He wore his usual dark suit, its jacket unbuttoned and flapping undignifiedly as he ran up to Ilona.

She smiled at him. "It's all right, Ghulam. It's good to see you again. It's good to be home."

The butler stood before her, puffing slightly, his face showing surprise and delight. "Welcome home," he said, as he buttoned his jacket with trembling fingers. The two maids who had rushed out with him stood absolutely still, although neither of them could refrain from smiling broadly.

Ilona introduced Millard and her crewmates, then said, "My guests will be staying here for several days, at least."

"I'll have rooms prepared for them, Baroness."

"Thank you, Ghulam." And Ilona led her four companions into the castle.

After a quickly prepared lunch Ilona spent the rest of the afternoon showing off Castle Magyr. When they reached the central ballroom she pointed out the paintings adorning the walls. "This one," she pointed to one of the huge canvases, "depicts the Magyr victory over the Huns, in the fifth century."

"I don't see a painting of the Battle of Mohi," Millard said, his head swiveling to take in the room's display. "Thirteenth century, wasn't it?"

Suppressing a frown, Ilona replied, "There is no depiction of the Battle of Mohi. The Mongols defeated us, they slaughtered the cream of European chivalry."

Millard's brows inched upward a notch.

"We don't celebrate defeats," Ilona added, feeling nettled at Millard's effrontery.

"I see," he said. "Sorry if I offended you."

Struggling to regain her equanimity, Ilona put on a smile and led the little group out of the ballroom.

Ilona showed her guests upstairs to their bedrooms. They oohed and aahed at the splendor of the décor, the luxurious bedcovers, the sweeping views of the countryside through the wide windows.

Then it was downstairs again to cocktails and dinner in the oak-paneled dining room that could accommodate fifty with ease. Ilona allowed Ghulam to seat her at the head of the table, Millard at her right, Humbolt at her left, Jan and Francine opposite each other.

The servants brought in the various courses: pheasant and venison and noble Hungarian wines. Humbolt started telling stories of his journeys through the solar system, Meitner spoke of his college days, even Francine talked about her dreams of joining the Council's scientific staff one day.

Then Millard said, "The council scientists must be having a difficult time of it."

"Difficult?" Ilona asked, from her chair at the head of the table.

"We've confronted the astronomical community with startling new concepts."

Meitner chipped in, "The confirmation of intelligent life, the idea that Uranus was knocked over into its present orientation only two million years ago, not four billion."

Nodding, Millard added, "By extraterrestrial invaders."

"That's the sticking point, isn't it?" Humbolt asked. "Extraterrestrial invaders."

Francine piped up, "It does sound sort of strange . . . fantastic."

"Like something out of a dream," said Humbolt.

"But it's true," Ilona insisted. "We have solid evidence of it."

Millard smiled sadly. "I'm afraid that what we believe to be solid evidence is undoubtedly very difficult for the non-scientific people to accept."

"They can't deny the evidence we've brought back from Neptune," Ilona declared.

"I wonder," said Millard. "It wouldn't be the first time that even the scientific establishment turned its back on a new idea."

Meitner said, "Like Wegener's concept of continental drift."

"Or Mendel's study of genetic inheritance," Francine added.

Shaking his head glumly, Millard said, "We're going to be challenging the astronomical community's bedrock ideas. We're going to be daring them to face a new concept that flies in the face of all they believe to be true."

"But we have the evidence to prove it," Ilona insisted.

"We'll be challenging their faith," Millard countered.

Frowning, Humbolt said, "You make it sound like we'll be facing the Spanish Inquisition."

Millard shook his head. "You know, back in the twentieth century some obscure writer said, 'Knowledge is always based on faith. The verb *to know* depends on the verb *to believe.*'"

The table fell silent.

"We're not going to have an easy time of it with some council members," Millard insisted. "Be warned."

THE ASTRONOMICAL ASSOCIATION

For two days Ilona showed her guests through the castle's extensive gardens and monuments. On the third day the Astronomical Association's board of advisors convened at Castle Magyr.

There were fifty of them, Ilona saw as she greeted them at the castle's main entrance. Mostly men, mostly old, balding, overweight, secure in their positions of authority and power.

Harvey Millard stood beside her and introduced each of them, with a smile and a handshake. Ilona felt slightly uncomfortable among them. She could sense the questions that lay in their minds through the seemingly endless introductions:

Who is this woman acting as hostess to our meeting? A baroness, they say. But she's not an astronomer, she's not even a scientist of any stripe. Why are we meeting here, in this ancient castle?

It was late in the morning, almost lunchtime, before all fifty of the astronomers were seated in the spacious main ballroom. The chairman of the board of the Association, Dr. Lin Macao, slowly climbed the four steps to the bandstand, stepped to the slim lectern standing at its middle, and turned to the assembled astronomers. Then he smiled warmly.

"Welcome to this special assembly of the Astronomical Association's board of advisors. I'm delighted that you could all leave your regular duties to attend this important meeting."

Macao was slight of stature, his face soft with wrinkles, his kind eyes dropping at the sides much like his ancestor the calm Confucius. Yet his voice was strong, penetrating, authoritative.

"We are here to discuss the implications of the information brought back from the planet Neptune by the Baroness Magyr's mission. You have all received and hopefully reviewed the data files and preliminary report of her investigators. Our purpose here today is to decide what recommendations we should make to the Interplanetary Council."

Sitting on the bandstand stage behind Macao, with Millard, Humbolt, Meitner and Francine Savoy arrayed on either side of her, Ilona studied the faces of the assembled astronomers. All of them seemed very old. Apparently hardly any of them availed themselves of the rejuvenation therapies that were available throughout the worlds. Then she thought, Or maybe they have gone in for rejuvenation and they've outlasted the therapies. They must be ancient!

With video clips displayed on the screen at the back of the bandstand, Macao swiftly reviewed the Astronomical Association's findings about Ilona's mission to Neptune. A duplicate screen at the rear of the ballroom showed the same displays, so that those on the stage didn't have to turn around to see them.

Still standing at the podium, Macao said, "Those are the data files that Baroness Magyr's mission returned to us. Our review of the data has shown no objections to it. It appears to be valid."

A portly, balding, white man sprang to his feet and shouted, "We certainly can't recommend anything to the Council based on these findings! They fly in the face of everything we know about the history of our solar system!"

"Do they?" Macao replied mildly.

Ticking points off on his stubby fingers, the astronomer said, "Wreckage of an alien space station was found on the seafloor of Neptune. Yes. It has been dated at two million years old. Agreed. But to jump from that to the conclusion that aliens invaded our solar system and sterilized the planet Uranus is a leap into the unknown! Where is the evidence for that conclusion?"

Millard rose to his feet and asked Macao, "May I respond to that, please?"

"That man's not an astronomer!" barked the speaker.

Macao said mildly, "Harvey Millard is executive director of the Interplanetary Council. I think we can listen to what he wants to say without losing our purity."

A few chuckles rose from the assembled astronomers.

Millard went to the podium as Macao stepped to one side for him.

Clasping his hands together on the podium's slanting top, Millard said, "Accepting new concepts is very difficult, I know. But refusing to accept them can be a cardinal failure."

The audience made no response, although several members shifted uncomfortably in their chairs.

"I believe Dr. Gomez's research was our first evidence and now Baroness Magyr's missions have uncovered significant more evidence that confirms that the planet Uranus was deliberately sterilized by twelve-foot-tall alien invaders about two million years ago—"

"Four billion years ago!" came a man's shout from the rear of the ballroom. "Uranus was struck by a major planetesimal, four billion years ago!"

Millard smiled placatingly. "And what is the evidence for that?"

"It makes sense! The solar system was filled with planetesimals back then."

"But where is the specific evidence that Uranus was struck back at that time?"

Ilona saw that the speaker was a relatively young astronomer, with thick dark hair and a stubborn jaw.

"How the hell can we produce specific evidence of something that happened four billion years ago? We see that the planet is tilted sideways, we know the solar system was filled with planetesimals zooming all over the place in that early era. What do you want: fingerprints?"

Millard's smile widened a notch. "I believe that Baroness Magyr's mission has found the fingerprints."

"Nonsense!"

Lin Macao stepped to Millard's side and said calmly, "We must consider the possibility—"

"We have considered the possibility, and we have found that this idea of an alien invasion is pure conjecture!" the astronomer said.

"Is the wreckage of an alien space station that's been found in Neptune's ocean pure conjecture?" Millard snapped.

"No," answered the astronomer. "But to jump from that to a scenario about an alien invasion is."

Millard shook his head dolefully. "There are none so blind as those who *will* not see."

DECISION?

The astronomers spent the morning arguing—
sometimes vociferously. Then Macao told them it was
time for lunch. The debates and arguments contin-
ued though the meal, and then the astronomers reassembled in the
ballroom and spent the afternoon arguing even more stridently
about the idea that alien invaders had sterilized Uranus and smashed
the planet sideways a mere two million years earlier.

Ilona watched and listened as she sat in her chair on the ballroom's stage. They don't believe us, she saw. They don't *want* to
believe us. We're challenging the views they've held for generations
and they don't want to change those views.

But more than that, she sensed fear among the quarreling, conten-
tious men and women. Cold fear. They ridiculed the idea that aliens
had invaded the solar system, but inwardly they feared that the invaders might return.

Macao kept a slim hold on the proceedings, allowing the astronomers to speak their minds freely. Too freely, Ilona thought. They're
closing their eyes to the truth.

Finally, as the setting sun cast long shafts of light through the ballroom's tall windows, Macao said into the microphone on the podium,
"Thank you all for speaking your minds so openly. I will appoint a special subcommittee to draft our report to the Interplanetary Council."

The assembled astronomers got to their feet, some obviously glad
that the quarrelsome meeting was at last ended, others still arguing
heatedly with one another.

Ilona followed Millard as he went to Macao's side. "You've earned
a drink, sir," Millard said, with a slight smile.

Macao shook his head. "Hemlock, perhaps?"

"Come with me," said Ilona, "where we can have some peace and
privacy."

Glancing at the departing throng of astronomers, Macao said

dolefully, "I don't think I should be seen going off by myself with you."

Millard's smile broadened. "Ah! You're afraid that your cohorts will think you're sleeping with the enemy."

Macao grinned back at Millard. "Something like that."

"Then let's go to the dining room with all the others," said Ilona.

"Yes!" Millard agreed. "By all means."

Accompanied by Humbolt, Meitner and Savoy, Ilona led Millard and Macao to the castle's spacious dining room.

The stately old room was filled with astronomers, all of them armed with various cocktails or nonalcoholic drinks, all of them arguing passionately. Ilona winced at the noise, but she led her little procession through the throng and up to the makeshift bar that Ghulam had set up beneath a painting of a World War II battle scene.

The drinks didn't calm the astronomers. Their arguing simply became louder, more intense.

"You mustn't take any of this talk personally," Millard half shouted into Ilona's ear. "Science is a very human activity, you know."

"Yelling at each other?" she questioned.

"Scholarly debate," said Macao. "Sometimes it can get painfully loud."

Humbolt pushed through the crowd toward her. "It's like a barnyard carnival! Jabber, jabber, jabber!"

With a nod, Millard agreed. "Quite often the one who wins the argument is the one with the loudest voice."

"Or the most determination," said Macao.

Looking almost dazed at the throng of arguing, gesticulating astronomers, Meitner said, "It's like a zoo full of angry monkeys!"

Francine added, "Is this the way science policy is really done?"

Macao almost laughed. "The alcohol doesn't help."

Ilona shook her head. "What we found at Neptune is going to be washed away by a tidal wave of liquor."

With a shake of his head, Macao contradicted, "No, I think not." Gesturing with his free hand toward the arguing astronomers, he said, "They'll settle down. I'll pick a few of the steadiest among them to write our report to the Council."

Millard's brows rose. "Can you really—"

Macao interrupted him. "Remember the dictum: 'Power is not with the man who votes. Power is with the man who counts the votes.'"

Millard broke into a chuckle. Meitner and Humbolt both looked puzzled, Francine thoughtful.

And Ilona understood. This quiet chairman is on our side, she thought. His report will support our conclusions.

Then she added to herself, I hope.

THE MORNING AFTER

Ilona woke when the drapes over her bedroom windows automatically rolled back to allow warm sunshine to flood across her.

The shreds of a dream fluttered away into nothingness as she sat up in her luxurious bed. Something about Father, she half remembered. But the more she tried to recall her dream the more it dissolved into oblivion.

She called to her phone to order breakfast in bed, but the phone's automated voice replied, "Director Millard has invited you to breakfast with Captain Humbolt and your other crew members at oh-eight-hundred hours, in his suite."

Ilona glanced at the phone's clock display: 7:12 A.M. Throwing her bedclothes back, she hurried for the bathroom.

When Millard showed her into his suite—on the floor below Ilona's bedroom—Humbolt and the others were already seated around the breakfast table. A pair of man-sized robots were placing dishes of steaming omelets before Francine and Jan Meitner.

"Come right in," Millard said to Ilona, smiling brightly.

"We're having a victory celebration," Humbolt called from the table.

"Victory?" Ilona questioned as she sat at the chair Millard held for her.

"A sort of victory," Millard said, going to his own chair. "Macao phoned me first thing this morning to tell me that his committee's report will recommend follow-up missions to both Uranus and Neptune."

"That's good news," said Meitner, holding a forkful of omelet in one hand.

Ilona felt less than elated. "He could hardly have done anything less, could he?"

As he picked up his napkin and tucked it beneath his chin, Millard said, "It's a step in the right direction, an important step. He's asking the Association to review what you've found on Neptune. That will lead inevitably to confirming your findings."

"And our conclusions, as well?" she asked.

Millard reached across the table and patted her hand. "One step at a time, Baroness. One step at a time."

"They'll come around to our way of thinking," Meitner said. Then he added, "Sooner or later."

"Macao's on our side," said Francine, smiling.

Ilona looked at the four of them. *They all think this battle is won. But it's really just beginning. That young astronomer was right: we really didn't discover anything that concretely connects the wreckage on Neptune with the sterilization of Uranus.*

Or did we?

Once she went down with Millard and the others to the castle's main floor, Ilona saw that the astronomers were in the process of leaving Castle Magyr.

She was surprised—almost shocked—to see the usually unflappable Ghulam perspiring and flustered at the entryway to the castle's main entrance. A line of cars, ranging from bright-colored taxicabs to somber black limousines, was arrayed outside in the courtyard.

As she approached her chief butler, Ghulam hurriedly pushed back a lock of hair that had fallen across his forehead.

She asked, "Ghulam, is everything under control?"

"Barely," the butler replied. "It seems that no two of these fifty people want the same flight to the same destination. Even the head of the Budapest Observatory is scheduled for a flight to Rome that departs in less than an hour!"

Ilona suppressed a smile. She had never seen Ghulam rattled before. *Astronomers,* she thought, *can be worse than operatic divas. Or tenors!*

Ilona spent the rest of the morning helping Ghulam and the other servants pack off the astronomers. It was almost fun, although some of the scientists became quite short-tempered. Each of them seemed to feel that his or her flight was the most important and the other forty-nine could wait until his or her transportation had started on its way to the airport.

I wonder what a boiling pot of stew the airport will be like, Ilona thought.

At last the fiftieth of the astronomers was packed into a car and left Castle Magyr. Ilona breathed a sigh of heartfelt relief as she turned from the driveway and headed back into the cool and calm of the high-arched entryway.

She was surprised to see Dr. Macao standing there, looking slightly amused.

"They can be quite a handful, can't they?" said the chairman.

Nodding, Ilona said, "Like frantic schoolchildren."

Macao agreed with a nod of his own. "You mustn't forget, however, that they have been among the most brilliant astronomers in the world."

Ilona noticed the chairman's "have been" wording. She decided not to inquire further.

It turned out that Macao's flight back to Copenhagen was not until early evening. Ilona asked Ghulam to have a late-afternoon meal prepared.

After spending more than an hour showing off the formal garden to Macao, Ilona saw Ghulam—looking much more like his usual imperturbable self—nodding at her from the head of a hedge-lined walkway.

As she led Macao toward the dining room Ilona wondered what a late-afternoon dinner should be properly called. In the English language, meals between breakfast and lunchtime were known as "brunch," she knew. But no one had invented a term for a meal between the usual lunch and dinner times.

Millard, Humbolt and Meitner were already in the dining room as Ilona entered, with Macao at her side.

"Where's Francine?" she asked as she went to the head of the table.

"Off to Copenhagen," replied Humbolt. "She has to report in person to her superiors."

Ilona glanced at Macao, who said, "She was the Association's representative on your second mission to Neptune, after all."

Millard added, "The committee wants to hear what she has to say about your findings."

With a nod to indicate she understood, Ilona took her seat at the head of the table, saying to herself, I understand, but I don't approve. How much pressure is the Astronomical Association's committee going to put on that poor girl?

As if he could read her mind, Meitner blurted, "I should have gone with her."

Millard asked, "Why do you say that, Jan?"

"She's got to face the committee all alone! I could at least have confirmed her findings."

With an almost paternal smile, Millard said, "It won't be like facing the Spanish Inquisition, Jan. They'll be fair with her."

Meitner was not relieved. "Still . . ."

"Still," Ilona said, "you'd rather be with her than here with us."

Meitner said nothing, but his face flamed red.

Darbin

macao left castle magyr shortly after their meal, as did meitner, who was scheduled to give his own personal report to the Astronomical Association in copenhagen. Ilona could see that Jan was anxious to be with Francine again.

It's not merely sex then, she wondered. They must have truly bonded, she thought somewhat regretfully.

The next two days were empty, as far as Ilona was concerned. Humbolt left for his home in New Mexico, after inviting Ilona once again to visit him there.

"Most beautiful scenery on Earth," he told her as they went together in the elderly limousine to the airport.

"We'll see," said Ilona. "After all this fuss with the Astronomical Association is settled."

"Aw god! That could take months. Years!"

Ilona smiled and shrugged. "We'll see," she repeated.

Millard remained at the castle with her after Humbolt left, but no news—no information at all—came from Copenhagen.

"What is Macao going to do?" Ilona wondered as she and Millard walked slowly along the hedge-lined paths of the formal garden.

"If I know our chairman friend, he's trying to get the Association to accept your findings. All of them."

"Including the confirmation of the alien invasion," she said.

Millard nodded wordlessly.

Ilona's wristwatch buzzed softly. Looking at its tiny dial, she saw the face of a young woman. The legend inching across the tiny screen below her image said OFFICE OF THE PRESIDENT, INTERPLANETARY COUNCIL in glowing letters.

"Baroness Magyr," the woman was saying, "President Darbin has just left Copenhagen. His plane should arrive at the Budaörs airport in half an hour."

The little screen went blank.

Looking up at Millard, Ilona said, "I suppose he expects us to meet him at the airport."

Millard broke into a tight smile. "Rank has its privileges—and its expectations."

"Apparently so."

"I recall reading that some motion picture director, back in the twentieth century, had a chair boy follow him wherever he went on the filming set."

"Chair boy?"

"Whenever the director wanted to sit, he sat. The chair boy's job was to have that chair beneath his rump in time."

Ilona did not laugh.

Ilona and Millard arrived at the airport as Darbin's sleek blue-and-white swept-wing jet rolled up to the ramp that fronted the executive travelers' hangar, its twin engines' shrill howl winding down to silence.

The two of them got out of her aging limousine as the plane's hatch opened, its stairs unfolded, and Yancey Darbin came stomping down to the ground.

He walked straight to Ilona and Millard, as if he had totally expected them to be there to meet him.

"Baroness," he said, engulfing Ilona's extended hand in his own. Then he turned to Millard. "Harvey."

There was no trace of happiness in Darbin's hard-bitten expression.

"You got that little chairman Macao all riled up," Darbin growled as the three of them turned toward Ilona's limo.

They got into the aging limousine and the driver started back to the castle. Darbin sat across Ilona and Millard, radiating fury like a volcano spewing red-hot lava.

Before either Millard or Ilona could ask another question, Darbin spouted, "That damned Macao wants to submit a report that says our solar system was invaded by giant aliens two million years ago and they sterilized the civilization on Uranus."

"But that's the truth!" Ilona blurted.

"Maybe it is and maybe it isn't. Either way, it's not going to be published. We're not going to tell the public that twelve-foot-tall aliens invaded our solar system two million years ago and that's final."

Millard said, "You can't keep that from the public!"

"The hell I can't!"

Ilona saw grim determination etching hard lines across Darbin's rawboned face. And she knew that the president of the Interplanetary Council had the naked power to silence Millard. And herself.

MILLIONS FOR DEFENSE

+++
+++++++++++++++++++++++++++

They rode back to Castle Magyr in tense silence. Ilona tried to read the expression on Darbin's face but all she could see was grim anger. Millard, sitting on the Council president's other side, looked tense, almost frightened.

The limousine pulled into the castle's sunny courtyard and the three of them got out. Ilona led them to one of the quiet little office-like rooms off the ballroom. Ghulam was right behind them with a tray of drinks and refreshments.

Darbin looked around the small windowless room, then turned to face Millard.

"Harvey, we've got a situation here," said the president.

"And you want to keep that information a secret," said Millard.

"We've got to!" Darbin snapped. "We can't go scarin' the whole damned world with stories about an alien invasion!"

For a long moment no one said a word. Then Millard asked, in a near whisper, "Why not?"

"Why not?" Darbin shouted as he ran a hand through his thick white hair. "Because the people will go nuts, that's why not! We'll have riots, demonstrations, demands that we do something!"

Nodding, Millard said, "Can you blame them?"

Jabbing a forefinger at Millard's chest, Darbin snarled, "I'm not goin' to have my administration destroyed by a bunch of scared ig-noramuses!"

Ilona's eyed widened. He's frightened that this might force him out of office! she realized. The whole human race is threatened, but his first worry is about his own career.

She stepped up to Darbin and said forcefully, "The people have a right to know."

Darbin wheeled on her. "Yeah. And they have a right to over-throw the government, to toss me and my people out on our asses."

Strangely, Millard smiled. "It doesn't have to come to that, Yancey."

"Doesn't it?"

"No, it doesn't." Pointing to the commodious leather-covered chairs lining the room's rear wall, Millard said, "Let's sit down and look at this situation calmly."

"Calmly," Darbin muttered. But he went to the chairs and sat in one of them.

Millard pulled another one out from the wall and turned it to face the Council president. Ilona, feeling ignored, forgotten, took a third chair and sat next to Darbin.

Calmly, soothingly, Millard said to Darbin, "There's no need to get all worked up over this, Yancey. You can tell the public what the baroness and her team found at Neptune—if you also announce what steps you're taking to meet the situation."

"Meet the situation," Darbin repeated, dully.

"Yes. I should think you'd want to send bigger and better-equipped missions to Uranus and Neptune."

"That's what Macao wants," Darbin said.

"And you should announce that you're asking the old Space Force to review its needs, in light of this new situation. It's mission will be to scan the stars. Search for signs of alien activity. Build up the Force's capability to meet potentially hostile aliens."

"Get ready for war."

"Be prepared," Millard agreed. "Don't let a potential enemy see us as weak."

Darbin nodded.

"You're going to have to increase defense spending, Yancey."

"Yeah. Sure."

"Show the people that you're ready to meet this new challenge."

Darbin sat up straighter in his chair. "Meet this new challenge."

"That's the spirit," said Millard, with a smile.

Ilona thought the smile looked forced, but Darbin didn't seem to notice it.

"You'll be regarded as the savior of our people," Millard encouraged. "They'll build statues of you."

Darbin huffed. But he didn't contradict Millard. To Ilona, it seemed that Darbin liked the idea of having statues raised in his honor.

His smile shifting slightly, Millard added, "I believe it was some

American politician who once said, 'Millions for defense, but not one cent for tribute.'"

"Millions for defense," Darbin muttered.

"You could combine the defense and research budgets, possibly," Millard continued. "Make our astronomical research a part of our defense effort."

Darbin started to shake his head, but hesitated. "Harvey, we don't even know if we're really bein' threatened. This is all just speculation."

"It's based on rather strong evidence, Yancey. The threat is too big to ignore."

"Millions for defense, but not one cent for tribute," Darbin repeated.

"That's the ticket," said Millard.

"Lemme think about that."

"Of course."

NEW EARTH

Darbin returned to Copenhagen, leaving Millard at Ilona's castle.

As the sun was setting, Ilona told Ghulam she wanted to have dinner with Millard on the patio outside the formal dining room. It was a lovely late summer evening, and the sky overhead glittered with the splendor of the stars.

Sitting across the small table from Ilona, Millard pointed to a particularly bright star twinkling near the horizon.

"That's Sirius," he said.

"The Dog Star," Ilona remarked, to show that she wasn't totally ignorant of the heavens.

She expected Millard to smile. But his face remained stony, troubled. "The astronomers have found an Earthlike planet there."

"So I've heard," said Ilona. "The news media are calling it New Earth."

Millard repeated softly, "New Earth."

Ilona said, "I understand the Astronomical Association wants to send a mission to it."

With the slightest of nods, Millard murmured, "An Earthlike planet, orbiting Sirius A."

"Close enough for us to reach."

"The mission will take nearly a century to get there."

"The stars are so far away."

"Yes," said Millard. "But that planet has no right to be there."

"No right . . . ?"

Millard glanced down at his dinner plate, but didn't pick up his knife or fork. Looking back at Ilona he explained, "The planet orbits Sirius A, the major star of the Sirius system. Sirius B is a dwarf star. The astronomers reckon it exploded in a supernova eruption several million years ago."

Ilona nodded.

"That explosion would have blown away any atmosphere around the planet," Millard said. "By all that our astronomers understand of the stars, that planet should be nothing more than a blackened, burnt-out cinder."

"But it has oceans, clouds, an Earthlike atmosphere," Ilona countered.

"Indeed it does. It shouldn't be there. By all that we understand of the heavens, it *can't* be there."

Ilona whispered, "Yet there it is."

"There it is," Millard echoed.

"So the astronomers want to send a mission there?"

His voice gaining some strength, Millard said, "Indeed they do. And now what you've found means they will also want to send more missions to Neptune."

"And to Uranus."

"And to Uranus," Millard agreed.

As she reached for her wineglass, Ilona said, "No wonder Darbin is so troubled."

"He's being stretched in several different directions," Millard agreed.

Ilona took a sip of the wine, then smiled and asked, "Who was it that said, 'The universe is not only queerer than we suppose, but queerer than we *can* suppose'?"

Millard made a sound halfway between a laugh and a grunt. "Haldane. J. B. S. Haldane, twentieth-century British geneticist."

"Looks as though he was right."

"I can't believe that," Millard said, with an intensity that astonished Ilona. "We can learn. We can understand. There's nothing in the universe that we can't figure out." Before Ilona could react, he added, "Eventually."

Ilona blinked several times, then decided to shift the focus of their conversation. Picking at the salad before her, she asked, "What do you think Darbin's going to do?"

"Yancey?"

Ilona nodded.

"His first instinct was typical of a politician: keep the information secret."

"But you think the people have a right to know."

Millard made a bleak smile. "They're going to find out, sooner or later, one way or another. What you found at Neptune is too big to be kept a secret for very long."

"But . . ."

"The news is going to come out, I can guarantee you that. The best way for it coming out is for Darbin to announce it, calmly and fully. And to announce also the steps he's asking the Council to take in light of this discovery."

Ilona nodded her understanding. "That will avert a panic."

"I think so," said Millard. "I certainly hope so."

"And it will show the public that Yancey Darbin's administration is on top of the situation."

Millard's smile turned bitter. "It will save his backside from getting fried."

CABINET MEETING

For two more days neither Millard nor Ilona heard anything from Darbin at Copenhagen. But on the third afternoon, as Ilona was sitting at her viewscreen reviewing Ghulam's monthly budget for the castle's grocery provisions, she heard footsteps clattering down the hallway outside her door.

She got up from her desk as someone started knocking on the ancient oaken door. A glance at the viewscreen set at one side of the entrance showed it was Harvey Millard, banging away at the door excitedly.

"Door open," Ilona called out as she stepped toward the entrance.

Millard was standing just outside, his chest heaving, a wide grin splitting his normally imperturbable features.

Holding a flimsy sheet of paper in one hand, he announced, "It's from Darbin! We're to meet with his inner cabinet in Copenhagen tomorrow!"

Ilona broke into a smile of her own. "At last," she said. "At last."

Ilona expected a grand meeting of the Interplanetary Council's membership, a spacious assembly hall filled with the solar system's political leaders.

She was bitterly disappointed, therefore, when she and Millard were led by a single female subordinate through the Council's stately central assembly building, up a mirrored elevator, and ushered into a smallish conference room nestled just under the edifice's slanting roof.

Barely a half-dozen Council members were sitting around a rectangular table, all but one of them male. Yancey Darbin sat at the table's head. The walls were bare, but glowing softly. Viewscreens, Ilona realized; none of them in use at the moment.

They all rose politely as Ilona and Millard were ushered into the conference room. Darbin greeted them cordially, then introduced each of the Council members, one by one. Each Council member smiled graciously, but Ilona thought there was no warmth or friendliness in their smiles.

She had forgotten their names by the time everyone finally sat down. She and Millard were placed at the end of the table.

"We're here," Darbin began, all traces of his "down home" Texas accent gone, "to discuss how we need to handle the information that Baroness Magyr and her team brought back from the planet Neptune."

Nods from several Council members.

Darbin said, very seriously, "our council scientists and Dr. Macao's astronomers have verified the mission's findings. As far as they can tell, our solar system actually was invaded by giant aliens two million years ago, and the intelligent civilization on the planet Uranus was wiped out."

Ilona blurted, "And the Pleistocene ice age here on Earth was initiated."

That started a debate. Was the ice age caused by the aliens or was its onset at that time merely a coincidence? If the aliens caused the ice age, did they do so to wipe out the ape-like creatures who eventually evolved into the human race?

"If that's what they were after," said one of the councilmen, "they failed. They goofed up!"

Smiles and nods around the table.

Darbin did not smile. "Whether they succeeded or not, it appears that the bastards did try to eliminate us."

"Before we even existed?" countered one of the councilmen. "Come on, Mr. President!"

Darbin's chin went up a notch. "That's what Macao and the astronomers believe."

The argument went around the table, more than once. Ilona sat, watching and listening, as these politicians argued about scientific evidence.

At last Darbin slammed his knuckles on the gleaming tabletop. "All right, that's enough. We've got Macao's report from the astronomers. No sense debating it."

That snuffed out the argument.

"What we've got to decide is, how do we react to this information?"

"Maybe they're comin' back."

"That's ridiculous!"

"Is it? How'd you feel if they showed up tomorrow morning?"

"They sterilized Uranus," Darbin said. "Maybe they'll come back to finish us off."

"That's preposterous!" snapped the woman member of the Council.

"Is it?"

She blinked at Darbin several times, but said nothing more and looked away.

Folding his hands on the tabletop before him, Darbin said, "I think we ought to at least try to prepare ourselves for the possibility."

"Prepare ourselves? How?"

With a slow smile sneaking across his weathered face, Darbin answered, "A little more than three hundred years ago, an American political leader said, 'Millions for defense, but not one cent for tribute.'"

"Who said that?"

"Robert Goodloe Harper," said Darbin. "United States senator, in the year 1789."

"Ancient history!"

"What the hell's it supposed to mean, Yancey?"

"That we've got to get ready to defend ourselves."

"Against aliens?"

"Who haven't been here for two million years?"

Darbin nodded patiently. "Against aliens who haven't been here for two million years. Because if they come back and we're not prepared for 'em, we're toast."

That started another round of heated discussion. Ilona saw that most of the Council members were torn between a fear of an alien invasion and the realization that the fear was based on something that had happened—or might have happened—two million years ago.

Darbin let them talk themselves out. When the members started repeating themselves for the third time, he suddenly slammed his open palm on the tabletop. Everyone twitched in their seats, startled, even Ilona and Millard.

"Awl right," Darbin said, lapsing back into his Texas drawl, "here's what we're gonna do."

All eyes along the table focused on him.

"We're gonna reinvigorate the old Space Force, a branch of the armed forces that has gone idle, and we're gonna rename it the Star Watch. Its job will be to patrol the space around our solar system and search for any signs of extraterrestr'al life. We will build their capabilities in the event those giants are planning on headin' our way."

"And if they find anything?" a councilman asked, his voice trembling slightly.

"We'll be ready, at least better prepared to figure out what they want, why they're in our vicinity."

Millard raised his voice. "Do you think we'll be able to communicate with them?"

"We'll try, by damn. We'll try our best."

Dead silence fell across the table.

Then the lone woman among the Council members said, "So you want to create a sort of space patrol, armed and ready to do battle with any aliens they find."

"Any *hostile* aliens," Darbin amended.

"Sounds crazy," said the oldest man at the table, bald, overweight, grim-faced.

Darbin challenged, "You got a better idea?"

The man scratched at his sagging cheek, then meekly shook his head.

"We're gonna increase our military budget and rebuild the Space Force, now Star Watch, program," Darbin said.

"And a recruitment program," added a councilman.

"That's right," Darbin agreed. "We want our best and brightest people in the Star Watch."

No one raised an objection.

"Okay then," Darbin said, his voice hard, demanding. "I make the motion that the Interplanetary Council shall create a Star Watch Program. We will convene a task force later."

The Council woman followed, "I second it."

"All in favor, vote 'aye,'" said Darbin.

For several long moments no one stirred. Then the bald overweight councilman shakily raised his hand. The woman did the same, and within half a minute all the other Council members joined them.

Darbin nodded, satisfied. "Okay. It's unanimous. Good. We start the Star Watch program. Thank you."

AFTERMATH

Ilona remained seated as the council members filed out of the conference room. Most of them seemed to be in a trance, astounded at what they had just voted for.

Harvey Millard got slowly to his feet and walked the length of the conference table, to its head, where Darbin was standing.

"Good work, Yancey," he said.

Darbin shrugged. "What the hell else can we do?"

Millard asked, "Do you think you'll be able to get this Star Watch idea through the whole Council?"

"I'm sure as hell gonna try."

Ilona rose from her chair. "President Darbin, if there's anything that the Magyr family can do to help, don't hesitate to let me know."

A thin smile inched across Darbin's craggy face. "I will, Baroness. I shore will."

It was early evening as Millard and Ilona left the Council building. He led her through the courtyard and out onto the street, crowded with people and vehicles inching along the broad avenue.

"I know a pleasant little bistro not far from here," Millard said, his voice raised over the buzz and chatter of the crowd. "Would you care to have dinner with me there?"

Ilona easily agreed.

The bistro was intimately small, in a cellar with a low ceiling. Although it was early, every table seemed to be occupied.

As Ilona and Millard stood just inside the front entrance, a short, pleasant-faced man in a dark suit and bow tie bustled up to them.

"Director Millard!" he boomed. "We haven't seen you in several weeks!"

With a smile, Millard replied, "I've been rather busy, Antoine."

Casting his gaze across the crowded bistro, he added, "It looks as if you are, as well."

"The price of success," replied Antoine happily. "But we will never be too busy for you, sir."

With that, Antoine raised one hand and snapped his fingers. As if by magic, a pair of waiters appeared, bearing small table and a pair of chairs. Within minutes Millard and Ilona were seated—close enough to other couples to be almost touching elbows.

The veal française was excellent, and Antoine personally brought to their table a bottle of white wine and opened it for them. It was crisp and cool and delicious.

Despite the bistro's noisiness, Ilona enjoyed their meal. It was difficult to hold a meaningful conversation, but once they finished their dessert of baba au rhum and thanked Antoine for his gracious attention, they found the street outside to be much quieter.

As they strolled beneath the streetlamps back toward Ilona's hotel, she asked, "Do you think you're doing the right thing?"

Millard hunched his shoulders. "Only time can answer that question."

"When I stop to think about it, to look at the question clearly, it all seems so unbelievable . . . preposterous, almost."

"So were tales of the gorilla, when that beast was first seen by Western explorers."

"But . . ."

He stopped walking and gripped her shoulder. "If we prepare ourselves for a possible conflict and nothing happens, we haven't lost anything. But if we don't prepare and we're suddenly confronted by invaders, we could lose everything. It will also revitalize some industries and we can be more inventive. Humans always love a challenge."

Ilona gazed at Millard's face. In the wan light from the streetlamps, she could not make out the color of his eyes. But she could see the set of his jaw.

He said, "I believe it was the first American president who said that the best way to avoid a fight is to be ready to do battle."

"Against an enemy who may never appear."

"Let's hope they never appear. But let's also remember what they did on Uranus."

The next morning Ilona flew back to Castle Magyr. For more than a week she waited there, fidgeting nervously, striding through the castle's ancient halls, walking alone through the gardens and hedge-works outside. Millard phoned every afternoon, even though he had very little to report.

"The Council is working its way through the astronomers' findings and Darbin's request to create a Star Watch."

"The Star Watch," Ilona said to his gloomy image in her phone's screen.

"Melodramatic, isn't it?" said Millard, with a wry smile.

Ilona nodded.

At last Millard's call was more excited. "The Council passed the authorization for the Star Watch!" he told Ilona.

Sitting at the desk in her office, Ilona broke into a wide smile. "At last!"

Darbin cautioned, "It's only the authorization. Funding the organization will take another vote."

"But they'll vote in favor, won't they?"

"Yes, but *how much* in favor? That's the question."

The news media carried not a word about the debate and decision over the Star Watch. The Council's action was taken in secret sessions.

The Council announced that President Darbin would give a major public address in three days. Millard invited Ilona to be his guest at the special Council meeting, and she swiftly accepted.

ACTION

++
++++++++++++++++++++++++++

Even though there was no special publicity about the council's special meeting, somehow everyone seemed to know that Darbin's upcoming speech was of particular importance.

The news media gave the announcement of the speech no extraordinary coverage, yet Ilona could sense the public's excitement and expectation the instant she stepped off her private plane at the Copenhagen spaceport. As she rode through the city's crowded streets to the Interplanetary Council's headquarters she could fairly sense the anticipation and ferment among the people on the streets outside her car.

Or is it merely me? she asked herself. I'm excited, so I'm projecting my emotions onto the people on the streets.

But once she got out of the car and started up the grand staircase of the Council's meeting hall, Ilona knew it wasn't just a projection of her own anticipation. A thick crowd of people was streaming up the steps, and they were excited. She could feel their expectation, see it in the animated conversations all around her.

Wearing a brand-new knee-length dress of sky blue that nicely complemented her eyes, Ilona hesitated at the entrance to the Council's meeting hall as she stood watching the crowd that was pushing, jostling, hurrying toward the waiting rows of seats.

An usher in a uniform studded with bright silvery buttons came up to her.

"Baroness Magyr?" he asked, over the buzz and chatter of the crowd.

"Yes."

"This way, please. President Darbin has reserved a seat for you."

Pleased but not totally surprised, Ilona followed the young man down to the tenth row of the vast, crowded, bustling auditorium. An empty aisle seat waited for her, and Harvey Millard was in the seat next to it.

Ilona thanked the usher and sat down. Millard half rose as she did so, and smiled a welcome to her.

Glancing back at the rapidly filling auditorium, Millard said as he sat down again, "It looks as if Yancey will be speaking to a full house."

"It's exciting," said Ilona.

Millard grinned slightly. "The last time Yancey spoke to the Council, we had to empty half our offices to fill up this barn."

Ilona suppressed an expression of surprise and replied, "No such problem today."

"No," Millard agreed. "No problem at all."

The stage was empty except for a single slim podium standing in its middle. Its rear was sheathed with handsome deep blue curtains. Darbin won't be showing any audiovisual aids, she thought.

Ilona assumed that the nine rows before them were reserved for Council members. Each seat was already filled.

The crowd's chatter went on uninterrupted. Turning to look across the auditorium, Ilona saw the side aisles were filled with TV crews. Someone has let out a pretty strong hint that this will be an historic occasion, she thought.

At that moment, Yancey Darbin came striding out from the wing of the stage, tall, rawboned, his expression dead serious.

The vast auditorium fell absolutely silent. Ilona could hear the clicking of Darbin's boots across the stage as he walked to the podium.

Gripping the edges of the slim lectern with both his big-knuckled hands, Darbin began:

"Afternoon, ever'one. I have momentous news to announce to y'all. Prob'ly the most important news in the history of the human race."

He paused. Ilona could see the tension in the backs of the Council members seated in front of her, sense the stress among the huge audience behind her.

Making a self-deprecating, lopsided grin, Darbin went on, "I got good news and bad news for ya." A moment's pause, then, "The good news is that we've found unequivocal evidence that intelligent life exists elsewhere in space."

A great heartfelt sigh rose from the audience.

Darbin waited for the moment to pass, then went on, "The bad news is that they're a bunch of murderin' homicidal fiends who wiped out the intelligent civilization that once occupied the planet Uranus, and someday might come back and try to destroy us."

The crowd's sigh morphed into a groan, a gasping sound of fear and shock.

Darbin raised his hands in a calming gesture. The auditorium quieted.

"So here's what we're gonna do," he said, allowing a small, determined smile to spread across his lips.

For most of the next hour Darbin explained what Dr. Gomez's research on Uranus and now Ilona's missions to Neptune had uncovered, and the conclusions that the Astronomical Association had drawn from them.

"So the Council has authorized the creation of a military force, to be named the Star Watch, to prepare us to meet any threat from hostile space aliens."

By the time he finished, Ilona had to agree that Darbin had given his audience the facts, and presented an agenda for facing them squarely. The audience rose as a single entity when he finished and applauded lustily.

Turning to speak into her ear, Millard half shouted over the audience's roars of approval, "Now comes the hard part."

reaction

++

ALIENS DESTROYED INTELLIGENT
CIVILIZATION OF URANUS
London Times

WE ARE NOT ALONE:
ALIENS THREATEN HUMAN RACE
Chicago Tribune/Examiner

ALIEN INVADERS
CAUSED ICE AGE
TV Today

ARE SPACE ALIENS
AMONG US TODAY?
Beijing Investigator

SPACE ATTACK COULD BE IMMINENT,
SAYS RETIRED ASTROPHYSICIST
Cairo Intelligencer

Ilona clicked off the news screen in her snug little office in castle magyr. nothing but fear-mongering stories about space aliens coming to attack earth.

One gram of truth and a few megatons of sensationalism, she said to herself.

Millard had not called her in several days. She realized that he must be up to his eyebrows in Council meetings and discussions with Darbin and other key Council members.

The vote for funding the Star Watch was due for this afternoon's Council session, Ilona knew. She remembered Millard's bleak assessment of the situation.

"Some of the most influential members of the Council," he had told her, "want to keep the funding as low as possible."

"How can that be?" Ilona had wondered.

With a grim smile, Millard had answered, "They see the possibility of an alien attack as pure fantasy. They're willing to vote a minimal funding, claim that they've done their duty, and go on to more realistic problems."

"More realistic . . . ?"

"Such as pork barrel projects for their home districts."

"But the alien threat is real!" Ilona had said to Millard's image on her wall screen.

With a weary shake of his head, Millard had replied, "Even if that's true, nothing might happen for another thousand years. They'll all be safely dead and out of office by then."

"And we'll be unprepared."

"That's democracy in action, Ilona. The threat has got to be believable—and *imminent*—before some politicians are willing to act."

She had nodded wordlessly.

Ilona could not sleep that night.

Every time she closed her eyes she saw the wreckage they had found on Neptune's ocean floor, pictured the cities and structures the civilization on Uranus had built over the ages, saw it all destroyed by the invading aliens.

She had read and reread Gomez's article. The civilization on Uranus never developed spaceflight, she told herself as she lay wide-eyed on her broad, sumptuous bed. Their clouds hid the stars from their sight, they never realized that they lived on a planet that circled a star, that there were millions and billions of other worlds, other creatures, other civilizations. They thought that the clouds above them were the edge of the universe, with nothing beyond them.

Then the aliens penetrated those clouds that masked their sky and utterly destroyed their civilization, down to the last spark of life.

And the aliens also came here, to Earth, and triggered the ice age, thinking that would destroy the human race before we were even born.

But we were born. We survived. We achieved intelligence. And now we look out at the stars not in wonder, or awe, but in fear. The enemy is out there. How soon will they return to destroy us?

As the sun cast its first warming rays through her sweeping bedroom windows, Ilona gave up on all efforts to sleep and got out of bed, red-eyed, stony-faced, determined to somehow face the future unafraid.

* * *

By the time she showered and dressed and called Ghulam to order breakfast, Ilona was almost ready to face the day.

And do what? she asked herself as she went down the curving staircase that led to the dining hall. She hesitated at its wide entrance. Her ancestors stared at her from their portraits lining the walls.

I'll have to commission a portrait of Father, she told herself as she walked down the length of the dining table and took her place at its head. Ghulam was already there, of course, holding her chair for her.

"Good morning, Ghulam," she said as she sat down.

"Good morning, Baroness. Did you sleep well?"

"I didn't sleep at all," said Ilona.

The butler sighed gently. Then he asked, "Shall I serve breakfast?"

"Please do."

"You received several telephone calls during the night."

"Anything important?"

"One. From Jan Meitner. He was quite excited. The Star Watch has offered him a commission as a science officer."

That stirred Ilona's interest. "And he's accepted?"

"Most gladly. He'll be accompanying the first Star Watch mission to Neptune."

Ilona wondered how Francine would react to Jan's news. "Anything from Francine Savoy?" she asked.

Ghulam shook his head. "Nothing."

A small, almost bitter smile edged across Ilona's face. That's the end of their romance, I suppose. Too bad.

Ghulam reminded her, "The fencing group will be here at ten o'clock."

Ilona had almost forgotten about the fencers. "They've been meeting here while I was gone?"

"Every week. Young Janos Kadar has taken charge of them in your absence."

"Really?"

"He's been quite effective, apparently."

"Really?" she repeated.

As one of the kitchen maids delivered a tray bearing her breakfast, Ilona decided she wanted to see how the fencing group had progressed under Janos's teenaged direction.

THE FENCERS

++

++

Wearing her white fencing uniform, Ilona entered the gymnasium, where her group of students waited for her, similarly clad. They all sprang to attention as she strode purposefully into the gym.

"Good morning," Ilona called to them. "It's good to see you all once again."

Janos Kadar—young, bright-eyed, gangly—made a stiff little bow. "It's good to see you again, Baroness."

Smiling at the teenager, Ilona said, "Ghulam tells me you have been meeting regularly while I was away."

Janos dipped his chin in acknowledgment.

One of the younger girls smiled as she asked, "Was your trip to Neptune a success?"

Ilona stared at her for a moment, wondering how she should answer that question. At last she said, "Shall I tell you about it?"

"Yes!"

"Please!"

The twenty-five youngsters gathered around her, all thoughts of their usual fencing lesson flown away.

Ilona motioned for them to sit on the wooden floor as she herself sank down in front of them.

"Where to begin?" she wondered aloud.

"At the beginning!" shouted one of the youngest fencers.

More than an hour later, Ilona ended her impromptu recitation with, "So we recharged our thrusters with the hyperbattery that the rescue craft had brought, and flew up from the ocean's ice pack, through the clouds, and back home to here."

The youngsters, sitting in a semicircle on the floor, stirred and blinked as if coming out of a trance.

One of them asked, "And Captain Humbolt, where is he now?"

"In his home in New Mexico," Ilona replied.

"And Jan and Francine?"

"Jan has joined the Star Watch, Francine Savoy is at the Interplanetary Council's headquarters, in Copenhagen."

"I've joined the Star Watch, too," said Janos Kadar.

Ilona stared at him. "You have?"

With a smile that was almost shy, the teenager replied, "I've been accepted as a junior officer trainee. In January I'm going to a school in the United States. It's called West Point."

Ilona's eyes misted with tears. She had known Janos since she'd started the fencing academy, when he'd been little more than nine years old.

"That's . . ." Her voice caught in her throat. This was almost like losing a son. Forcing herself to keep from weeping, Ilona said, "That's a brave thing to do."

Janos's smile widened happily.

And Ilona suddenly realized what she had to do. She called Derek.

SZENT FERENC KÓRHÁZ <SAINT FRANCIS HOSPITAL>

He's a handsome man, Ilona said to herself as she sat down before the desk of the hospital's chief of obstetrics, Dr. Rizwan Tolna.

Tolna's facial expression was serious without being grim. Clean-shaven, he had piercing sky-blue eyes, a strong chin, straight nose, and short-cut salt-and-pepper hair.

Looking straight at Ilona, he said, "What you've requested is rather out of the ordinary."

"I suppose it is," she said.

Folding his hands atop his broad, dark mahogany desk, Dr. Tolna said, "Reproducing a human being is not a procedure to be under-taken lightly."

"Lightly?" Ilona huffed. "I've flown out to the planet Neptune—twice—to find my father. All that was left of him was these few scraps of DNA. A few molecules. Nothing more."

Ilona felt tears welling up in her eyes. Good! she thought. Let the tears flow. Let him see how much I want to have Father return to me.

But Dr. Tolna did not seem moved. "Baroness," he said softly, "reproducing a human life is a serious matter."

"I'm aware of that," said Ilona, as she pulled a tissue from her purse. "That's why I'm talking with you . . . it's why I'm pleading with you."

As she dabbed at her eyes she saw that Tolna looked uncomfort-able.

She went on, "I was told that Saint Francis Hospital has the finest facilities for such a procedure. And the finest staff."

"That's true, but . . ."

"But what?" she snapped. "What's wrong with wanting to bring my father back to life?"

Tolna spread his arms. "There are some very intricate ethical problems involved."

"Ethical problems? What ethical problems? My father died out there on Neptune. You have the knowledge and the facilities to bring him back to life! Where is the ethical problem?"

"The man is dead," Tolna said firmly. "Is it morally correct to bring him back to life?"

"Is it morally correct to refuse to do so?"

With a bleak shake of his head, Tolna answered, "That's a question that the Holy Father in Rome should address. Not me."

"You refuse to help me?"

"Only until you can get Holy Mother Church to agree to allow the procedure."

Ilona stared at the doctor for a long, silent moment.

A voice in her mind snarled, This is medieval thinking! I have to get the Church's blessing to revive my own father?

"Why must the Church be involved?" she demanded.

"Yours is an unprecedented request," Tolna said.

"I want to bring my father back to life!"

"Yes. You've made that quite clear. And we have the facilities and experience to do that, with a high probability of success. But—"

"I'm not interested in your facilities," Ilona interrupted. "I intend to carry the baby to term myself."

Tolna's eyes widened. "In your own body?"

"Of course. I don't want him gestated in one of your artificial wombs. That's unnatural."

"But . . . but . . ." Tolna sagged back in his chair, seemingly out of words.

Her patience nearly spent, Ilona demanded, "Will you do it, or must I go out of Hungary to have it done? Japan, perhaps?"

Tolna did not answer for long, silent moments. At last he said, in a near whisper, "Go to the Church. Get their approval."

Saint Stephen's Basilica stood bathed in autumn sunlight. Its walls had withstood invading armies and rebelling Hungarians for many centuries. But Ilona paid scant attention to the basilica's long, often blood-soaked history.

She stood in the private office of Cardinal Horvath, waiting for His Eminence's appearance.

Like Ilona herself, Horvath was the child of a long Hungarian lineage. Ilona had met him on a few social occasions, but this meeting was the first time she had asked for a private audience.

His office was small, its walls filled with bookshelves, except for the single window that looked out at the cathedral itself. A bright blue sky glowed out there, dotted with puffy white clouds. The trees lining the street beside the cathedral were decked in brilliant autumnal reds and golds.

Ilona had been ushered into the office by a Church official, wearing a dour black suit that hung on the man's frame as if it had been borrowed from a larger, more robust man. Then he had silently retreated back through the office's door, leaving Ilona standing before the cardinal's desk, alone.

Clutching her small purse in both her gloved hands, Ilona stared at the office's other door, waiting for the cardinal to make his entrance.

The old game, she told herself. Let your visitor wait, impress on her your importance, the loftiness of—

The door abruptly opened and Cardinal Horvath stepped in, smiling heartily.

"Baroness Magyr!" he exclaimed. "How good to see you again!"

Ilona stepped forward, knelt and kissed the cardinal's jeweled ring.

The cardinal was a smallish man, many centimeters shorter than Ilona. Slim as a saber blade, with a thick mop of dead white hair and a face that could sometimes seem as if it was etched in granite. But he was smiling beatifically at Ilona.

Gesturing to the small table in the far corner of the tiny office, the cardinal said, "Please sit and make yourself comfortable." His creaking voice reminded Ilona of a gate whose hinges badly needed oiling.

Once they were both seated and facing each other, Ilona said, "I'm here to ask your approval—"

"To bear a baby," said the cardinal. "A baby who happens to be your own father."

Ilona nodded, realizing that the cardinal had been well briefed for this meeting.

"Dr. Tolna said I need to get the Church's approval for such a procedure."

Cardinal Horvath smiled genially. "Tolna is very conservative. I think his wife influences him too much."

Surprised, Ilona could only say, "Really?"

Spreading his hands wide, the cardinal said, "Holy Mother Church has reached a point where she needs to reexamine her positions on a number of issues. The world marches ahead, and from time to time we of the Church need to catch up."

Ilona blinked with surprise.

Horvath went on, "Three months ago His Holiness celebrated twenty years in Saint Peter's chair. He'll be eighty-six years old before the year is out."

"And he refuses life-extension therapies," Ilona said.

The cardinal raised an admonishing finger. "All the princes of the Church refuse such therapies. It would not be wise to have a Pope reigning for centuries, would it?"

Ilona could only murmur, "No, I suppose not."

His smile returning, Horvath said, "But you are here to address your own problem."

"My father . . ."

"You must love him very much."

Ilona felt tears welling. "Yes," she whispered. "I do."

"You are a good daughter," said the cardinal, also in a whisper.

"Is it wrong? To want to revive Father?"

Horvath went silent, his expression grave. At last he said, "Love is never wrong. Jesus Himself told us that."

"Then . . ."

"Let me see what I can do. It may take a few months for the matter to work its way through the Curia, but I'm sure that Holy Mother Church will not be so asinine as to refuse your request."

Ilona sank to her knees and kissed the cardinal's ring again. But in the back of her mind she remembered all the charities and special programs that Magyr money supported.

Is his approval based on Magyr money? she asked herself. And the answer was that she didn't care if it was. It didn't matter. All she cared about was his approval.

Ilona woke up in a cold sweat, the dream already slipping away.

Drenched in sweat from the agony she'd been through, Ilona lay on the hospital bed, her newborn baby at her breast.

The boy's eyes were closed as he suckled, but Ilona had seen them wide open a few moments earlier. Black as midnight, the same as Derek's, and just as her father's flashing eyes had been. Good, Ilona thought as she looked down on the tiny, busy face. His genes are strong.

A nurse entered her room, silent as a wraith, and smiled down at Ilona and the baby.

"Everything is well?" she whispered.

Ilona nodded. Everything is very well indeed, she thought.

Ilona glanced at the mirror atop the room's dresser. She looked pale, drained, weary. But she smiled. "I'll have to get washed up and fix my hair."

With an understanding nod, the nurse said, "We'll have a team here when you're ready."

"Good. Thank you."

"You're very welcome, Baroness." And the nurse turned and left Ilona's room, still silent as a wraith.

Ilona looked down at the baby. He seemed asleep. "Miklos," she whispered to him. "Miklos Magyr XVII." The family tradition, carried through the centuries.

She raised her face to the room's only window, where a bright summer sun was rising to begin a new day.

A new day, Ilona thought. A new world. Alien creatures exist beyond the limits of the solar system. Hostile aliens, cruel and merciless. You will have to face them, my son. You will have to deal with them.

Someday, she knew. That is your heritage, little Miklos. Your future. Your responsibility.

Someday.

But for now, sleep and rest. Grow strong and wise. Meet the future when the time comes. For now, cling to me and let me mother you. That is my future. That is my responsibility.

Father and daughter. Mother and son. We will face the future together.

aCKNOWLEDGMENTS

This novel could not have been completed without the generous help of my editor at Tor Books, Melissa Ann Singer. I also thank Dr. Martha Dávila-García, and my granddaughter Ilyana Rose at the Barbara Bova Literary Agency, for reviewing and editing the text where required. If there are any inaccuracies, they are entirely my own doing.

I thank all of the countless others who, over the years, provided many valuable insights and ideas. They have helped me make this novel of the planet Neptune as accurate as possible. As every author must, I have taken poetic liberties with the basic facts, here and there. Now, on to Neptune and the mysteries that lie within.

Ben Bova
Naples, Florida